Bloodline

"Another magnificent winner from America's newest Queen of Mystery……" Mid-Atlantic Book Reviewer

~*~

"***Wish I had written this one………..."*** J. Jackson Owensby, Author

~*~

"Another gripping thriller from a first-class mystery writer…." Midwest Book Reviewers

Whispered Dreams

"**Samantha Shu** brings an original and freely-imaginative approach to popular fiction that is refreshing. She comes out of a long and venerable line in British and American literature that includes such diverse antecedents as Edgar Allen Poe, Arthur Conan Doyle, Ambrose Bierce, Dashiell Hammett, Agatha Christie, Dorothy L. Sayers, and Raymond Chandler. Her writing particularly suggests Arthur Conan Doyle, in terms of its use of deductive reasoning and logic, and Dashiell Hammett, in its strong characters and narrative pacing. This latest work displays all the classic features of her unique approach, which blends hard-boiled investigation and relentless sleuthing with realistic dialogue and brilliant description. At a fundamental level, the novel explores a theme as old as the Bible – the conflict between good and evil – but the work transcends that conventional premise and brings us directly into the current, post-modern era, where people face existential decisions that define them as much as the provident or improvident actions they take."..............................John Murrray, (Colorado) author, *The Indian Peaks Wilderness Area: A Hunting & Field Guide*

~*~

"***Loved it!***.........." Kathy Lane (Texas) "Loved *Whispered Dreams*, didn't want to put it down. I can hardly wait for Shu's next one. I will be buying it as soon as it is released."

~*~

"***Awesome!***........." Sheryl A Brown (Parker, CO) "What a great read. Could not put it down. A must read for anyone who loves a good Romantic thriller."

~*~

"***Masterfully engineered!***........." Macelin Cane "Macelin" (Colorado) "Once again the words and rhythm of Samantha Shu have successfully tackled the art of a suspenseful thriller. From the very beginning, an intricate and mesmerizing tale of mystery and mayhem. As soon as you feel comfortably footed on solid ground, she sweeps you at the knees, leaving you gasping for more. Don't put it down - you won't be able be able to function in everyday life until you know………"

~*~

"Thrilling!.........." Jill K. Ross (Golden, CO) "What a thriller! Through every twist and turn, you won't be able to put it down. And who doesn't love a good heroine? Fantastic! A great read. Get this book! You'll love it."

~*~

"Spine-tingling page turner!.........." D. D. Morehead (Denver, CO) "A great read! Shu's characters are edgy and smart. Her dialogue is snappy and her plot complex and enjoyable. This book has it all for lovers of suspense, with a surprising ending that will shock you to the core. A must for your library!?

~*~

"***Supermom!***.........." Margaret J. Dolan, *Lover of Vamp Fiction* (Fort Worth, TX) "I loved this thriller! Samantha Shu is an excellent writer and *Whispered Dreams* is a fantastic achievement! Truly the right genre for her.

~*~

"Truly outstanding!........." Mid-Atlantic Book Reviewer "Samantha Shu takes her place among the top quality writers of suspense, romance and action."

~*~

"Top drawer entertainment!........J. Jackson Owensby, *N.C. Writers Assoc.* (North Carolina) "Shu has produced a book that is impossible to put down. I did, and you will, read deep into the night as she keeps us on the edge until the last thrilling word."

BLOODTHIRSTY

By

Samantha Shu

Argus Enterprises International, Inc
North Carolina***New Jersey

Bloodthirsty © 2010
All rights reserved by Samantha Shu

No part of this book may be reproduced or transmitted in any form or by any means, graphic, electronic, or mechanical, including photocopying, recording, taping, or by any informational storage retrieval system without prior permission in writing from the publisher.

A-Argus Better Book Publishers, LLC

For information:
A-Argus Better Book Publishers, LLC
Post Office Box 914
Kernersville, North Carolina 27285
www.a-argusbooks.com

ISBN: 978-0-9842596-9-4
ISBN: 0-9842596-9-4

Book Cover designed by

Printed in the United States of America

ACKNOWLEDGEMENTS

When I began the long journey of delving into the psychopathic serial killers thought processes, I was knee deep in earning my bachelors degree. I am now about to graduate with a BA in Criminal Justice. During this eye-opening, many times demanding, overwhelming and mind-blowing experience, I met and became friends with many extraordinary people. Several of these great thinkers and truth seekers are represented in this novel, (you know who you are.) It is these inhabitants that I wish to thank. Without them this experience would be one dimensional. I hope that after reading, you will acknowledge that the depth of character is only matched by the genuine article.

Mark Leone, Thank you for teaching me to think critically, allowing me to learn the true nature of the criminal mind; I would also like to thank you for showing me how closely the criminal mind resembles that of the other side.

Leslie Minor, without your gentle nudging my writing would not be what it is. Thank you for supporting me as a teacher and a fan.

Joey, as always, you help me to organize my brain when it is firing on all cylinders at once. Thanks for keeping me grounded. I cannot wait to see you flourish as you have helped me to do.

Ray, you continue to astound me with your ability to find the flaws in my work and point me in a better direction.

Bill Connor, my publisher. You have had an effect on my existence that only a wise guru could, changing my path into a dream while keeping me on track with your humorous prodding and down to earth approach.

Thank you, forever.

Finally I would like to thank the office staff and all of the professors at Westwood South Campus, Denver Colorado. Without their constant support and guidance, this book would never have been finished.

Thank you all, I will never forget the past few years, with you standing at my side.

For

Will, Silver, Rayne and Rose

"We are what we repeatedly do. Excellence then, is not an act, but a habit."

'Aristotle'

Greek critic, philosopher,

(384 BC - 322 BC)

Prologue

Slaughter was the decadent dessert on an otherwise appalling menu. Payton stared at the oversized moron and wondered how he could do what he was doing and not feel completely ridiculous. He was naked, sweaty and humping her leg. It wasn't even the upper part of her leg; he was pressing his lotion-covered cock against her shin and grunting like a hog.

She smiled and opened her mouth slightly, encouraging him to finish. "Does that feel good, baby?" She didn't wait for his answer, she kept talking. "Come on, baby; spread your sweet juice on my hot leg."

She tried not to gag as she said the words. Those feelings had no place here. Pushing them away, she smiled a sexy smile. He groaned loudly and she felt a hot stream of wet fluid slide down her calf. He fell onto his side, and then readjusted himself pressing his soft belly into the bed. For just a second she looked at him with pity. How had he gotten to this place? How had he… then she stopped herself. She didn't give a damn about this freak! She had work to do, things to accomplish; plus without him there would be no game. She couldn't have that. The game was all there was now. She needed the game; it was the ultimate fantasy.

For years she'd considered it, thought about the possibilities. Could she really do it? Would it be easy? Would she get caught? Then she had realized she couldn't get caught, not the way she was planning it. This was the moment. This was the beginning of the most exciting time in her existence.

His meaty, sweat covered hand came up and rested against her thigh and he said, "That was the coolest thing I've ever done."

Payton laughed, it sounded shrill to her. She felt as if she were standing on a precipice and wondered if her next moments would send her over the edge. She felt herself beginning to fall as she reached under the small hand towel lying on the table beside her bed. Her hand wrapped around the slick handle. She pulled it out. Looking at the long blade she saw her reflection .Her teeth looked massive in the warped image and she realized that she must have been smiling.

"Good" she said in a sweet voice as she raised the blade high. "You're gonna die happy" His head started to come up as she gripped the handle with both hands and slammed the blade into his back. A shock shot up her arms as the blade impacted with bone, she fell back, releasing the handle. Her eyes glistened as she took in the amazing sight of what she had done.

A scream and a gag shot from him as he rolled off the bed onto the floor. Payton scrambled further onto the bed trying to create distance. He was trying to grab the blade; twisting and reaching as if he could only get it, he would be fine. His eyes were big, his mouth open. He was on his knees now and she watched fascinated by what was happening.

"Sorry" she said and she realized in awe that she actually meant it. This was a spectacle she could do without. She closed her eyes briefly and wished for him to hurry and die. Her eyes opened, she stood on the bed pressing herself against the wall.

He looked at her and stopped moving. He was like a statue kneeling before her. "Bitch" he said in a clear voice. Blood flowed from his mouth as if the word were signed now in an ancient form of blood ritual. His hands fell to his sides and he crumpled to the floor.

Payton stared at the man laying in the sticky accumulation on the floor of her small bedroom and wished she had chosen any carpet color other than white.

Ok, baby, time to get to work, she thought and jumped off the bed, grabbed the knife and yanked hard. It made a gross scraping sound and a pop as it let loose, blood flew from the blade splattering the walls; she felt a drop fall just above her upper lip. She shuddered and wiped it with the back of her hand.

"Okay… okay… okay!" she chanted. "You're really in it now, girl. No turning back, no hesitation, no mistakes. Game On!" She knelt down beside the bloody, sweaty man and focused on the future.

Chapter One

Timber Byrne shook her head in dismay. *You guys are the stupidest motherfuckers in the gene pool,* she thought.

Taking in the sight before her, she wondered how these guys ever solved a crime. There had to be twenty uniformed officers traipsing around, screwing up the scene. A few plainclothes detectives stood talking at the corner of the dark alley. Several crime-tech guys were kneeling beside the body, taking pictures and slipping evidence into baggies; spraying chemicals on fluids to ascertain their type; blood, semen, water, and whatever else might be there. She knew these guys could find that proverbial needle in a haystack even if it was made of human hair.

What she didn't understand and never would was the need for so many damn cops standing around chatting about what could have happened.

As she moved closer she groaned, recognizing the detective standing there and casually sipping his coffee. *Robin Blake*, that's all she needed. *Why am I even here?* She thought.

Her division wasn't needed for a simple dead body. Even if it had been a murder there was no reason she should be pulled out of bed and called to a murder scene. As she approached, Blake looked up. She saw no surprise in his eyes. She knew immediately who was to blame.

She stomped up to him and said, "You're an asshole, Blake!"

"Good morning to you too, Agent Byrne" He was grinning and she wanted to punch him in his stupid perfect mouth.

"It's not even close to morning." she snapped "Why am I here? It's obvious you had me called in. Are you sleeping with someone at the agency now? Is that how you pulled this off?" She knew she was out of line and yet, she didn't care.

Blake grabbed Timber by the upper arm and yanked her a few steps away from the other detective. "Hey!" he said in a low growl, "That's bullshit! You're about to make a fool of yourself over some ancient crap between us?"

Timber looked at his hand on her arm. She was so shocked by his actions she almost couldn't bring herself to speak. When she did, her voice was calm and controlled. "You better remove your hand from my person right now or I swear to God, Detective, I will bust your ass for sexual harassment and, before I do, I'll shoot you in your dick for assaulting me. Are we clear?"

Blake's eyes hardened and he took a step back, dropped his hand and said. "I won't touch you again."

He turned his back on her and began walking toward the body "Take a look at this. Tell me you don't want to be involved and I'll let you go back to bed."

As Timber followed she realized she was shaking. This was the only man that could elicit those explosive emotions from her. She was wired a little tight. She knew that, yet she had always attributed that to the fact that she was a woman in a field where men reigned. There was the matter concerning her stature.

Timber was a small woman. Not just compared to a man but compared to anyone. She was a five foot-one, one-hundred and ten pound "firecracker". According to her four brothers, she'd never failed to live up to the nickname. The part of Timber that gave her the most trouble was the fact that she was utterly beautiful. She had done things to tone it down, cutting her naturally golden hair so short that she could jump from the shower, rub it with a towel and be done. He blue eyes were almost too large for her face and whenever possible she kept them covered with sunglasses. She wore clothing that deliberately made her look anything but sexual. Jeans and baggy sweaters were her casual wear. For work she kept to black slacks and white button-down blouses. No frills, no heels.

What she didn't realize, and what none of her co-workers had cared to share for obvious reasons, was that all of the things she did to make herself less sexy only made her more adorable. The guys at work had started calling her *'pixie girl'*. If she knew that, her cute little pixie head would have shot from her body in a fabulous, exploding fireworks extravaganza.

Living in her delusion that she was a tough non-sexual being that could rival any man on or off the job, she angrily strutted after Blake, mumbling under her breath.

A tech looked up as they approached. Blake nodded his head. The tech pulled down a small white cloth that had been covering the dead man's face.

This was the job, dead bodies, blood, it's all part of the deal; but there are still times that you want to turn and empty the contents of your stomach on the dirty pavement. Timber swallowed the bile rising in her throat and knelt down for a closer look.

One eye was swollen shut and yellow with a black ring around it as if he had been hit with something perfectly cylindrical. His other eye was missing. The hole was hollowed out like it had been cleaned. His lips were pulled back from his mouth and something was shoved inside. Timber took a pen from her shirt pocket, grabbed a baggie and wrapped it over the end of the pen. She slipped it inside the mouth and moved the object just enough to see its origin. "Oh" she said and looked at Blake

He nodded and knelt beside her. "There's more" he said and took her pen from her hand and used it to slide the shirt open. The breast tissue had been completely excised from the body.

"Did you find it?" she asked, referring to the missing tissue.

"Not yet, but I'm guessing by what's in his mouth, we're going to find it."

"In autopsy?" she asked

"That would be my guess"

"Yeah, unfortunately mine, too" She looked closer and noticed that the slices on the chest were clean and sharp, no hesitation marks. She shivered and said, "I need to make a call"

"So, you in?" he asked, a smirk starting at the corner of his mouth

"Oh shut up" she said and pressed a button on her phone. The line began to ring and she turned away from Blake as he laughed and said, "I'm just asking,"

Chapter Two

Payton thought about the next kill. She was excited now. Looking forward to it. She was going to be spontaneous. That would be the smart way to start. The first had been so well planned. She laughed and twirled around her small apartment, dancing, moving, swaying. Music played loudly in the small space, Anna Nalic's songs about loss and love, but mostly about power; the kind of power that comes from living in pain. She liked Anna, but not as much as she enjoyed 'MoZella'. That woman knew love. She knew what it really felt like to fall apart. Give yourself over completely and recover better than ever. Her favorite MoZella song was *'Light Years Away'.*" That one really covered it; referring to the loss of her mind. She laughed; shrill and high, then slapped a hand over her mouth.

Sometimes she imagined going to her ex-boyfriend's house, breaking in, tying him up. She would make him listen to that song. Then maybe, while she's singing along with the chorus, *'I don't blame you anymore, that's too much pain to store',* she would cut his heart out and lay it on his crotch.

"Now that's a solid plan." she said aloud and giggled. This time the sound was closer to what a laugh should sound like.

She was aware on every level that killing Keirnan was never an option. Never kill someone you know. Never kill anyone who can be traced back to you.

That sucked! So many people she would annihilate if she could. So many useless pieces of shit wasting air that could be consumed by more deserving individuals.

She flopped down on her couch, slapped her bare feet on the coffee table, and let Anna's voice wash over her. She may not be able to erase her foes but she could imagine it fully. *Maybe I'll find lookalikes, which could be fun.* She tilted her head back against the cushion and started planning her next adventure. A small smile curved her sensuous lips as she imagined her lover screaming her name.

Today was a day to make money, to prepare for the next one. The next one would have to be different, something to completely throw off everyone. It was time to slow down, take a few days off, and confuse the egocentric police agency and all of their stupid profiling fuckers. Her thoughts were interrupted by a knock at the door.

She glanced at her reflection, placed a firm hand on the doorknob and smiled as it opened. A young man stepped through the door and into her small living space. His height reached approximately six feet-three inches. He was well-muscled, young and had a sweet smile. "Hi, welcome, my name is Payton." She held out her hand and it was immediately engulfed in his larger one.

"Hi" he replied, "I'm Ben" He smiled a big goofy grin and pumped her hand up and down twice before releasing it.

"Come on in, sweetie, and make yourself comfortable." As he slipped out of his jacket, Payton closed and locked the door, turning to Ben, happy smile in place.

"We need to take care of your donation first, baby." She said her standard line that indicated she wanted her cash. Cash was key, after all.

"Oh sure." His hand slipped into his front pocket and a wad of cash slipped out. He handed her two crumpled hundred-dollar bills. Payton slipped the money into her purse saying "Take your clothes off and hang them on the gentleman's rack." She pointed to the wooden structure. Ben undressed and following her instructions, lay down on the bed, face down.

He had nice skin, tan, smooth; she paused a moment, enjoying a look at his fabulous body. This was the body of a man in his formative years, with baby skin that covers a nicely muscled structure. She had seen once too often how cruel time could be, slowly causing youth to fade away as age takes its ugly grip. She moved beside him, and began. Her hands followed the curves and valleys bringing just the right amount of pleasure. Fingers traced down to the center of his thighs, lightly tickling. He moaned and his ass rose off of the bed.

Payton smiled. Not a smile of pleasure because this was never pleasurable, merely a smile of accomplishment. This was the job, make them squirm, make them want it; make them need the pleasure more than they want the money. The goal is always to make them forget about the money.

Touching, rubbing, groping, smells that are not pleasant, witnessing things that made her want to gag were all part of the gig. Forty-five minutes later, Payton was slipping into her small turquoise dress, already thinking about the next few hours. His voice broke into her thoughts and shattered all of her well-laid plans.

"I'm gonna need that money back" He said it so casually that she heard the words, yet did not understand the meaning

"What?" her tone also casual.

"I'm gonna need that money back. I'm only seventeen and if you don't give me my money back I'm gonna call the police and you're gonna go to jail."

"You are not seventeen." She was transfixed by the situation. She couldn't believe that was all she'd thought to say, although it was quite obvious he was lying.

"My father is on the city council and I know the laws" he stated smugly.

"Really? You know the laws?" On what planet is it legal to get service and then not pay?"

He shrugged and said, "I'm really sorry, but I need that money. I'm driving across country and I need that money for gas." He didn't sound in the least apologetic. He was using the words like they had power with no feeling behind them.

Payton was astounded by his audacity and she stammered in her anger "So …ssso you knew, coming in here you were going to rob me?"

"No." He shook his head vehemently and then began to justify his answer by saying, "I was going to ask you to make me a deal, but when I saw you and you were so beautiful, I just wanted to …"

"Rip me off? She shot out demanding an answer, "So, if I were some skanky bitch, you would have offered to pay me less, got a shitty session and left happy?"

"No, I probably would do the same thing. I really need that money."

"I don't want to give you the money back, because I need it too. I worked for it and it's wrong for you to take it back. You do realize it's my money now and if you take it back that it is stealing?" She wanted him to acknowledge that he was a liar and a thief. She wasn't sure why, but it seemed important.

Her heart was beating a rapid tattoo, pressing her chest wall and the surrounding area in on itself. Her eyes burned with unshed tears, not from sorrow but rather from anger. Anger at the turn of events, anger at how her mood had been so high moments before. Her mind was whirling, the tornado of thoughts trying to get out. He was big, strong, and he was going to take her money. She knew she could fight him. Fight and defend if need be, keep the money and win. But he would tell, he would call the cops and then the real stress would begin. The questions, the harassment, the only way this worked was if her scenario continued to retain its complete secrecy. This person… no, she corrected her thought. This miscreant was threatening to ruin all that.

Anger was ripping at her. He was probably bluffing but even if he was, he might complain to a neighbor, call the cops anonymously; all of the possibilities were there and she knew them.

Fight or flight? Fight or flight? Fight or flight?

Then he made the decision for her. He took away the reasoning and the doubt with a few simple words "I could have your license taken away, I've done it before."

All mental negotiations ceased. "You've done it before?" she asked and waved her hand to stop him from answering. She smiled up at him and sighed, "You never know who the bad guys are going to be. It's always a shock, isn't it? You think it's going to be obvious. They'll wear a black hat; maybe speak with some antiquated accent. You'll immediately get a bad feeling when they touch you or maybe the hairs on the back of your neck will stand up." She moved a step closer to him and said, "It's always a shock to come face to face with evil and not have even an inkling that you're looking into the eyes of something so dark."

He looked at her with a small patronizing smile turning up the corners of his wide mouth. Shaking his head, he said, "I'm not a bad guy."

She interrupted with a small laugh "Oh, I wasn't talking about you."

Before he could respond her foot came up hard between his legs. A puff of air and spittle flew from his mouth and burst onto her skin. While he was catching his breath, she grabbed a candle set in a thick glass jar and slammed it into his face. Fortunately, his hands were busy comforting his groin. His features had no protection from the crushing blow. As a geyser of blood flew from his crushed nose and sent large hail-sized spatter around the room, Payton used the momentum from the first swing and came back around slamming the glass into his cheekbone. A resounding and satisfying crack accompanied the action. *Mister Tall and Cocky* fell to his knees and made some small, incoherent noise before his eyes shut and he slipped into oblivion.

"Well, now, that was satisfaction on a stick!" She laughed, looking at the candle she held in her hand. The cover on the jar depicted an apple pie with a large scoop of vanilla ice cream melting seductively on top. Payton giggled and dropped the jar on the floor beside the bloody man. "Well, you don't get more American than that, murder and apple pie"

She stepped back and took in the sight of her small space. This was not good, unplanned, bad. Luckily, this preposterous man couldn't be linked to her as far a she knew. Payton grabbed for his coat and retrieved his cell phone. First things first, she thought. Her fingers moved over the keys quickly erasing all numbers associated with her. Then she took the phone into the bathroom and gently washed her fingerprints away. Suspicion could cause anything to happen, so a clean cell phone was not an option. She took the unconscious mans hands and used them to contaminate the phone once again. This time she was careful not to add any of her own contaminants. Another problem was she had just spent time with this man, so she was all over him. That had to be remedied. Not to mention the blood.

He was going to be dead soon anyway so a little blood wasn't an issue, but this blood was not good. This blood was in her apartment and it could have her DNA in it. Time for cleanup. "ICK!" she moaned and went to the bathroom for her rubber gloves and something to keep him unconscious till she decided how she would kill him. The glorious part was that this was definitely getting easier.

Chapter Three

The next week Payton kept her eyes open. She would stick to her plan. It was a good plan but if she happened to cross paths with someone who looked like him… well then maybe she could give herself a little counseling while taking care of business. She had always loved the two bird theory. Unfortunately she met no one who even resembled the bastard. When her opportunity arrived it was as she expected it would be. A useless piece of shoe shit pranced into the room and began removing his clothing. Payton smiled sweetly and sat on the bed watching his movement. He was a big man. Very tall, broad-chested and bow-legged.

She was glad that he was big. Big was good.

"So, you're gonna go out with me soon." He said it like it was a statement, no question in his voice. She looked at him standing there in all of his glory, his golfer's tan visible in the dim light.

"Come on over here, baby," she purred, and patted the bed beside her.

"I'm a good looking guy. You wanna go out with me." he said again confidently, with a large smile on his stupid, flat face.

"Of course you're good looking." She put out her hand. "Come here." Payton knew this was a risk. She hoped it wasn't messy. Ok, so she knew it would be messy; she just hoped she wouldn't puke. "You want a date? Then sit and have a drink with me."

"I don't want to have a date now. God, are you dumb? I wanna fuck now. I wanna date later."

She could feel the anger building up inside her. When this loser asshole had walked into her apartment he was just a tool. He was quickly becoming something more. If she hadn't already done the slice and dice, this dick would be the perfect candidate.

Stick to the plan, stick to the plan, stick to the plan, she chanted to herself and smiled, chanted and cooed.

The glass of red wine sat on the edge of the small glass table. "I'm gonna make you feel so good. Have some wine."

"Jesus! What's up with the stupid drink?" He picked up the glass and held it out as if it were a challenge.

She continued to sit on the bed, tilted her head demurely and began twirling a lock of her long hair. She knew she appeared bored and beautiful. It's not at all what was going on inside.

Her guts were churning; butterflies chased their tails inside its acrid stew. She couldn't take her eyes off the glass.

He took another step towards her and said in a very petulant voice, "I don't want to drink with you because you don't want to date me."

"Really?" she said sweetly, and stood pressing her hands against his bare chest. She was experiencing a feeling of excitement.

An opening had presented itself and she wasn't wasting any time. "Baby, have a drink with me and we'll go out afterwards."

He looked down at her like she had lost all her senses. "I don't want to go out now. I want to go out tomorrow."

She wanted to laugh and scream at the same time. "Whatever you want, you're so sexy," she cooed. "I've wanted to go out with you for awhile. You're the best-looking friend I have." She ran her hand down his chest, her voice a sexy vibrato. "I've been playing hard to get. I guess I took it too far." She looked into his eyes. "Forgive me?"

He laughed, tilted back his head and drank the entire glass in one gulp.

Chapter Four

Blake adjusted his tie and scanned the dark precinct's parking lot. He was tired and edgy. Too many hours chasing shadows had put dark ones under his eyes. He squinted as a breeze caused a small box to slide across the pavement before tipping and rolling as only a square could roll. It thumped along the pavement propelled by the elements. Blake could have sworn it was moving with intent in his direction. He thought about walking toward it. Save the time and trouble of the extensive quest in the small item's future. Yet, he didn't move forward. He stood in the dark parking lot staring at a small box blowing in the soft breeze. He laughed as it blew past his boots and continued on its way.

"That could have been wicked," he said aloud, imagining how cool it would have been if the box had stopped at his feet. Still, it seemed odd. As it had rolled past he noticed a green ribbon tied with a large bow. The box itself seemed simple, old cardboard. Maybe something a small trinket would come in. He looked around at the parking lot. A half dozen cars remained; no one around to drop anything and it was late. He glanced at his watch: after midnight.

'Man oh man, do I need to get a life outside of work'. Again he looked at the box. It had stopped its movement across the pavement and now sat illuminated by a small beam of light at the corner of the parking lot. Eerie.

As he approached the object, it became clear that this was something special. The green ribbon wasn't ribbon at all but an iridescent tube. The bow had been built in some factory from the ordinary fare that would eventually be sold as a small Christmas ornament. Someone had used hot glue or super glue to apply it to the tubing. The cardboard was covered in dark lines; he couldn't tell exactly what they were, maybe marker.

He bent and took a closer look, suddenly fascinated by it. The lines appeared to intersect in several different places. He reached inside of his coat pocket and pulled out a latex glove, slipped it on his left hand and carefully picked up the box. It was heavier than he had imagined and as he turned it there was a subtle feeling of liquid inside.

He stood and quickly walked back into the building. On his way in, he looked to his left and right, taking in as much of the street as possible. He had been contemplating the mysterious item for only a few minutes; still the person or persons who had placed it in the parking lot of his precinct must be long gone.

He took the stairs, hoping to avoid those nosey graveyard guys still in the bag, or as the civilians like to say, chained to the patrol car. Whether using cop slang or civilian speak, it all shook out the same. Sometimes the bitterness and jealousy could get very old. Blake was young for a detective. He was thirty-nine, although he appeared to be at least ten years younger; a curse instead of a blessing. Blake had spent the better part of his career proving himself. Yet, he continued to do things that puzzled those around him and made it harder for people to take him seriously. Making jokes at inappropriate times, talking just a little too fast when dealing with a suspect. Then there were his ties. Every day for three years he had dressed for success. Shined black leather police issue boots, black or dark blue suit, cut to fit. A slick and ironed shirt usually in burgundy or blue, but occasionally he'd fall into the status quo and wear white. But his ties were always the sticking point.

Blake had a collection of over six hundred ties. They ranged from Batman to Mickey Mouse. He had collectors' ties and ties that he'd tripped across in Wal-Mart.

The collection had started his first day as detective. As a joke he had worn a Superman tie and it had gotten such a good response he wore a Batman tie the next day. Soon girlfriends were buying him ties and people he hardly knew were adding to the collection. Now he had the wonderful capacity to wear a different tie every day. He thought of it as his mutant super power.

Standing in his office looking down at the small box on his desk, Blake considered his responsibilities and weighed them against his curiosity. After all, there really wasn't anything sinister about the box other than its simple existence. Otherwise it was just a found item. He shook his head and pulled his phone from his jacket pocket. Covering his ass wasn't a new experience. As he dialed he wondered at his choice. He smiled as a female voice made itself clear on the end of the line.

"Fuck, Robin. What do you want? I'm sleeping!"

He knew she'd be asleep and the satisfaction of waking her was apparent in his next words. "No kidding? I thought you'd be up training your flying monkeys."

"Ha, Ha! You're so goddamned funny! WHAT DO YOU WANT?" she yelled into the phone.

He pulled the phone quickly away from his ear and laughed. It was amazing that while she was bitching a blue streak, he was picturing her in her tiny white underwear and silky tank top. Of course, he had no way of knowing she was wearing that particular outfit. Yet, he would always remember her the way she was the last time he had walked out of her bedroom - her short hair a mess, one strap falling off her shoulder and sparks of blue fire shooting from her eyes. He imagined those sparks flying from her eyes now. Enough time had passed, he'd finally moved past the anger and into acceptance. Now as he listened to her bitch and moan, all it brought from him was mild amusement.

"Honey, I found a box. I want to open this box and I don't want to wait around till morning. I don't want to call in forensics until I'm sure it's not a box of candied walnuts someone dropped by accident." He waited, half expecting her to comment on the use of the word 'honey'. She didn't.

"Do you think it is walnuts?" she asked.

"No" he stated flatly.

"Why?" She was intrigued now. He could tell by how monosyllabic she had become. No quip, no diatribes, she was curious.

So he told her the simple truth. "I have several reasons but the most important is it's making the hair on the back of my arms stand up."

She made a noise that sounded like a snort.

"Hey!" he said, insulted

"Fine, stop whining. I'm getting dressed."

"Don't do anything drastic," he teased.

"Tell me Robin, have you always been such a funny guy?"

Before he could come back with some witty repartee he heard the distinctive disconnect loud in his ear. He sat down in his desk chair, rested his boots on his desk and stared at the mysterious thing resting on his desk.

Ω

Timber walked into the office of the Denver Police Department, flashed her badge and passed the patrolman behind the front desk.

The elevators faced the west side of the building. Instead of going in that direction she headed for the stairs, still feeling a little groggy and in need of a heart rate boost. She took the stairs two at a time, kicking up endorphins and sharpening her mind.

As much as she loved to give Robin Blake a hard time, it was all for show. He was a good cop and she knew it. There were valid reasons for his success in the department. He trusted his gut. She had seen him get flack for it, had seen him press the issue and come out of a pile of shit smelling like chocolate ice cream with a cherry on top.

Tonight he had found something. Something that she would have dismissed had anyone else called in the middle of her slumber, especially to come look at a box.

As she ran up the four floors she felt more energized and could actually feel her synapses start to fire. Her mind was sharpening. She pushed open the door from the stairwell. As she heard the door close behind her she looked around at the empty offices.

Memories of different times washed over her. She quickly shook those thoughts away and walked directly to Robin Blake's office. As she walked in she didn't mince words.

"Okay, Blake, show me!" She put her fists on her hips and took a defiant stance.

"What happened to 'Robin'?" he asked, swinging his feet off the desk and standing.

She lifted her shoulders and shook her head. "Too personal, we're working now."

"We weren't working on the phone?"

"I was half asleep. Don't make a thing." She slipped too easily into a comfortable place with this man. The last thing she wanted to do was admit that.

He smiled knowingly and shrugged "Ok. I like Blake better anyway. Especially the way it rolls off your tongue."

That was exactly what she needed. Irritation flooded her. "Oh fuck off, Blake!" She put the emphasis on his name, practically spitting it. "Get to it, show me the damn box and let's see if we're going to be intrigued or if we're going to be eating fancy walnuts."

"I'm hoping for the nuts." he said, staring down at the box.

"Me, too," she said. "Let's go."

They both slipped on latex gloves. She opened her kit and pulled out a small vile, two baggies, and a sheet of plastic. Blake lifted the box and placed it on the plastic sheet. He took a small pair of snips and cut through the green plastic tube.

A hissing sound emanated from the small opening and they both took a step back,

"A gas?" he queried.

"No... Smells like..." She paused. "What is that smell? Man, it's lilac." she said triumphantly and grinned his way.

"Are you sure?"

The grin dropped away. "Come on. I'm not a big guesser. I'm a..."

He finished for her, "Pain in the ass?"

"My God, you just keep getting funnier. No. I'm a 'Knower'."

"That's not even a word." He shook his head, laughed out loud, and leaned in closer to the box. "You're right; lilacs."

"I told you... 'Knower'."

He ignored her and began opening the box, first carefully removing the tubing and bow, then slowly removing the paper it was wrapped in. "I wonder why lilacs?"

"Well," Timber said, staring down at his handiwork. "Maybe the walnuts are a gift and the recipient likes the fragrance of lilacs."

"Maybe." he mumbled.

"So if it's walnuts we gonna eat 'em?"

"I hate walnuts."

"Yeah, they really are the worst nut. But if they're coated in sugar..." she knew she was babbling.

He cut her off, "Look at this."

He had spread the wrapping out on the desk and held down the corners.

Timber looked over his shoulder and said, "Oh... I don't think it's walnuts. Is that...?"

"Yeah," he said slowly "This is a map and that red 'X' is where we found *Mister Missing Parts*."

"Shit. Fuck!" She grabbed the phone and began dialing.

An angry voice answered. "Byrne if this is your idea of…" Having no idea what he was going to say and not really caring, Timber interrupted.

"Sir. We have a situation down at DPD. We need forensics and a team. He's communicating"

Her S.A.C, special agent in charge, John Grady, responded as she expected. "Do what you need to do and make the calls. I'll be there in 20 minutes."

"Yes sir." she responded.

Grady asked, "Why DPD?"

"Detective Robin Blake found the item."

"Is he the local in charge of that case?"

"Yes sir." she said. "He's the one who brought us in."

"Makes sense that he'd find… what was it?"

"A box."

"What's in it?"

She looked at Blake and smiled a wide toothy grin. "Rather not say on phone, sir."

" Good idea. Well, whatever it is, step back. Stick to protocol."

"Yes sir. Of course, sir." She hung up the phone and quickly dialed again. It only took a few moments to make the other calls. When she pressed 'End' she looked Blake directly in the eye. "We have twenty minutes 'till the Cavalry arrives. Open it."

"You don't want to wait?"

"Hell no. I want pictures. I want details. Details I may miss with 30 people in the damn room. Open it." she demanded.

Blake grinned. "I knew there was a reason I called you." He bent forward once again and sliced through the tape. Inside nestled in a bed of green grass was a dark red cylindrical object.

"Is that grass?" Timber asked.

"It would appear that way." He ran his fingertips across the tips of the grass. "Feels real but I'm wearing latex and well…"

She raised an eyebrow and he continued. "It looks like it's a root system, like it's actually a patch of sod." He reached his gloved hand inside and gingerly pulled out the item inside.

Timber peered at the odd thing looking for details, traits that would give away the sender's identity. It appeared to be a red apple, stem and two tiny leaves included. She couldn't tell from her vantage point the material, maybe ceramic or glass. In the middle of her musing, Blake tilted the apple and the movement shifted a thick liquid inside. The apple wasn't red; it was a thick hollow apple, filled with what looked like a lot of blood.

Chapter Five

The body was placed exactly where the 'X' had told them to look. The two officers, Sebastian and Cable, had secured the scene and called the Medical examiner before Blake and Timber arrived. Upon discovering the second 'X', they had both scrambled to get patrolmen on site to check it out. Both had been hoping for radio silence. No news is always good news. When the first crackle came over the radio they were so engrossed in the blood-filled apple seated in the patch of grass, they were startled.

"Detective Blake, Patrolman Cable here. We have an adult male on scene, 'D.R.T.' The young man's voice was strong and clear. No mistaking it. The slang that cops used may seem insensitive to the average person, but to cops the proclamation was old hat. The patrolman's statement that the latest victim was dead right there was read loud and clear by both Timber and Blake.

"Well, fucky, fuck, fuck!" Timber said and slipped into her brown leather jacket.

Several of the crime scene techs now preparing to move the mysterious item looked up at her, amused. She had been desperately hoping that the second 'X' was just a goose chase, a perpetrator sending them chasing their tails. This seemed too soon. Escalation like this usually didn't happen in the beginning. Only a little over a week had passed since they had both stood looking down at the mutilated corpse represented by the larger of the two red 'X'es.

"Guys, bag and tag this mess and type that blood. I want to know what the hell is in that apple ASAP."

The CSI standing closest to Blake glanced at her.

"Oh, sorry." she said. "Just do it and call Blake with the results." She wasn't accustomed to being second on a case with local police.

When the guy still looked to Blake for confirmation, Blake nodded and sat down heavily in his chair, shaking his head in dismay "I had a quiet night planned. I was really looking forward to heating up some pasta and watching a little *'Family Guy'*." He lifted the radio and spoke in authoritative tones. "Contain the scene, follow procedure, I'm on the way." He let go of the talk button and slipped the device into his belt clip.

Timber said "I prefer *'South Park'*. She moved through the door and Blake followed, laughing. "You would, they all talk like you."

"Nah, I'm much worse. And anyway, you should be watching it, too. Those are local boys, gotta show support to the local talent." Timber passed the elevator doors and headed for the stairwell.

Blake followed and looked longingly at the elevator doors as he passed. "Bullshit!" he said "You watch that show because it's the most politically incorrect crap on TV"

"Fine! Like you don't watch *'Family Guy'* for similar reasons?" she challenged as she took the stairs two at a time.

Blake watched as her firm bottom moved with each long step. "Hell yeah, I watch *'American Dad'* for the same reason. But we were talking about you, not me."

"Ah," she said as she made the last step in a long leap and turned to face him.

Blake came up short, almost slamming into her.

She looked up into his face and sneered, her blue eyes snapping "Yeah, we wouldn't want the subject to land on you." Her back pressed into the door, pushing it open, and the distance between them increased in more ways than one.

Confused by how quickly the air between them had thickened, Blake opened his mouth but quickly shut it again. He never knew the right thing to say; best to keep things professional. That's what she wanted. *Women!* he thought and slowed his step to stay behind her. The view is better here.

Ω

Twenty minutes later they drove up to the site. Crime scene tape was being placed and the medical examiner had arrived. Suzette Meeker was a tall, broad-boned, albino, black woman. She was the descendant of a long line of law enforcement professionals. Attorneys, cops, judges and even a few feds peppered her lineage. Amazingly, not one of those had the creamy white skin or the stark white hair of Suzette. The texture of her long dread locks was an effect of her heritage. This startling configuration was held together as always in a thick leather band. She was kneeling over the body creating a striking picture of peculiarity and extremes.

As they approached, Suzette looked up at them and the twinkle in her pale eyes belied the casualty that lay before her. "Well, well." she smirked "I wouldn't have believed it if I wasn't looking right at you. Did you two just emerge from the same vehicle?"

"Come on, Zet." Timber said imploring her friend to stop what she was implying. "Let it go."

Suzette smiled showing large, straight teeth and one not so straight one, just to the right of center. She called it her witch's fang and refused to have it fixed. She loved to say that someone as perfect as she should have one flaw. Zet had always been able to make Timber laugh, but looking at the man lying on the broken pavement, she wasn't in a jovial mood.

"Well" Zet said, looking from Timber to Blake and back again "You can bet all the royal jewels that I will not let it go," she shrugged "But for now…"

Timber heaved a big sigh of relief as they all squatted down in tandem. "Okay, my initial finding is poisoning." Suzette said.

"What?" Blake asked, confused.

"No way." Timber chimed in.

"Really?" Blake asked stupidly.

"Man, that's weird." Timber said and looked at Blake.

"I know" He was nodding his head and making varied confused grunts and mumblings.

"Why, am I suddenly not speaking the native tongue? Don't people get poisoned in your line of work?" Zet asked.

Before Timber could respond, Blake stepped in and said "The last body was stabbed and cut up, genitals removed, eyes burned out."

"So? Different killer." she stated matter-of-factly

"Yes," Timber said. "Has to be." Even as she said it, she knew that was the wrong track.

"Sorry, guys." Zet was looking at Timber who could see that Zet was aware of a greater confusion. "This poor guy wasn't stabbed or shot. I can't be sure till I get him to the morgue, but there is evidence of poison."

Timber said "Oh. Did you look at his dick?"

Blake laughed and Zet raised her eyebrows, "I always enjoy your couth, Agent Byrne, Yes, I did a preliminary check and as far as I can tell he still retains all of his parts."

"Weird" she said

"You said that already," Zet replied. She smiled and said "So I'll take him with me, do a tox and call you as soon as I have results. I'll do him first thing tomorrow."

"Thanks Suzette" Blake said, "I appreciate the priority"

"Are you kidding? The sooner I have the answers, the sooner you two will tell me all the details."

"Well it's simple." Blake started "I found a box and..."

She cut him off "No, Not that. I wanna know about this." Her finger wagged from him to Timber and back again.

Timber groaned, turned on her heel and headed for the car. "You coming, Blake? Or am I leaving your skinny ass here?"

She choked down a laugh when he said "Hey! I'm not skinny!"

Chapter Six

Timber sat in the chair across from Blake. He watched her as she ticked off the reasons that she believed there would be more killings. "It's obvious this is the same unidentified subject. I mean, come on! A moron could see it. The map on the box should cinch it. The weirdness of the first body is directly linked to the apple."

"Why are you so worked up?" he asked, finding it odd that she was reacting so strongly to a case. Despite the depravity he knew she dealt with on a consistent basis, here she was behaving as if this were a personal attack.

"I'm not sure… Wait! I know. You're an asshole," she said, squinting at him.

"What's that about?"

"You know what."

"No, really. I have zero idea why you're so pissed." He didn't and as the day got shorter so did his patience.

She grabbed her jacket and turned toward the door. "Does this look familiar?" she asked and put her hand on the knob.

"Hey!" He stood, slamming his hands down on the top of the desk. "Are you saying I walked out?"

She stopped and turned. "Amnesia? Surely it wasn't that long ago." She sneered at him. "We had sex and then you walked out. Wait… more like ran."

Memories swept past, elusive yet vivid. "I called you that night and hour after…"

She cut him off. "Yeah, I remember. I think you said 'Thanks for a great night. I hope you had fun'."

His mouth fell open slightly. "You remember what I said?"

"Yes. I'll never forget it. I also remember the next time we talked, because it was five days later!"

His gut twisted. "Yes, I remember. You told me you didn't have time for me, or something bizarre like that. We had a great night and then you lost your freaky little mind."

She started to respond and he stopped her.

"No! You're going to listen to me. I waited to be with you, I was patient, I was tolerant. I put up with your crap on the job. Then, Eureka, finally!" He raised his arms in the air. "Finally! We hook up. Let me assure you I will never forget it." Images from those moments flashed in his mind's eye making the words burn in his throat. "But, that's all I got. You shut me down so fast that I felt the wind in my hair. Since that day, you have acted like I broke some cardinal law. Tell me Byrne, what was my crime? Wanting you? Needing you? Having you? Or was it the fact that I made you scream?"

While he was talking, she stood. Blake was sure she would begin a tirade explaining her behavior and in the process making him feel guilty for some imaginary transgression. She opened the door and walked through it, saying over her shoulder just loud enough for it to reach his ears. "You made me cry."

The door closed with a loud click and Robin Blake stood with his hands splayed open on the desktop. His mouth was slightly open, his back straight and tense. He could feel the anger, confusion, and stunned dismay raging around inside his skull. Trying to wrap his mind around the idea that he had actually hurt her was almost too much to handle. For a long time after, he was bitter and then he had been hurt. Now, every time he saw her he was reminded of all that could have been and never was. Also, for what was and how quickly it had disappeared. The idea that there was something he'd missed was difficult to take. The confusion at the time had been paramount. Had he caused the rift? Had he done some stupid guy thing and lost his chance at…?

"No!" He slammed his fist against the desk. He hadn't done anything. He had followed the rules. Yet, somehow in the midst of it all, he had hurt her. His jaw clenched as he imagined tears slipping from her big blue eyes. The vision made him want to kill the cause of those tears. The problem was, according to her, he was the one, the cause, the asshole that had made her cry.

"Damnit!" Blake ran his hands through his hair. That time in his life had been dark. Not long after the rift opened up between him and Timber, his most devastating investigation knocked the breath from him. Blake had watched a colleague almost lose her life, because of his incompetence. Although no one held him accountable, Blake felt it was his slow deductive approach that ultimately led to the catastrophic assault of a fellow cop. Now, as he looked back, he realized he may have been blinded by those events. He considered what would have happened if his night with Timber had happened at any other time. He was disgusted when the realization hit him. If he hadn't been so wrapped up, he would never have let her walk away. He would have fought to keep her in his life. That knowledge took his knees out from under him and he fell back in his chair. He couldn't change the past, but he swore, as soon as the case was closed, he would alter the future. Robin Blake had no intention of letting Timber Byrne walk out of his life a second time.

Chapter Seven

A Colt automatic pistol lay on the small glass table surrounded by miniature tea-light candles. The silver handle glinted with the reflection of the tiny ginger flames. Payton sat between the legs of a common-sized man with the hairiest back she had ever seen. His ass arched in the air in an attempt to convince her to touch it. She almost laughed. The absurdity of the situation was a little too much to bear. Her mind began to wonder, as it often did at times like these. A trick of compartmentalization she had learned early in life. The man lying on his stomach enjoyed the touch of her fingers as they glided over his hairy skin. Payton wasn't thinking about adding to his pleasure; she was thinking about how bizarre it was that he hadn't noticed the gun. Initially she considered hiding it, but the idea of having it sitting out in plain sight was too tempting to pass up. She hadn't really planned on what she would say if he did notice.

The idea of shrugging her shoulders and pretending like it was the most normal thing ever to have a handgun sitting out on display was intriguing. *After all, aren't we in America?* She grinned at the idea of what his face would have looked like. How long would he have stared at the offending weapon before he decided a naked girl was more appealing than the fear of a small gun sitting innocently on a pretty table, surrounded by tiny candles? Unfortunately, he had walked in, took one look at her full red lips and tight little body and overlooked everything else. His clothes hit the floor hastily and soon his hairy ass was high in the air, completely unaware that he could be in danger. In what galaxy had it become safe to call an ad in the paper, speak to a total stranger, make a deal, go to a location of the stranger's choice, give that person money, get naked and give up all your power, in the hopes that at some point, you may get laid?

A condom sat on the table next to the gun. Payton couldn't remember in what textbook she had read that a condom was as good as a silencer. She sat the condom next to the gun hoping that if he noticed the gun he would also notice the condom. If it should have happened, it could have gone two ways. He would see the gun, then see the condom and have to make a decision: sex or death? There was also a chance that he would see the condom and react badly. Maybe he read the same book or web site that she had. Maybe he would know she planned to slip that condom over the end of the gun and not his tiny little dick. Considering all of the funny things that she could have said were making her feel a little giddy. Sometimes just imagining a thing could cause a rush of adrenaline to begin. Her heart began to speed up with just a glimpse of those possible scenarios.

The loud snore startled her and then made her giggle. Only moments before, the bastard had been wriggling his ass and now he was snoring. She pressed her palm into his lower back and used it as leverage to slide off of the bed without rubbing her naked buttocks across his legs. There was little fear of waking him. The dose she had given him was enough to keep him down for a few hours. She hadn't wanted to go overboard, especially after the last time. The sedative she found on the Internet was perfect for sedation, but not so great for murder. After the previous disgusting event, Payton went back online; sure she must have done something wrong. She was embarrassed by the discovery that she had not done the appropriate amount of research. The drug she chose clearly stated all of the unfortunate side effects. Ick! She shivered, remembering.

He snored again and she turned up the volume on her iPod. Harry Nisson's voice rang throughout the small space, explaining how it was important to put the lime in your coconut and drink it all up. She slipped the condom onto the barrel of the gun. Her hips began to sway to the Cajun rhythm of the upbeat song.

Bob, the sleeping man, was snoozing with his mouth open, a trickle of spittle sliding onto the sheet under his face. She grabbed a pillow and laid it gently over his head. She set the gun down on the pillow and went into the bathroom to pee. As she sat down, she wondered if the process would get easier. The relieving of her bladder didn't calm her or make her heart beat any slower. She slipped on a cotton tee-shirt and panties and returned to Bob and his hairy back.

She climbed onto him, her rear pressing into the hollow just above his ass and picked up the gun. She pointed it at the pillow, just above where his head would be, rose up on her knees for a better angle and pulled the trigger. The concussion of the gun was loud. The recoil jerked her wrists exactly as she knew it would. The condom hadn't worked as well as the book had implied. The pillow took much of the impact noise. Blood gushed from the side of the bed as if the mattress were hemorrhaging. The smell of urine and gun smoke filled the small space.

"Gross!" She groaned and shivered, cleaning up was always the worst part.

Chapter Eight

"So, what is the current situation with you and Robin?" Suzette was standing over the body of a middle-aged white male cadaver, his balding scalp peeled back to reveal the skull underneath. A white mask covered her mouth muffling her words slightly. She held a small electric tool in her left hand. The blade was circular and looked like a torture device in one of the horror movies that were so popular these days.

Timber smiled at her friend and made a disgusted sound before saying, "Doesn't anything distract you?"

"Well, normally, I am prone to distraction, but how could I pass up anything as juicy as this?"

"Liar." Timber said, knowing that the woman before her was distraction proof. The medical examiner could focus on a problem while contemplating ten others, all the while dissecting a corpse as if she were casually preparing a meal.

To punctuate her point, Suzette flipped a switch and the blade on the small tool began to spin with a dull, whirring noise.

Timber remained by the door a few feet away. She raised her voice above the noise. "Couldn't you wait to do that?" She let a small whine enter her voice.

"No." Suzette said, as metal met bone and the sound changed.

Timber pressed her shoulder blades against the wall, crossed her legs at the ankles and waited. She was always amazed at the ability to deal with all of the muck that was left over when a person died. Timber had no problem looking at the aftermath, analyzing it and categorizing it.

What she could not do was cut it open and see what was inside.

Zet on the other hand, had always been fascinated with the destruction of the human body. Knowing how it all worked was enough for her. She had to see it, feel it and cut it open. Timber watched as Zet switched off the skull saw and gingerly lifted away a triangle of bone. "Ah..." she breathed dramatically. "The core of man." She said and looked up at Timber. Suzette slid her mask down so that it was resting on her throat and smiled, showing of her slightly imperfect grin. "So, are you going to gossip or is this visit all business?"

"Business." Timber stated with flat affect. She didn't want to discuss how confused she was and she knew if she was not very careful, the woman staring at her would see through her and dig at her open wound. It was difficult to focus on her calm expression. She was relieved when the other woman looked away.

"You, my dear, are a true killer of fun" Suzette said, with a knowing smirk on her lips.

"So I hear!" Timber snapped, irritated. "What did you find?"

"Well, in number one," she said, referring to the first victim, "we have COD as stabbing. The fatal wound was through the bone and into the heart."

"Ouch." Timber said and added, "Simple." By the damage done to the body, she had been certain death had taken a tad longer and been far more complicated. She felt some relief for the victim.

Suzette was shaking her white dreadlocks in subtle denial. "By that time, shock had set in. There were seventy-two stab wounds. Some with hesitation marks."

"Oh," Timer's heart sank. "You don't think the fatal wound came first?"

Suzette frowned. "Can't say for sure; they all happened in rapid succession. But hesitation marks usually come first, so…" She looked at Timber, letting her come to her own conclusions.

"Okay, so… maybe not as angry as we first assumed." Timber said.

"That was my take, although, the overkill was dramatic."

"Strange." Timber was calculating the evidence with what she knew.

Zet interrupted her musings, her tone casual "It gets stranger."

"Great."

"There were two places where flesh was excised, the groin and the breast tissue."

"Uh huh," Timber nodded; she knew this from the crime scene.

"And," Suzette continued, "we found the groin tissue in his throat."

"Let me guess, the rest was in his stomach?" Timber asked.

"Not quite." Suzette said and stepped to the side of the body. She placed a sharp blade at the center of the chest and pressed down. The skin began to open in a straight line. No blood accompanied the slice. The heart of the poor man had long ago stopped supplying the pressure needed to push the dark life force through his vascular system.

"What?" Timber asked, fascinated as always, by the bizarre sight.

"Well, there was also significant damage to the trachea and the esophagus. I found wood splinters throughout along with the remainder of the missing tissue."

"Wood?" Timber felt her stomach tighten before she brushed the prevailing images from her mind.

"I'm no detective, but I could guess that a wooden handle of some kind, maybe a broom was used to shove the tissue down his throat."

"Was he alive?" she asked, her face twisting with expectation. Even after all of her time on the job, she still could not contain her emotions. Whatever she was feeling invariably showed on her fine features, leaving little of her thought processes to the imagination. Too late she wiped away the expression and cringed when her old friend laughed knowingly.

"Not for most of it, thankfully," Suzette said and continued. "The first bite went down while he was dying. Blood was still flowing when the tissue was excised."

"This fucker is seriously sick!" Timber said. "And now, what about door number two?"

"Well, oddly enough, I was correct on my initial finding; poison."

"Really?" Although the initial guess had been poison, Timber was sure the M.E. had been wrong. The idea that a killer could change his mode of operations was not completely foreign, but it was rare and it never reversed in intensity.

"Yes, Ma'am. Simple, good old-fashioned poison, slipped into red wine, the oldest party trick around," Suzette confirmed.

"Digression," Timber mused. "Any chance that the order is wrong?" she said, grasping at a random straw.

"Nope." Suzette countered, "Number one died first."

"What the hell?"

"Don't know a thing about hell, but I can tell you the how. The blade for number one was twelve-inch butcher knife with a thick serrated blade and a slanted tip. Two was chloral hydrate. A few drops can cause sedation and unconsciousness."

"Have you checked number one for the drug?"

"Yes, ran tox, clean."

"So we have an executioner that starts out with a bloody slaying and escalates to a nice gentle poisoning?"

"Well, if it's any help it wasn't exactly gentle." Suzette said.

"No?"

"No. There would have been nausea; confusion, vomiting some bleeding and loss of bladder and bowel control; all before unconsciousness occurred."

"Nasty." Timber grimaced, imagining the macabre death.

"Very. It's not a pleasant way to go. The cardiac arrhythmia associated with overdose can be… well," she shrugged, "not fun."

"Wow! You," Timber pointed at Zet, "are eloquent," she said sarcastically, then asked, "Any fibers? Hairs? Did crime techs get anything useful?"

"No, the body appears to have been cleaned."

"That's just fucked! I hate a neat criminal." Timber complained.

"Maybe the mess offended your killer."

"Unfortunately, that could be the case. Was the other one cleaned?"

"No. Just the vomiter."

"Okay. I'll call Blake and fill him in." Timber said.

"No need. He was here at six." Suzette looked up, gauging Timber's reaction.

Timber failed the test and asked, exasperated, "This morning?"

"Well, since six p.m. hasn't arrived yet …Yeah."

"Smart ass! Robin was here at six in the morning?" Timber asked, shocked and a little pissed.

Zet shook her head, a small white lock falling over her pale shoulder. "Didn't we just do this?"

"Shut up! He didn't call me." Timber said, after all of his whining about how he needed her and now... She pushed down her anger before she let too much show.

"I figured as much when you waltzed in." Suzette said, just loud enough to hear.

"I don't waltz!" Timber snapped.

"You're right, I meant strutted."

"Fuck off, Zet!" She turned and headed for the door. There wasn't much more here and she needed to think about what had transpired so far. Suzette's voice stopped her before she pressed her palm into the iron door.

"Okay. Hey, wanna grab lunch?" Suzette asked.

"Sure." Timber said, the idea suddenly sounding very appealing. Suzette had been great at brainstorming for as long as she could remember. The issue would keep her off the topic of Robin Blake.

"All right. Let me clean up and I'll meet you."

"Where?" Timber asked

"Let's do Fresh Fish. I love their crab cakes."

"Okay, but I'm not talking about Robin," Timber said, her face serious and set in a frown.

"Yes, you are." Suzette said confidently.

"No, I'm not."

"Yes, you are."

"See you in twenty," Timber said, waving away the silly back and forth.

"Twenty-five, I need to jump in the shower and wash the dead off me."

"Lovely."Timber pushed through the door and left the acrid smells behind her.

Chapter Nine

Grady looked at the report in his hands. "Poisoned?"

Blake nodded and wondered if this seasoned federal agent had any real answers. "Yeah. Strange, right? You ever known a serial to change in mid-flight?"

Grady shook his head confirming his own thoughts. "No. And he's not a serial. If this is the same guy, it's still only two."

"Well, it's a certainty that it's the same guy. There were two indicators on the original contact map. One was where we found vic. number one and the other we found poisoned guy," he said, indicating the map tacked to the evidence board.

"Okay." Grady conceded. "We know it's the same guy, but we have no real evidence. No connection. That mark on that piece of paper is flimsy at best. And serials aren't serials until there are three."

Blake grumbled. He knew the deal. He'd run into this kind of bureaucracy before. It still frustrated the hell out of him.

"Anyway," Grady continued, "you should be happy as long as they're not connected and there isn't another. You're still lead."

"I don't give a fuck about that and you know it." Blake snapped.

"You know, I heard rumors that there was a detective that cared more about solving the case than his own self interest. Can't say I believe such an animal exists."

Now Blake was getting pissed off. This wasn't the first time he'd gotten flack for doing the right thing, the just thing, even if it slowed him down.

"Look," he said, ignoring the agent's last comments. Sometimes convincing others of your intentions just wasn't worth the time. He believed in actions. Soon enough, Special Agent in Charge, John Grady would realize just what kind of cop he was. In the meantime he'd try to ignore his ignorant comments and obvious oversights. "I know all the signs. Overkill, displaying the body where it could easily be found, making contact, giving us a map to vic number two. This is a serial and we need a task force. The bodies are going to start piling up and we need to be prepared."

Grady shrugged. "Body three comes in and you get your task force. Until then, work with your team and keep Byrne in the loop if you want. That way, when and if …" he paused and shrugged. "She's already up to speed."

"So you really want me to sit on my hands until someone else is dead?" he said angrily.

"No, Detective, I want you to do your job. Investigate, solve the murder, and put the bad guy away."

"You know that's not an issue. I'm doing my job, but we don't have the resources you have. The computer techs, the profilers, the manpower needed to do what needs to be done quickly."

"Man oh man." Grady whistled through his teeth and ran his hand over his round gut. His thumb dug in under the roll of fat at his waist and hooked into his belt. "I have never met or laid my eyes on a detective so hot to work with us stuck-up feebs."

Blake knew the FBI got a terrible rap. Most guys on the job hated them. They wore nice suits and were better educated. Shit, most of them were lawyers so they knew the law in a way that cops couldn't even contemplate. Plus, they made more money and the public actually liked their image. As he looked at the man before him Blake couldn't understand the bullshit of that perception.

It wasn't until much later he watched a hot-tempered blonde burst into his office that he faced the real reason he was so hot to get a task force going and why Grady's attitude was so irksome.

Ω

"Hey, so why ya going behind my back, Sherlock?" Timber said, addressing Robin Blake. Timber wasn't really angry about anything. After having drinks with Zet, she actually felt relaxed and somewhat malleable. This was a state that she was generally unfamiliar with. The venting session had done a world of good. Her typical high-strung feelings were smoothed out by a few glasses of Merlot and a walk down memory lane. As much as she had assured her friend that she would not discuss her love life that is exactly what she had done. For a full hour Timber had vented about how the sexy detective had brushed her off and then sent her mixed signals, before finally ignoring her completely. Maybe Freud hadn't been as nuts as all of his contemporaries claimed. She wasn't ready to analyze her dreams or talk about her oral fixations, talking really had turned out to be cathartic.

Timber had previously been unaware of her need for a sympathetic ear. The beauty of the situation was that Zet seemed to sense this and refused to allow her the senseless glory of wallowing under her carpet of denial. They drank and talked, snacked on shrimp cocktail and pâté. It was precisely the atmosphere Timber had been desperate for. She wasn't looking to relive the experience any time soon, but it had certainly done the job for now. A genuine smile turned up the corners of her mouth and she felt none of the usual confusion that came with the simple action.

"I always saw myself more along the lines of Mike Hammer," Robin said, looking at her with a bit of confusion on his face.

Timber found it funny and wondered at his expression. "Really? Mike is so rough and such a dog."

"I can be a dog." he said, still searching her face.

"No, you can't." Then she remembered that he could be and she shook her head and laughed. "Oh yeah, you can, but not 'Hammer' dog."

"I really don't know what that means."

"So how come you were all super spy this morning?" she asked, feeling light and breezy. She could see how high-strung personalities became alcoholics. The tranquil factor alone would be worth many of the horrible side effects.

"Super spy?"

Timber had never noticed before how much he seemed to enjoy pushing her buttons. Without effort, the smile remained on her face as his slipped even further away. "Why didn't you tell me you went to the morgue?"

"This is the first time I've seen you. Plus, officially, you're not on this."

She ignored the last part, choosing not to take the bait. "Awesome, tell me now." She pulled out a chair giving her legs room to stretch and fell back into a high-backed chair in front of his desk. She stretched her jean-clad legs, crossed her black boots at the ankles and waited. She watched as he took her lead, walked around the desk and sat in his chair. He made the space look less huge. His desk, a family heirloom passed down from father to son, was far too big for the office, but with Blake sitting behind the oak monstrosity, it didn't look so ridiculous. Timber could tell he was shaken by her casual attitude and his inability to cause any reaction this time.

He said, "I was having a hard time sleeping, so I decided to stop fighting it. I got up early, didn't want to interrupt your beauty sleep so I left you alone." He slid a notepad across the desk and said. "Notes."

She stayed where she was and said "Talk, I don't wanna read."

"Say please."

"Please." Timber added a sexy smile to her lips.

Eyes full of suspicion; he asked "What is wrong with you?"

"Nothing, I'm just feeling relaxed and I'm not allowing you to irritate me."

"I always irritate you," he said and leaned forward, examining her face.

"Not today" she assured him. She realized he didn't believe her and it showed, but she had bitched about this man for over an hour, felt vented and was almost over it. Not completely over it, but enough to let it go. Maybe it was that time.

"Are you drunk?" he smiled, relaxing. He leaned his elbows on the oak surface and looked at his notes. "I'll read."

"What? Why would you ask that?" she said and sank deeper into the soft chair.

He pointed at her with his entire hand, the index only slightly in front of the other four "Oh my god! You are." He was obviously amused, yet she remained calm.

"Nah," she denied. "I'm just relaxed."

"How many glasses of wine did you have while you were relaxing?"

"You're such a know-it-all."

"No. I just know you."

"Just read!"

He shook his head in dismay and began to read aloud. "Cable and Sebastian did a canvas of both body dumps, no witnesses." He continued to eye her suspiciously.

What's wrong with having a glass of wine? Timber thought, trying to focus; after all she wasn't working today. It was supposed to be her day off. She wouldn't even be here if she hadn't found out he went behind her back. Plus, he was right. She wasn't even on this one. She had her own cases – no evidence, no witnesses.

"Surprise, surprise." Timber really hadn't expected any evidence of significance. Bodies were usually dumped for a reason. Blake read and she listened to the details she already knew. Sometimes repetition could lead to something.

"The first was a forty-six-year- old American Indian-Asian mixed heritage. The guy was basically an Americanized melting pot. He was a computer tech from Ohio, here on business for two weeks. Vic two: thirty-three-year-old Caucasian. Trust fund baby; spends his days playing golf and enjoying the local county clubs. He owns a home in Hawaii and is only here through the holidays. Had a few locals as ex-wives."

No new insights revealed themselves and despite her wine-induced relaxation, she began to feel hollow. "Guess he's gonna miss them this year."

"Good guess." Blake said

"Bummer." Timber mumbled; "Kids here?" she asked.

"Yeah, both; but no connection."

"Damn! You're sure?" she said, hoping to stumble upon something.

"As sure as I can be. Different schools, different friends; so far nothing, but the digging continues."

"Who's on this?" Timber asked

"I told you."

"No, which dick?"

"I wish I knew what you meant when you ask that."

"You do." She disliked both of the detectives currently assigned to the case; she trusted Blake and his instincts were good, so she allowed for the discomfort. Plus she didn't hate bossing around guys that pissed her off.

"It's Carter, he's handling Cable, Sebastian and Peterson." Blake said.

"I think we should try and find a connection between these families." she suggested.

"That's a long shot"

Timber nodded, "Yep, most of them are."

"What about with the map?" Blake asked.

"It's at the lab now. I am really crossing my fingers on that front."

"Think there's something there?"

Timber thought about the night she first looked at the strange scribbles on the aged paper. They were both so transfixed by the 'x marks the spot' and its significance, they may have let something more subtle slip by. "Maybe. If there is something, the lab will find it."

"Hope you're right."

She snickered "Usually am."

He shook his head and flipped the small notebook closed. "I have a chain of custody listed for the sod and the blood. I need a report on those as soon as…"

"Got it." She interrupted. "There with the map and the box, it was a package deal." She immediately saw the pun and snickered again, "Hey, I'm really funny today."

Blake didn't seem convinced.

She pulled her legs in and sat up straighter. "You really are not any fun at all today." she whined and stood up, bracing herself on the edge of the desk.

"I don't think I've ever been fun as far as you are concerned." Blake said

"Now, that's just not true." Timber knew she was swimming near a waterfall. She needed to get out of this office before she climbed up on the desk and grabbed his hair, forcing him to kiss her the way she remembered he could. He was leaning forward, deep dark eyes searching hers when she realized how pregnant with tension the air had become. She turned abruptly and walked to the door suddenly feeling sober and a little confused. "I'll call you as soon as I know anything."

When she grabbed the door handle his concerned voice slowed her for a single step, "You're not gonna drive, are you?" Then she pushed through the door and shut it behind her without responding. She would have yelled a 'fuck off' over her shoulder, but she was still wrapped up in her fantasy of his kiss and she was afraid her voice would crack from unexpressed tension.

Chapter Ten

Carter looked at the students all gathering inside the classroom getting ready for the lecture. He tried to focus on the topic for today's class and kept finding his mind wandering. A beautiful young student sat in the front row. Her long blonde hair was pulled back in a tight ponytail; small strands cascaded over her forehead brushing the tops of her eyelashes. Green eyes, full pink lips, high cheekbones and creamy pale skin created a startling amalgamation. He had been finding it more and more difficult to concentrate lately. There were strict rules against fraternizing with students, yet he desperately wanted to break the antiquated regulation.

As Carter began to speak his eyes repeatedly wandered in her direction. Invariably she was paying attention to his every word, locked in on him, focused and attentive. While the other students whispered amongst themselves, took notes or just doodled on their otherwise empty paper, she was watching him. Whenever he managed to look away he would feel the pull of her green gaze. At times when their eyes locked, he felt the room melt away and it was as if he were speaking directly and only to her.

The topic for this class was the psychologies of the aberrant mind, primarily the sociopath and the serial killer. This was a topic that usually filled his classroom. Fascination with serial killers had become popular in recent years and the influx of criminally-based television shows and serial-murder movies had filled the criminal justice departments in most universities across the country. His classes were no exception. Carter loved being a professor. He enjoyed sharing his knowledge with intelligent inquisitive minds.

For fifteen years Carter Graydon had been an active member of the Denver Metropolitan Police Department. His title and pay grade had changed over the years, but his passion and dedication to the job never had. Now teaching part time, his eyes had been opened to a whole new world and he looked forward to slowing down. Spending more time in the classroom and less time on the job was a pleasure he found almost decadent. He held a masters degree in Criminology and a Ph.D. in Psychology, a title he did not use. He preferred Detective. A young co-ed once told him it was sexier than Doctor.

As Carter moved across the floor, speaking and interacting with his students, he was constantly aware of the beautiful woman that sat in the front row. He wondered if he would ever get over his need to taste the delicacies his secondary career offered him. He was contemplating this when the pager on his phone began to vibrate. The code for a homicide flashed on the dark screen. Looking around the room he located his TA and waved the tall young man over. As he explained the situation he noticed the pretty blonde staring at him. It wasn't hard to figure out what her eyes were suggesting. Maybe he could wrap up the scene and pawn off his paperwork on a rookie. The dead asshole lying in a ditch somewhere didn't care if he got some pussy before closing the case. After all, he wasn't going to suddenly wake up, was he?

Chapter Eleven

The phone pealed in his ear as he raced down I-25 South. The call was for a 187, homicide, possible gunshot. Gang-related was the buzz. It had been a few days and his gut was saying it wasn't that cut and dried. The last homicide was discovered at approximately the same time. The neighborhood was upscale and an alley shootout was not a typical crime scene in Jackson Farms Estates.

Blake let the phone ring until the machine answered and then he hung up and hit redial. He did this three times before the voice he was waiting for came on the line. "Why is it always about interrupting my sleep? Don't you have any reverence for sleep?"

"No, I really don't. Why are you asleep so early?" he smiled into the phone as usual, picturing her while they spoke. He never pictured what she was now. He pictured her then: pliable, sweet, almost needy. Not what she had become; angry, defensive and difficult. Her voice when newly awake, she was unguarded and reminded him of the past. He sighed and let the image of her slip away. "I am headed to a possible body dump in Jackson Farm."

"Jackson Farm?" Her voice was ramping up now, adding the edge she had sharpened it to. "Are you sure it's a dump and not a leave? Maybe it's a domestic."

"Maybe." He waited knowing what the next question would be.

"Got hint to COD yet?"

"Gunshot."

"In Jackson Farm? You sure?"

"That seemed off to me, too."

"How far out are you?"

"Ten."

"I'm on my way, text me the address and don't let Zet run off with the vic."

"Will do. See you there." Before he could press 'end' on the phone, she said "Blake?"

He was surprised by the almost whisper and automatically responded in kind. "Yeah?"

"Thanks for the call; I know you didn't have to do that. Not yet."

Before he could answer the line went dead, leaving him wondering what he would have said. The woman was a complete conundrum. If he was too kind, she didn't respect him. If he responded too sharply, she acted wounded; and if he ignored her she became combative. He had decided long ago, avoidance was the only answer. Unfortunately, he could not avoid her now and he knew that she was going to over think her response and arrive on scene, irritated by her lapse into kindness. He groaned as he slowed his car, pulled into the taped-off lot and typed in the address, hitting send. She would arrive soon.

Blake stepped from the car and felt the gravel move under his feet. The parking lot was old. In an area where everything was new and rebuilt, this was a throwback to darker times. This neighborhood was high end but it hadn't always been. Was it possible the creep was familiar with the neighborhood and would know the perfect dump spot? If you were looking for a dump this would be it: dark, no street lamps and no views from the streets nearby. Two big dumpsters in a line blocked the view. As he came around the corner, flashlights and standing lamps lit the scene. Patrolmen were snapping shots, using markers for scale.

A detective was sketching the body, a measuring tape dangling from one of his Dockers' many pockets. As Blake walked up the man shook his head. "You trying to catch all the kills in town, Detective?"

"No, sir, I am not. Just checkin' out a theory." Blake said and took in the scene.

"That gut talking again?" Detective Graydon asked and walked over, gloved hand extended.

Blake gripped the other man's hand and nodded "Yeah, havin' a hard time shuttin' it up."

"Really? What's it tellin' you now?" Carter asked.

"I'm not ready to share. Are you?" Blake nodded toward the body lying face down on the broken pavement. When the detective didn't respond immediately, Blake assumed he was going to have some trouble. The man was powerful in the department and even though he was moonlighting as a professor at a local prestigious college, everyone knew he was dedicated and excellent at his job. As far as adversaries went, Detective Carter Graydon wasn't on the top of his list.

"Is that Charlene Morgan?" Carter asked.

He followed the detective's eye line, relieved that he was wrong about the detective's silence. Just as rapidly, relief ebbed away and emotional Drano retched on his Superman tie. Standing at the edge of the police tape, leaning as far as she could without falling over and holding a large camera in front of her face, was Charlie Morgan, reporter for the Denver Post.

Blake made a growling noise low in his throat and answered through his teeth. "Yes, the one and only. Is she the only press?" Blake asked

"So far." Carter answered and then added, "Where're you going?" as Blake walked toward the brazen redhead snapping pictures and wobbling on the heels of her imitation leather boots.

"Hey Charlie!" Blake yelled, "Put down the camera and come on over."

The camera came down and a big goofy grin spread over her face. "Can I get a few candids first?" she asked, excited anticipation in her tone.

"Not a great idea." Blake said. He was trying to keep his voice stern, but her excitement was humorous and he felt the corner of his lips starting to turn up. As much as he hated the press and despised the idea of dealing with them, at least this one he could anticipate. *Better the enemy you know ...*

"Come on, Detective, give a girl a break," she whined.

"You don't need a break. Anyway, I could have you thrown out," he threatened.

She laughed. "No, you can't! I'm behind the barricade and this is public property."

"Fine, stay there," he said and turned away.

"No! No, wait. I'll leave the camera. But are we on the record?" Charlie asked, and ducked under the tape.

"Not yet. Just talk."

Charlie smirked knowingly. "Great, let's talk. I've really missed our long talks."

Blake shot back, "Have I mentioned how much I love you guys down at the Post?" He gripped her upper arm and pulled her to the side of the tape that had very little view of the body beyond the dumpsters.

She craned her neck and tried to pull away. "What's up, really?" she asked, shuffling after him. Blake wanted to ask her why she was wearing five-inch heeled boots to cover a crime scene. Then he decided he didn't really want to know and said simply, "Dead guy."

"How?" she asked

"COD appears to be gun shot." Then he asked what was bothering him about Charlie's appearance on this particular scene. "This is small stuff. Why does the Post have you on this?"

"We heard something?" she said, guilt peppering her expression.

Blake shook his head in confusion. "Is that a question or an answer?"

"We heard something." she said, more definitively

"You heard what?" he asked, his curiosity piqued. A small feeling of dread was creeping into his consciousness.

What she said next twisted his gut and made him wish for a world without journalists. "That this is the third victim in a possible serial murder case." She spoke the words so fast he was about to ask her to repeat them when a southern accent with a distinctive tone rose over his left shoulder.

"Well fuck me! I'm a few minutes behind and you tell the press everything. Jesus, Blake, way to keep it close to the vest!" Timber accused.

Blake considered trying to explain her mistake and it occurred to him that she would figure it out without his help.

"So it's true?" Charlie said, her eyes darting from Blake to Timber. Her pupils enlarged and she looked like she was about to jump up and down.

He shook his head once and shot a dark look Timber's way. "We don't know anything at this point. And what I'm itching to figure is why you seem to know more than we do."

Timber followed the looks and asked "What? You didn't just spill?"

Blake turned on her and threw his hands into the air, his frustration starting to boil over. "No, brain trust! I didn't! You did! Congrats, maybe she'll use your name and you can be famous for leaking information about the creeper to the press."

"The creeper?" Charlie asked and slid a small silver recorder out of her pocket and held it up. Her thumb pressed a button and a small green light began flashing.

Before Blake could respond to the action Timber asked, "You gave him a name without me?"

Blake shook his head in dismay. He felt like he was playing the lead character in a farce, "Well, not officially..."

Charlie spoke up, pressing the device closer to Blake's face. "The 'creeper,' I like it. That's not what he calls himself though."

"What?" Timber and Blake asked in unison.

"Genesis," Charlie said simply. As Blake continued to stare at her open-mouthed, she said, "He says his name is Genesis and he's bloodthirsty."

"He who?" Blake said and snatched the recorder from her hand and slid it into his shirt pocket.

"Hey!" Charlie screamed and then shut her mouth tight, biting her bottom lip as he held up a finger to silence her.

He kept his voice low and level "How did you come by this knowledge and does it by any chance connect to your appearance here tonight?"

She nodded and made a pained face "I got the address from the letter sent to the Post," she said, using her speedy voice again.

Blake was dismayed, "You received a letter about a murder and you didn't call the police?"

Charlie shrugged and took a few steps back, crossing her arms in a defensive posture. "I thought it was a hoax. I checked with legal and they said I had already opened it, so I could check for validity and write my byline before I called."

"Where is this letter?" Blake hoped the intensity he felt was coming through in his tone. He wanted to spin her around and put handcuffs on her, stuff her into the back of a police car and send her downtown. He also wanted to wring her neck. Instead, he held out his hand and hoped for her sake she had something to place in it. For a moment, she held his stare, her arms crossed, her eyes flinty. He met her gaze and held. Quickly, her resolve began to dissolve and her hand dropped; she grunted as she pulled a Ziploc baggie out of her purse.

Blake snatched it from her grip and said "You cannot print this; it'll throw the city into a panic."

"Arrest her." Timber said, stepping between Blake and Charlie. Her hands were fisted at her waist. "That'll shut her up."

Blake agreed. He knew it would be a waste of time as he explained the obvious. " It would only be a few hours before her brother comes down, bails her out and writes an editorial about the Denver police stepping all over her first amendment rights."

"Blah, blah, blah! Timber responded "I'll arrest her under the Patriot Act and seal her up in a cell until we catch the fuck face and then I'll forget she's there until I have fat grandbabies and one of them happens to have red hair." Timber used her fingertips and fluffed her short locks mockingly. "Then I'll say, 'hey remember that red-headed bitch that tried to fuck with my case? Whatever happened to her?'" She leaned in and looked up at Charlie "How does that sound?"

The expression on Charlie's face slid from confident to confused, finally settling on amazed. "I get the point." she said and sneered.

Blake felt like laughing. It was moments like these when he remembered why he was so attracted to the tiny flaxen bombshell.

Timber made a satisfied sound "Good. Now blaze on out of here and be…"

Blake cut her off. "Oh no, she's not going anywhere."

"What? Why?" Charlie said, looking worried.

"Stick her in your car." Blake said to Timber, choosing not to explain. The single reason he had his irritation under control was the women's interaction. He needed time to get where he needed to be, without emotions juggling his thoughts like ping pong balls.

"Okay. Why?" Timber said as she slipped her handcuffs out of her back pocket and clicked one onto Charlie's wrist before she could pull away.

"Now why did you do that?" Charlie whined and shook her wrist.

Timber smiled and winked at Blake. "Don't worry, I'm going to leave the other one off and open. Take off and you have stolen federal property. Go sit in the passenger side of my car."

"That's sneaky."Charlie said snidely

Blake opened his mouth then shut it as they continued to banter. He turned and headed back to the body. As he walked he snickered. He was impressed at how easily Timber was able to handle any situation.

"Thanks."Timber said to Charlie, her voice full of pride.

"And you wonder why no one trusts the feds?" Charlie yelled, as she followed Timbers orders.

"I don't wonder." Timber mumbled as she jogged to catch up with Blake. He was still laughing under his breath as she stopped at his side.

"What's so funny?" she asked.

"Nothing."

"Okay, what is the COD?'

"Don't know yet." he said.

"Do you know anything?"

I know that you're beautiful and I want nothing more than to take you home and... He walked faster, trying to ignore her sweet smell. *What is that, cotton candy? God!* "I know that this is number three and I'm about to get my task force." he said.

"You know that?" she asked, thankfully oblivious to his reaction to her presence.

"Yep, thanks to your detainee."

"Don't you mean my task force?"

He knew she was right and he honestly didn't care who was in charge. But he couldn't let her know that, so he played the game. "Oh, shut it!"

"Shut it? Really?"

"Really." he said. "Your detainee is actually a godsend."

"I was considering that."

"It would have been difficult to connect this one without this letter." He patted his jacket where he slipped the baggie.

"How do you know that?"

"Well... look." They stepped into eye line of the M.E.

She looked, and as she took in the obvious, she said "Oh, wow, gunshot?"

"Looks like. Of course, we don't know anything till Zet gets her hands on him…"

"Where is she?" Timber looked at the medical examiner's jacket draped on the middle aged man she didn't recognize.

"It's her night off." Blake said.

"They get nights off?" It amused him how insulted she sounded, then he almost laughed as she said, "That's unfair."

"Yeah" he agreed halfheartedly as they approached the very dead body.

"He is really hairy," she stated flatly.

"It's making me itch." he said looking down at the man covered in black curly hair.

"Send field notes to me. We just caught this case. Sorry, Carter," Timber said.

Carter looked up from his notes. "No way. You saying this is part of those other two?"

"'Fraid so." Blake assured him.

"That sucks… for you… I am on my way back to…well, anywhere but here. Here ya go!" he tossed his notepad to Blake, who caught it saying, "No, no, no, you are first detective on scene, this is yours for tonight."

"That only works," Carter argued,"…if I'm assigned to…"

"Yep," Blake nodded, confirming the detective's thoughts.

"Come on, Blake!" Carter begged.

"I'm going to request you anyway, so just volunteer," Timber added.

"I'll volunteer tomorrow." Carter promised.

"Great." Blake said, happy that he got what he wanted so easily.

"See ya!" Carter yelled, as he jogged from the scene.

"Early, Carter!"

"Yeah, yeah!" he yelled over his shoulder.

"You sure told him." Timber mocked.

"Didn't I tell you to shut it?" Blake said.

"I'll go talk to the media mogul and you handle this. Come by after, we'll compare notes and call my SAC."

"Sounds great, Bossy." Blake stared down at the body. How could a person deal with that much body hair? He scratched his arm as a phantom itch occurred.

"You mean 'Boss'?" Timber said.

"Yeah that's what I meant," he said absently.

"Give me that letter."

"No way!" He turned and patted his pocket again, "Mine."

"Come on, don't be a baby. It'll be mine soon enough."

"I have trust issues, get over it. Go interview her. I won't be far behind."

"You mean interrogate?" she asked.

"Noooo..I mean interview. Keep in mind, that's Nick Devon's woman. I don't need the CIA raining hell fire on my honeymoon."

Chapter Twelve

"Look, I brought you here because of your personal affiliation with… someone I…respect." Timber threw her keys into the glass tray that also contained sunglasses and various coins from the bottom of her pockets.

Charlie stood in the doorway, a startled look on her face. She was holding out her hand with the pair of handcuffs dangling from her wrist. "You mean fear?" she said.

Timber turned from the overdressed reporter and laughed, mocking her. "I don't fear anyone and don't play dumb." Timber looked over her shoulder and took in the ridiculous sight. Why was she wearing that? Her purple sweater and black tights were over the top enough, but the thigh high stripper boots really topped it off.

"So, now you think I'm not dumb?" Charlie asked and shook her wrist. "You going to remove these?"

"No." Timber said. "And no, I think you're an ignorant ass" She fell onto her couch and grabbed the bottom of her flat, thick soled boot and yanked, grunting with the effort. She had been on her feet for so long her toes had actually become swollen.

"Thanks" Charlie said and stepped into the room, slamming the front door behind her."

"You seem to be the type of woman to appreciate honesty." Timber said and yanked at her other boot.

"I am."

A white rustic dining room chair, sans table, sat just to the right of the front door. Charlie slowly bent her knees and leaned into the chair, her eyes staying locked on Timber. Her slow motion movements were obviously a statement.

Timber just didn't know what the hell she was trying to say. Maybe it was a power play of some kind. Like

'Screw you I'm not coming any further into your house'. Timber didn't really care what statement the bitch was making. She was a member of the media. As far as Timber was concerned, that meant enemy.

"Good, try this." Timber said snidely and leaned back, placing one arm along the rear of the couch and crossing one ankle over a knee. "That little conversation we had back at the crime scene?"

Charlie nodded, looking instantly more uncomfortable.

"I wasn't bluffing. And I don't care who your boyfriend is."

Charlie sat up straighter and shook her long red locks.

Timber was suddenly felt insecure about her short, blonde, shaggy mess of a head and reached up. She stopped herself from rubbing her head and rubbed her chin trying to cover the silly action.

"You are up in arms about something I haven't done." Said Charlie "So relax, Detective Blake has the letter and I will consider keeping it quiet," Charlie said

"Consider?" Timber asked.

"Well you haven't exactly offered me anything."

"Bullshit." Timber dropped her ankle off her knee and leaned forward at the waist.

Charlie smirked "Has anyone ever told you that your appearance and your tendency toward the obscene do not mesh well?"

Timber shot back "Has anyone ever told you that you they were going to rip off your high-heeled boots and beat you to death with them?"

To Timber's immense pleasure, Charlie looked appropriately startled as she replied, "No," then moved her bottom uncomfortably in the wooded chair.

"That's good for you." Timber said and stood up. She decided she'd made a strong enough impression. She grabbed the dangling cuff and pulled it up, Charlie's arm came with it. Timber was surprised that the action didn't elicit a painful outcry.

"So, to sustain my life all I need to do is?" Charlie asked.

Timber turned the key and the cuff clicked open. "Tell me everything and keep your pen still till we close the case." Timber said, slipping the cuffs in the small case clipped to the back of her black belt.

"No way!" Charlie said and stood up towering over Timber, her heels adding four inches to her already impressive height. "This is going to break and I want the exclusive."

Timber looked up unaffected by the height difference. She shrugged and said "Fine. But we control content." She was done playing. She wanted to finish this up get and back on track.

"Never going to happen." Charlie said and stomped one foot on the carpet.

Timber laughed loudly, turning away, dismissing the petulant reporter. "I can put a gag on you."

Charlie was furious and it showed in her voice. "No court in their right mind would…"

Shaking her hair as she walked away, Timber said loudly "No, I mean I could get a gag and put it over your mouth and stuff you in a closet." Timber began to climb the stairs to her bedroom. Pausing halfway up, she turned, yelling, "Sit down!" As she finished her assent, she heard a grunt from the woman still fuming in her living room. She felt it might take the edge off to give her a few moments to think about her situation.

The day had already been long and then the call, just as she was finally slipping into unconsciousness. Now Timber was on the edge. She knew if she didn't get a handle on it she might be digging a hole in her back yard. Her jeans and white tee shirt lay on the end of her bed. She shed her work gear and dropped her gun, badge and cuffs in the chair next to her bed. The process of changing was cathartic. And as she came back down the stairs barefoot and casual, she contemplated opening a bottle of red wine. Then she considered the idea of being that relaxed when Blake arrived and instantly dismissed the idea. Charlie was still sitting in the white chair when Timber came into view.

"This is abuse of power. I am going to expose your federal ass…"

"Oh calm down. I was just pissed. Stop fighting it and tell me what you know. You're a reasonable woman. I know this because you're with Nick and there is no way that could happen without a lot of compromise on your part. I may not be willing to throw your legs in the air and make you feel like a teenager, but I can protect you, so give."

Charlie's lower jaw dropped an inch and hung there, eyes wide. "Wow, you really have a way about you."

"I have heard that." Timber felt less stressed and ready to move this along. She waved her arm at Charlie to follow her in to the kitchen. "Tell me what you know."

She was pleased to hear the sounds of movement behind her. Then Charlie said, "The letter came to me."

"It was addressed to you?" Timber asked.

"Yes, and the headline was 'Dear Miss Morgan'."

"Personal," Timber said, then asked, "What else did it say?"

"I would show it to you … But then I'd have to..."

Timber started to laugh, "You're a funny girl. Have you ever heard that before?"

"A few times." Charlie suddenly looked extremely uncomfortable and Timber felt a little bad as she tried to contain her mirth at the other woman's expense. It didn't stop her from doing what needed to be done.

Ω

When Blake arrived at Timber's home many things had been hashed out. First and foremost, both women had come to the understanding that Timber was the alpha dog and Charlie was going along for the ride. As Timber managed to point out, she had the bigger gun. Although she was using the word 'gun' as a metaphor for the Federal Government, they both knew the meaning was also literal. Timber was moving toward a grudging respect for the focused reporter. She was also pleased to discover Charlie Morgan had a certain respect for law enforcement, a situation that was rare in her experience. Many factors culminated in a meeting of minds and, by the time Blake arrived, the women were sipping coffee and chatting like old friends. This was such a surprise to Blake that he stood in the kitchen doorway for several seconds before announcing himself, startling Timber into grabbing her gun off the counter and pointing it in his direction. "The door was unlocked," he said simply, looking at the weapon in Timber's grip.

"You could still knock." she said, slid her thumb to the safety and moved it, slipping the gun back in place on the counter, the barrel pointing away from them.

"You ever think about controlling those emotions?" he asked as he pulled off his coat and dropped it on the back of a chair, then joined them in the large nook. The seats were padded and high backed providing support and comfort. The kitchen was Timber's favorite part of her small two bedroom home. Its large corner nook was perfect for entertaining a small group while simultaneously preparing a meal and enjoying conversation. She smirked at Blake and watched as he slid into his chair, folding his long frame to fit in the small space.

"No, it's what makes me so charming." Timber said.

Charlie made a noise that could have been a laugh if it wasn't cut short.

"Too much of anything is bad, even charm." He dropped a piece of paper, obviously a photocopy, onto the table top and said, "Interesting reading."

"That's what I said" Charlie replied.

Timber picked up the letter. "Crime tech have the original?"

"That's what took so long," he affirmed.

Charlie piped up, "How exactly does that work? Don't you have to have permission to bring that here? And is this really three connected murders? What are the details of the other two? Are you going to build a task force? And why are you two working together if you didn't already know these were connected?"

Timber listened to Charlie as she asked question after question without waiting for answers. She sat back in her chair and exchanged an amused look with Blake. She glanced over the scribbled writing and said, "If we weren't sure before, we certainly are now."

"No kidding." Blake said

"Are either of you going to answer my questions?" Charlie asked.

"This isn't an interview," Timber said.

"It's an interrogation," Blake said, surprising her.

"I can ask firmer questions. Unfortunately, I don't have any needle-nosed pliers," Charlie mocked.

"You are hysterical." Timber said.

"You have uncontrolled emotional outbursts. I have humor." Charlie shot back.

"Oh, her outbursts are humorous?" Blake said.

"Okay, Abbot and Costello, can we focus?" Timber asked.

"Yes, let's focus on answering the questions." Charlie said.

"You are so pushy; cut it out!" Timber yelled.

"I'm a reporter."

Blake spoke up, answering a few questions, keeping the exchange moving, "No, it wasn't hard to get possession of the letter. The techs made a copy for me and I signed it out. It's protocol and chain of custody. They now have the original and I am lead."

"For now," Timber pointed out.

He nodded, a tolerant smile curving his lips. "For now, so I am privy to all the evidence."

"Was that so hard?" Charlie asked

"Can it." Timber said in a tone that implied threat

"When did you receive this?" Blake asked

"Two days ago." Charlie answered

"What?" Timber's question was more of an exclamation.

Charlie was quick to defend. "I didn't know what the numbers meant. I was out doing some undercover work and …"

"At a strip club?" Timber asked, looking pointedly at the other woman's outrageous attire.

Charlie caught on and, choosing not to take the bait, said "Oh! No. Anyway I received a call from a friend who was doing some research and he suggested the numbers might be a date, time and address; so I went with it and, 'voila'."

"Voila?" Blake said.

"Had it occurred to you that if you turned this over immediately, we could have made the connection sooner and saved a life?" Timber asked

"No." Charlie said flatly.

"Priceless." Timber grunted.

"The dead guy, was he killed there?" Charlie prodded.

"I am not going to discuss the case with you. You already have far more than you should." Blake said, frustration seeping into his voice.

"Isn't that why I'm here?" she asked.

"No." Blake told her.

Charlie shrugged, unaffected, "Okay, so I'm going to assume that he was not killed there. That means he was already all dead. This also means that even if I had turned it over you would not have…could not have saved anyone."

"We could have set a trap and caught the bastard." Blake pointed out.

"I don't…" Charlie began.

"Okay stop. We did this whole thing already while you were wrapping it up." Timber said

Blake looked at the letter and then at the two women, "Fine, but I'm asking the questions now. Do yourself a favor and answer without making things difficult."

Charlie opened her mouth and Timber watched amused as Blake shot her his patented 'shut-up look' and she complied. Timber wished she had the ability to stop someone with a look. She had to string together scathing comment and scary threats to get the same outcome. Sometimes things were very unbalanced in the universe. She spread the paper out on the counter and looked at the page. Charlie and Blake looked on.

> I am amused that the police have not connected my work. How about a name for me, it's early but its time. How about Genesis? You don't understand these things … but u will u will u will
> 2 down or is it 3? ? you u you tell me.
> 9221215kake1345gerard

"Cryptic and creepy." Blake said.

Charlie nodded, "We had a psychologist look at it. She said many of the factors of the note are inconsistent, but the gist is, it's a game."

"Yeah, that's obvious." Timber agreed.

"So," Blake said, "those numbers at the bottom I get the date and address but whats with the extra letters?"

"We have no idea."

"'K a k e'… the obscurity factor is pretty high," Charlie said.

"Maybe." Blake said, looking troubled.

"Got a thought you would like to share?"

"Not yet." he said and picked up the letter.

"If you get anything else…" Timber started.

"We'll call." Charlie assured.

"No waiting this time?" Blake asked.

"No waiting." Charlie nodded, then added, "And I get an exclusive."

"We will share as much as we can and after we close it the story is all yours." Timber promised.

"Great." Charlie was thrilled and it showed.

"I'll need to send a uniform to get an official statement," Blake said.

"No, I'll come to the station." Charlie volunteered.

"You're not getting in the war room," Timber flatly told her.

"Okay," Charlie shrugged as if it were of no consequence.

"I'm serious, Charlie. Try it and I will arrest you." Timber threatened.

"You guys are taking all of the fun out of my job," Charlie pouted.

"Perfect! That's what I was going for. You?" Timber looked at Blake.

"Yep, that's about all I focus on, making the press unhappy. It's a lifelong dream of mine," Blake said.

"Ha ha. Now who's Abbot and…whoever?"

"Costello," Timber said.

"Oh yeah." Charlie was not nearly as thrilled as she had been a mere moment before.

"You can go now." Timber said.

"Thank you. Do you…?"

"I have your number." Blake stood and grabbed his coat. "I'll give you a ride."

Chapter Thirteen

Payton ran, her feet hitting the pavement in time with the beat of the music being piped into her ears. Blue October announced their need to sink into the ocean and disappear. She did not understand the sentiment but she still enjoyed the tune. The beat and tempo kept her feet moving. She was running to think, a technique she had learned not so long ago. It was an accident really, a beautiful accident, like superglue and sticky notes, a beautiful fateful occurrence that had moved her in a new direction.

She had always hated to run before. Hated the impact and the way her hips felt for days after, like they would fall off or snap if she moved wrong. She tried everything: knee braces, new tennis shoes and vitamin supplements to help lubricate her joints. Still, running had not been for her. That was before number one. She liked to call them by their numbers. The order in which she killed them seemed to document their importance. Other than being a piece in her elaborate puzzle they were little more than meat to her, meat with a number.

When number one had finally finished dying; when his blood no longer flowed and she had pulled the broom handle from his mouth that last time, Payton had felt a moment's hesitation. For just a blink of an eye her plan faded away and she saw herself standing over the bloody mess. Wild-eyed with a man-made torture device gripped in her fists, she saw herself glowing with the deed she had just completed. She panicked. Dropping the broom, Payton grabbed a hoody, slipped it on and ran from the apartment. Her body was covered in blood, but she didn't care. It dripped from her fingers as she whipped them out in front of her body. Back and forth she pumped them, her feet moving at a pace that she could never maintain for long. And yet despite this past experience, despite the fact that blood matted her hair and mixed with the sweat dripping down her face, she didn't get tired. She ran; ran from the act, ran from the blood, and ran from herself. Eventually, clothing so thick with sweat and blood that literally they could be wrung out, Payton's mind began to clear. She no longer felt ashamed and afraid; she no longer felt guilty. She realized that, despite her ghastly appearance, no one had noticed her. No one had called out for the bloody woman to stop running. No one had assumed she was hurt and asked if she were okay. Despite her bizarre appearance and her state of mind, she had been seen by no one.

By the time Payton made it back to her apartment, she had known the truth. She was meant to do this. Required, in fact, to accomplish her goals. A higher power believed her righteous and true. There was no other explanation. She felt like a God as she walked into the apartment and looked at herself in the bathroom mirror. The mask of sweat and blood streaking her face was a testament to her discovery and she felt as if she were a God. A God in the business of redemption.

Now, as she ran through the streets so familiar to her, she felt none of the aches and pain she had felt before. Her body no longer restrained her. No; she ran because it gave her power. When she ran the universe spoke to her, guided her and helped her focus on her goals. Today was no different. It was time to change up the game. Time to create a scene without the body. Make them chase their tails a tad. She needed to drag things out a bit. The right pattern had yet to emerge and she couldn't kill just anyone. There were rules, protocol and if she lost her mission then, well she may no longer be a God. She picked up the pace as the song changed and a new cadence required her attention. Then a thought struck. She would send another letter. A letter with a more obvious clue. The last one had worked out so well. Then an even better idea wormed its way into her thinking, a distraction. If she could cause a big distraction, she would have time to complete her next few tasks. If she wasn't careful, that stupid fed and her boyfriend detective would solve the case. She wasn't fooled; she knew they were screwing. She also knew if something happened to one of them it would affect them both, much more so than normal partners. These two were connected. Payton knew she was on the right track. She knew she had to hurt one of them. The question was; which one? She smiled and felt her cheeks bob with the effort. Running and smiling was harder than it looked.

Chapter Fourteen

Charlie looked windblown and frazzled as she pushed a plastic bag into Timbers hand and said "I got another one. Read it!"

"Give me a sec," Timber said.

"No! Read it now!" the frazzled redhead demanded.

"Jeez woman, chill." Timber said.

"Yeah, Read it, then tell me to chill."

Timber unfolded the letter carefully by the corners and gaped at the blunt text.

> I leave clues at house with no home
> 3854 s Dartmouth. Don't wait bring a friend!
> Genesis

Timber gripped her phone and held down the button allowing direct contact with the person on the other end. "Blake?"

A snapping and a buzz came across the line as his voice replied. "Blake here, what's up?"

"Got something. Get some big whites over to 3854 Dartmouth, Denver. Might wanna hurry."

His voice came back, "On it. See you there."

As Timber pushed past her, slipping the note back into the bag, Charlie said, "I'm coming too."

"Just stay behind the tape," Timber said, already feeling impatient with the willful reporter. *Isn't it enough that a member of the media was embedded in my investigation? Does she also have to be so damn bouncy and excited about it?*

She looked at the note again. 'Genesis'. The name was obviously biblical. She considered the implications. *A beginning. A new start. Does the unsub think they are starting something new or is it a signal that it was only the beginning?* Timber considered these possibilities while mulling over several others. *Why were there extra letters in the message before this one? 'K A K E's another spelling for 'cake'? Call letters of some kind? The lab is analyzing the letter but you never know how productive a lab will be in these circumstances. Ciphers sometimes get solved and sometimes people get away with murder. It sucks but it's true.*

Minutes later, Timber pulled into the front of a small, nondescript, white house with brown trim. A realtor's sign was stabbed into the front lawn, announcing the sale of the property. A broad-faced man, smiling and looking downright cheerful, graced both sides of the sign. As Timber stepped from her car, Charlie jogged up to her. *Great!*

"You think that's what he meant by a house with no home?" Charlie asked, pointing to the sign.

"That seems like the most obvious answer," Timber muttered.

"I thought so, too. Seems strange. He hasn't been obvious before."

"So far…" Timber stopped herself as she stepped onto the lawn and turned abruptly.

"So far?" Charlie asked expectantly

Timber looked at the uniforms lining the walk and yelled to the young female officer. "Hey, Peterson. Tape off this scene and no press. Got it?" She looked at Charlie.

Peterson came running over and saying, "Yes, ma'am," was on her way to accomplish the task.

Charlie yelled at Timber's retreating back: "This isn't much cooperation on your part, Agent!"

As Timber walked across the well-manicured lawn, she noticed how quiet the neighborhood was. There were no 'looky-loos', no old women walking their dogs, no children playing in yards. A black sedan pulled up and

Robin Blake jumped out, slamming the door. His long legs brought him to Timber's side in a few easy jogging steps.

"Where'd the tip come from?" he asked.

"Her." She jabbed a finger over her shoulder.

'Wow, you must love that," he said, quietly chuckling.

"Sure do, I'm planning on putting her on my Christmas list." Timber said, deadpan.

"Let me guess, you're gonna buy her a muzzle."

"I was thinking a ball gag. But that's good," she said, then took the front steps in one leap, her adrenaline peaking.

Blake entered the front room behind Timber and they both stopped, staring for a moment taking in the sight before them. Two walls had writing on them. One looked to be blood, the liquid dried in a dripping pattern with streaks where it had been smeared to make the words 'death to pigs'.

On the wall adjacent to that one, the message was written in a different medium, but of approximately the same color.

For heaven's sake catch me before I kill more
I cannot control myself

"Think that is lipstick?" Blake asked.

"Sure do," Timber said.

Blake looked at the two officers, Cable and Sebastian, who were standing at the back wall looking up at the three words. "Where's the body?" he asked.

"Ain't one." Sebastian said.

"Come again." Blake said.

"Ain't no body. Just this," he said again.

"Well, shit." Timber said.

"Make sure you take photos of every room and print it all. Don't cut corners. This may be the crime scene from a past body dump," Blake said.

Cable took a step toward Timber, looking nervous. "Agent Byrne?"

"Yeah?" she answered.

"I heard you were putting together a task force and I wanted to tell you that I put in a request for me and my partner to be on the team." The uniformed officer looked as new as he sounded.

"Is this your partner?" she asked, motioning toward Sebastian.

The other man spoke up "Ah, no. I like to ride alone."

"You're Mike Sebastian?" Timber remembered seeing his name on a few reports. His writing was surprisingly better that his speech.

"Yes, ma'am," he replied.

"You want to work on this too?" she asked.

"Yes, ma'am," he answered.

Blake nodded at her, signaling his approval of the two officers.

"Process this scene. Crime techs will be here soon. Follow chain of custody and get it to me. I want everything. I don't care if one of you has to camp outside of the lab. Follow me?"

"Yes, ma'am!" Cable said, clearly thrilled. Sebastian only nodded.

Timber flipped open a small note pad and began writing down her impressions. The house was immaculate, save for the two walls covered in strange script. The tan carpet was clean and still retained the marks from a recent vacuuming. "Make sure you get the contents of the vacuum bag" she said

Officer Cable responded with another 'yes, ma'am'. Timber smiled at his eager face before checking out the other rooms. Nothing about the house was out of the ordinary. Blake had come to the same conclusion and said as much as they were leaving the scene. Timber asked, "Do you wanna call the realtor or should I?"

"Depends; are you getting a room together?" Blake was offering her a chance to set up the war room.

In her estimation she had enough work. "Nah. You do it. The team that's been working the individual murders should be on this. Let's keep the focus local," Timber said.

"That's mighty kind of you," Blake said.

"Don't sound so surprised."

"You just don't want to do the extra work,'' he smirked.

She found she wasn't surprised he had her number. She shrugged. "There is that."

"I thought so."

"No, really, there's something else. I need a day to shake out a few things so you can get it set up and..."

"Shake out?"

"It's not a big deal. I need to check in with my SAC and get some approvals; if I don't, you'll be swimming in feebs." Timber needed to think. She also needed distance from this super hunk that kept distracting her.

"By all means take care of that." Blake said.

"Don't be a slacker while I'm gone." Timber replied.

"Gone? Come on, you're just practically across the street," Blake raised an eyebrow in question.

Timber shook her head in disgust. "Stop being difficult and work up a war room. Those yahoos inside are gonna bring in all the evidence and paperwork from this. You'll want to pull them for the detail."

Chapter Fifteen

\

The woman that walked in the door was striking. It wasn't just because she was beautiful, there was that. Yet the most striking thing about this beautiful Amazon was the scar that traced an angry red thick line from left ear down across the front of her throat and ended just below her carotid artery. The case that had brought such a disfiguring scar into this woman's life was far behind her, but the devastation would always remain. The scar was a testament to that and sometimes Timber felt her old friend wore it with pride.

"Hey, Danielle!" Timber stood and slapped the woman on the shoulder, eliciting a grin. "What brings you to our strange and booming metropolis again?"

Danielle Devon had been living and working in Washington, DC for as long as Timber had known her. Her brief stint in Denver had left its devastating mark, literally. After her recovery, Danielle had left; no silly, sappy goodbyes, no tears, which was only one of the many reasons, Timber liked and respected Danielle.

"Came to see Quinlan. Heard about the case, thought I would stop by."

"How is he?" Timber could tell by the off-handed nature of the remark that they wouldn't be discussing Danielle's lost love in detail.

She wasn't disappointed when Danielle responded with a simple. "Same."

She quickly jumped to a less sensitive subject. "Oh.. Okay. Well, the case sucks! It's weird and the M.O. keeps changing and I'm working with Blake…" she immediately regretting the last, bit down on her tongue, turned to her desk and started gathering the case files.

"He's a good cop," Danielle said, curiosity blooming in her tone.

"Yeah..." came Timber's flat response.

"Something there?" Danielle queried.

Oh god this was her fault, why had she mentioned his name, "No!"

"Ah." It was a curious response and Timber felt defensive.

"Ah?" She turned, one hip planted against the desk piled with papers.

"Ah." Danielle said again, easily seeing through the situation, probably sizing it up with her big brain.

"Fuck!" Timber was embarrassed and Danielle could see it. It was obvious in the tilt of her head and the slant of her azure eyes. Luckily Danielle had less interest in Timber's personal life than most of the cops in her own town.

"Moving on." Danielle said, a small smile curving her full lips. "Can I help? Magraff gave me leave but I'm sure I could get on the task force."

Timber watched the other woman move. *Such confidence and grace.* She was easily a foot taller than she, with wiry muscles and a mane that would drive Timber crazy; yet she moved like she was a part of the world, not like Timber who was always bumping into it. She was curious why Danielle Devon, Special Agent from the Washington office, would waste time in their city. She expressed her curiosity, hoping she might find out what was really behind the stunning agent's sudden appearance. "You're not busy enough with your DC bag? Murder, capital and all?"

"Don't want my help? I can fade." Danielle's face changed.

It was clear she needed this. The 'why' didn't matter. Timber understood and had every intention of helping one of her own, even though she didn't really know what she was helping with.

"No. No, don't do that, I'm just giving you shit. It's what I do," she chided.

"Oh, I forgot." Danielle smiled halfheartedly, her eyes tracing the stacks of files on the desk.

"You used to give as good as you got. What's up?" Timber worried about any agent wrapped up in personal trauma. She wondered if her old comrade had recovered from the terror that had almost ended her life two years before. Most people could never get over that trauma.

Danielle's eyes remained glued to the desk. "Oh, I'm distracted." she said

"That's not good for us," Timber replied pointedly.

Danielle looked up, her cerulean eyes meeting Timber's. "I will get un-distracted." Her tone changed, all the murky distance gone now.

"That sounds good," Timber said, a big grin changing her elfin features into a mischievous sprite. "Need a focus? Here are the first three. Read up. You stayin' with Nick?"

Danielle answered, never taking her eyes from the files Timber was gathering. "Yeah. Charlie wouldn't let it go; she freaked when I mentioned a hotel."

"I could see her wanting to keep family close. She's a control freak." Timber said as she handed the files to Danielle and hoped she wasn't making a very big mistake.

Danielle laughed.

"What?" Timber asked

"Nothing," Danielle said and turned on the way out with her prize in hand.

"You're saying I'm a control freak, too?" Timber accused, knowing it was true. "You know Charlie is working this?"

"Yes." she said over her shoulder.

"Think there'll be a conflict?" Timber asked

"Nah. If she gives me trouble, I'll sick Nick on her," Danielle said.

"Hope it works, she's been a real pain in my ass," Timber said.

"Sorry 'bout that. I'm here wrapping up a few things. I'll call you tomorrow." Danielle said

"Let me know if you have an issue getting assigned."

"I'll call you as soon as I know." Danielle nodded, obviously distracted.

"Don't take those out of the building," Timber warned.

"Sure, I'll camp out in the cafeteria for a couple hours, do a skim and bring 'em back. You gonna be here?" Danielle asked.

"Nope. Just drop them on the desk." Timber suggested

"Sure. Talk to you tomorrow,' Danielle said and smiled

As an afterthought, Timber asked, "Does that hurt?" referring to the long ago injury.

"Nah. Itches sometimes," Danielle said and continued on her way to the exit.

"Makes ya look like a bad ass." Timber was impressed by the other woman's disinterest in hiding the massive scar. It was remarkable. But still she could tell the wound was far deeper than the tissue she could see.

"I am a bad ass." Danielle said, her face showing no emotion as she pressed her back against the door, opened it and slid out into the hallway.

"Crazy," Timber said under her breath. "That woman is fascinating."

Chapter Sixteen

Robin Blake looked into Danielle's eyes and it occurred to him that there was something missing from her gaze. The conversation was stilted in the beginning but things relaxed as soon as the food arrived. Danielle took a large bite of her guacamole burger and smiled as she chewed. It was the first time her emotions moved into the apex of her face. He watched as a small green spot was licked off her bottom lip.

"Yuck." He hated guacamole. If he really contemplated the situation, he would realize he disliked almost anything green.

"What is it with women and disgusting food?" he asked as his plate of fries was placed in front of him.

"Men eat crap, too," she said, and dabbed a napkin at the corner of her mouth where the green had been just a moment before.

"Crap, yeah," he said and shivered. "But that?" He pointed to the oozing green dropping onto the plate from her oversized sandwich. "What the hell is that?"

"Avocado." She looked at him like he was shy a few million brain cells.

He pushed a fry into his mouth, enjoying the salty flavor. "Mmmm. Now that's food."

"No. That's a heart attack," she said, and crunched into her mammoth sandwich.

"Nah. I'm in great shape," he said, and watched her chew. His eyes kept moving from her face to the scar, the scar that shouldn't be there, the scar that he felt more than partially responsible for.

"For now," she said, her full mouth causing her words to slur slightly.

"Nice," he said referring to both the comment and her overflowing mouth.

"Better take care of those muscles. Wouldn't want to get flabby before you get the gold," she mumbled.

"The gold?" He was confused and then surprised by her next statement.

"Timber," she said matter-of-factly and dropped her food back onto her plate unceremoniously.

His stomach dropped. "Shit! Isn't there anyone that doesn't know about that?"

"No." She leaned back and placed one arm across the back of the booth. Her body language was open as she watched his reaction.

"Great." He squinted at her. "Still the consummate professional. Why do you feebs advertise every interpretation?"

"Can't help it. Anyway, It's always all over your face."

"Mine. Why just mine?" he asked, insulted.

Robin watched as she seemed to contemplate her answer. A strand of black silk fell over her left eye, she brushed it aside absently. "The truth is, it's all over hers too, but she always looks like she's between agony and ecstasy so…" she shrugged.

He couldn't deny the truth in either of her observations. Timber couldn't hide much on her open face, yet she was so full of emotions they were hard to decipher at times. It was part of the reason he was so angry at himself for missing all of the signs. It was always there right in front of him, but he chose to see something different. "There's nothing left of it," he said and felt sick suddenly. The idea that Timber was part of his past and not his future didn't sit well.

"Bullshit." Danielle said

"Did she…?"

"Are you kidding me?" The voice of the dynamic woman across from him was full of scorn.

He was instantly embarrassed. He sat up straighter and crossed his arms across his chest. He knew how defensive he appeared, but he couldn't seem to help himself. He said simply, "Sorry."

"No." She shook her head, denying the tone. "I just meant we're not that close. Timber is more likely to punch me in the nose than confide in me. I was really surprised she was so eager to accept my help."

"Ah," he said, feeling stupid and childish. He dropped his arms and took a deep breath. He felt the strain of his shirt across its broad expanse, wished he felt as assured as he knew he appeared. Being well put together and self-contained was a skill he was proud to possess. Lately, his self-possession was being tested. He shoved a handful of fries in his mouth and chewed. His jaw muscles worked far harder than necessary.

She seemed to see through him. "But anyway, my guess is she isn't anywhere near over whatever happened." Daniele said.

He swallowed the fries; they stuck for a moment before he managed to push them down with a large gulp. He couldn't keep himself from asking. "How do you know?"

"Seriously? She vibrates whenever you're within a few feet of her." Danielle wiped a napkin across her lips. "Plus, no one gets that pissed at someone they don't care about."

He looked down at his plate and took a drink of his water. His stomach was getting twisted and the fries were starting to feel like weights floating in acid. Averting to a different topic was his only option. "Okay, I think if we discuss this anymore we are going to move into little old lady status."

Danielle laughed, "I was starting to feel myself age."

The air was immediately lighter. He mirrored her posture, slinging an arm across the back of his seat. He needed to know, needed to feel like she had been okay, after.

"So, how are you?" He tried to sound casual.

Her face changed "It always comes down to that, doesn't it?"

"I suppose," he said.

"I guess I could cover it up."

"You could," he said, knowing she was referring to 'the scar'.

"Seems like a lot of trouble, just to avoid the conversation," she said casually.

"True. So let's have the conversation," he challenged.

"Okay, let's go," she shot back.

"So, how are you?" he began again. He could still see her laying on the ground, a psychopath sitting on her, a knife pressing into her neck. The guilt from that moment still found its way into his dreams. In varying degrees, he blamed himself for Danielle's altered existence.

"I am great." Her response sounded pressed and hollow.

"Really?" He knew it was a lie, yet he pressed, hoping she would convince him. He was taken aback by her response.

"Yeah, I'm even dating."

His right eyebrow rose and he smiled, feeling hopeful. He wondered if it was possible that her words held more truth than her eyes. "That's interesting. Who is he, and more importantly does Nick know?"

"He's on the job, Washington P.D. He's in your line."

"A detective? Nice. Nick?" He pressed again.

"No. He doesn't need to know everything."

"That's gonna go over well." Robin had known Danielle's twin brother for as long as he had been a cop. The other man was a daunting figure and very protective. The idea that Danielle was keeping quiet about something so huge meant she wasn't just hiding from him. If anyone could see through your lies, it would most certainly be your sibling, certainly a twin.

"I realize that. I don't see any reason to bring it up." She looked down at her plate, seemed suddenly fascinated with her food, leaned in, lifted her fork and began moving the vegetables.

"Not serious?" he queried. A pause and her cheeks turning slightly pink alerted him to trouble brewing. "How serious?"

"I'm here to say goodbye to Quinlan." She looked up, her eyes meeting his. They were such an odd color, lighter than they should be, especially considering her otherwise dark coloring.

"Oh?" he said, unbelieving.

"Yep." She confirmed the seriousness of her statement, her eyes still locked on his.

"Have you seen him?" Again he flashed on her bloody form; a knife slicing her throat, Nick screaming, and the smell of gun powder in the thick, dark air. His eyes blinked, he sat back.

"Yesterday…The same." she said and scraped her fork on the plate making his teeth tingle. She dropped the offending utensil onto the plate and fell back into the seat. A defeated look passed over her pretty features, distorting them with a dull sort of pain.

"I went a few months ago. He's lost some size." Robin said clumsily.

She nodded. "A coma will do that."

Robin remembered the hulking reporter well. The man had been an irritant, but he could never have wished such an existence on anyone. He still didn't understand how Garrett Quinlan had ended up in a coma. As far as he knew, the reporter hadn't been anywhere near the scene. The clean up was Fed territory, ripped away from any police cooperation the minute the case was associated with CIA. Case closed. Robin remembered how frustrated he had been at the time, but no one was talking, Timber included. He remembered trying to persuade her to give up information before; fun, but unproductive. So, he chose to let it go. "This sucks. What are you going to do?" he asked.

"Well, I'm not sure. I don't know if I can be serious about anyone, but I need to say goodbye before I can consider moving on. I've waited. Something I never thought I would do. Wait for a guy. But I did; suddenly I'm having feelings for someone and the doctors say Quinlan is not waking up." She shook her head.

"This is shitty." It occurred to him that his situation wasn't nearly as dire as it could be.

"That's life. Well, my life anyway." She cringed and said, "Oh, that sounded pitiful. I did not mean that. My life is actually pretty damn good, considering."

He let it go, impressed with her bravado, but completely unsurprised. Danielle Devon was a force. He was suddenly very curious about the man that drew her attention away from the tragic figure lying in a hospital bed across town. "Your new guy, does he know what happened?"

She grimaced and nodded "Cliff notes. But really, who doesn't know? It was splashed all over the news and every flippin year they rehash the anniversary because of Garrett Quinlan, media dynasty. Shit, you'd think he was a Kennedy the way they behave."

"I think the publicity has a lot to do with the brutality of the thing," he said, remembering again. A permanent part of his landscape now.

"I guess." Her finger absently traced her scar.

Robin looked away, the image of her brother looking up at him as he leaned over the body of his dying sister, sweat slicking down his dark face, accusation ripping through the space between them, tearing at Robin, ionizing the air.

"Shitty," he said

Chapter Seventeen

This was perfect. The old man waved his left hand around while talking like he was conducting some kind of orchestra. "I own a few fur houses around town. We store furs for the summer for all the rich assholes that don't care about throwing away a hard earned dollar."

"Fur houses?"

"Just big refrigerators that keep the fur from rotting and cracking. It has a humid state and .. oh you're not interested in this junk. Such a pretty girl. Come over here and let me see those pretty boobies."

Payton giggled and stepped closer. "I'm very interested. Tell me more about those refrigerators."

Ω

Blake gathered the paperwork from his desk and pushed open the heavy stairwell door. Even with a burden he couldn't bring himself to take the elevator. He'd read once that by simply taking the stairs you could add years to your life. He knew it was absurd; since that day elevators reminded him of coffins and he did his best to avoid them. He had no fear of the space inside and although many of his fellow officers were sure he was claustrophobic, he wasn't. He simply wanted to live as long as possible. He didn't know what lay beyond this life and he was in no hurry to find out. His journey complete, he stepped into the large room, dropped his arms full of paperwork and motioned to the three officers in the room.

"Most of this is organized but file it and take notes. You've all got twenty-four hours to get familiar with all aspects."

"Yes, sir." the officers in the room responded.

The three began to sift through the papers busily getting ready for tomorrow's roll call.

Blake stood in front of the board attached to the back wall and tacked the Victim's pictures in order of the body finds. Under each photo of them alive he tacked a photo of the body. The last two photos were of the odd messages left on the walls of the empty house.

"Looks grim."

Blake turned and waved at the other man. "Hey, Graydon. Glad you could make it."

"No way I was gonna let you get all the glory," he mocked.

"Glory? That's not really why I'm here." Blake said.

"Sure, like leading a big case didn't put you next to the hottest tail you've ever tasted."

Blake felt a rolling form of anger that only came with insults to your woman. "Whoa! Carter, you might want to backtrack before you're digesting those pretty white teeth."

"Golly gee, Boss," Carter said, scoffing at his reaction.

"I am not playing," he said, his voice quiet and deceptively calm.

Carter rubbed his gut and snickered, not affected by Blake's heated reaction. "Sure, man, I can take a hint. So what's with the serial? You like anybody for it yet?"

"No. I spoke with the realtor and his alibi checks. I've run down about every lead. At this point I'm hoping some brainstorming might bring it together."

"That's always a good thing," Carter said and walked to the board.

"Don't you teach a class on this crap?" Blake asked. He knew the answer, hoping to make a point. The jab floated over Carter's head.

"Sure do," he said.

"Well, read up. We need all the help we can get. And Graydon……"

"Yep?" Carter Graydon said, still unaware of the tension he had caused.

"Keep your mouth shut about Agent Byrne." As he walked away Blake considered what would happen to his career if he had followed his instincts.

"Yes, sir, Detective Blake," Carter said, his tone still full of cocky mockery.

Blake felt his jaw clench as he left the room.

Chapter Eighteen

Timber looked at the shape of Robin Blake's chin; almost flat on the bottom, the perfect shape for a strong jaw, his cleft centered perfectly. The line of it was straight and solid. Small muscles jumped as he read the paperwork. His thick eyebrows occasionally arched and dipped with emotion. Unguarded, he was easy to read. The case was appalling to him, as it should be. She watched as his eyes became slits and his broad shoulders climbed toward his ears then rolled. expressing emotions turning physical. She watched, fascinated, as his face became animated with scorn and contempt. Spontaneously, Timber picked up a small pillow from her sofa and threw it at him, connecting with the jaw she had been fascinated by moments before. His head whipped back with the soft impact. Before she could jump up and escape he was on her, the papers scattered onto the floor. He grabbed her and lifted her easily, throwing her onto her back on the soft sofa and falling on top of her.

She giggled and pressed her hands to his chest. "You been workin out?" His body felt solid under her palms, but what she couldn't escape was the rapid beat of his heart.

She felt his hot breath on her cheek as he responded "Every day."

She looked into his face. He was grinning widely, a small dimple playing in his right cheek. His chocolate eyes were dancing. So good-looking. Her stomach did a little flip and something must have changed her countenance, because his smile started to fade, his teeth disappearing behind his full lips. She said the first thing she could think of. "Did you know your chin is actually square?"

He nodded slowly, a response that brought his face closer to hers. It was interesting how big he was. The way he lifted her so effortlessly reminded her of their night together long ago. She could see in his expression he was remembering, too. His face was unhurriedly coming toward her. The slow motion part of it was telling. He was giving her time. Time to stop him, time she desperately needed if she was going to survive. "Blake!" she said loudly. The descent stopped.

His jaw clenched and his eyes became smaller before he pushed himself off her and stood. He turned his back on her and ran a hand through his hair. She sat up and leaned over pressing her palms to her face. She quickly moved them, they retained his smell. She made a sound in her throat and stood. He turned as she was standing, both colliding. In an effort to scramble away, she stumbled and he had to grip her arms, firmly steadying her. His grip was strong and he held on. She could feel his eyes burning into the top of her head. She stared at the pearlescent buttons on his shirt and said, "Son of a fuck!"

He released her and stepped away. She let her eyes drop to the floor. Glossy photos of the dead lay scattered, like macabre art, on her dark gray carpet. Her pulse slowed as she took in the horrible sight. The photos were awful enough without the context of her screwed-up love life, but in the shadow of it, they were particularly obscene. She dropped to her knees and began gathering the files, slipping them back into their respective folders. She saw his shoes, the black tips visible in her periphery. He wasn't moving. He was watching her. She knew she was being ridiculous. Unfortunately, she didn't see any other option.

"Want me to make coffee?" he asked

Thankful for the reprieve, she sat back on her heels, a handful of paperwork pressed against her chest. "Yes. That would be superb."

"Okay, I'm on it." He turned and left the room without another word. The tension was still thick. She wondered how they were going to go on from this. This was the situation she had been trying to avoid. Work and sexual tension should not go hand in hand. She shook her head in disgust. The worst part was how incredibly respectful the man was. If he was anyone else she could simply have sex with him and walk away. In fact, that was exactly what she had tried to do before. Unfortunately, she hadn't been able to get that one fantastic night to leave her treacherous mind. Worse was the fact that she had asked him to leave her alone and he had. He had not even called. It was a game and she was ashamed for playing, but a huge part of her was still angry that he had been so willing to comply. For months after, she had seen him in every dark-haired man. If someone with a dark mane and broad shoulders passed in her line of sight, she found herself catching her breath in hopeful anticipation before the sad realization of the moment. Afterward, Timber was always ashamed of herself. The lie she liked to tell was simple. *I am strong and don't need a relationship to be happy.* Funny, it only began feeling like a lie after ***that*** night.

In an effort to behave like an adult, despite the debacle, Timber rose from the ground, her focus to take the sting out of her odd behavior. His back was to her as she crossed the threshold of the kitchen. The room was open to the front hall and the back stairway leading to her bedroom. Timber wondered how easy it would be to lead him to the latter. She knew the better idea was the former, not as appealing but definitely better.

"Do we need to talk?" she asked, hoping he didn't.

"No."

She was surprised. "No?"

"No," he said again.

"Really?" She knew that she was pushing it. *What are you doing? Leave it alone*! she thought.

Just as she was considering her error, he responded to her prodding. He dropped the coffee filter on the counter and turned. "Jesus, Timber! What do you want from me?"

His eyes were dark and snapping with unsuppressed desire and anger, a dangerous combination.

"Nothing." she said simply. She felt guilty for antagonizing him. Especially since she really didn't know how she felt. She was beginning to resemble a teenager playing games.

"That's clear," he snapped.

"What does that mean?" *Oh God! Shut up, Timber!*

He turned and swiped his hand across the counter, wiping the coffee filter and grounds into the sink. "I can't do this. Do not do this." he demanded.

Good; she didn't want this drama. "Cool. So we keep our distance and we don't talk." She realized that coffee was not happening and was looking at the mess in the sink when he turned. Crap!

If possible his expression was more intense "No."

"Can't make up your mind?" She laughed; it sounded awful and forced.

"There will be no keeping our distance."

Her heart jumped, an adrenaline rush blurring her mind. "Uh..I um..." she stuttered stupidly.

He sneered at her, "We work together; we're partners."

"We are not fucking partners!" Her childish response was reactionary. She was fairly familiar with her mouth opening before she had time to consider.

"My mistake. That should have been obvious."

"Funny."

"I don't think so; I think it's tragic."

"Funnier." What the hell was going on? Why was she acting this way, her blood was moving too fast. Her heart, pumping endorphins, causing her to react instead of respond.

"Yeah, I should have a routine." he said sarcastically.

She considered him a moment, standing there, looking so beautiful and angry, a chunk of hair falling over one eye as he looked down at her. She wondered if it was strange that she found his anger oddly sexy. She wanted to make this right. She wanted to take the fire out of his eyes and place it on her skin. What the hell. Why not use him. Why not get what she wanted for once. "So you just wanna fuck then?" she suggested.

"What?" His right eye twitched and his jaw clenched. "Are you just trying to get a rise out of me?" She could practically hear his teeth grind together in frustration.

Timber bit down on her bottom lip trying not to laugh at his reaction; she was feeling better now, more centered. "You said 'tragic'. And you don't want to talk, so my keen deductive reasoning tells me you just wanna fuck."

He shook his head and looked briefly at the ceiling in disgust. "You are a tragic figure."

She wasn't surprised by his response; still it stung. "Fuck off!"

"Original."

"I'm wrong?" she challenged.

"If I wanted you like that, I could have you," he said.

She knew he was right; still she didn't want him to know it. "Ha!" She spat and hoped it sounded convincing.

He took a step toward her. The kitchen was small and the step brought him too close. "You vibrate when I'm near you."

She felt he mouth fall open. "What? I do not!"

"Yes, you do. And you pay attention to the details."

She was falling off her axis. "You are so full of yourself."

"Yeah, me and my square jaw are terribly conceited." He used her words against her.

Oh Damn! "Chin. And it's my square chin and I." she said lamely.

"Thanks, I love it when you correct my grammar."

He was closing the gap, she could feel herself start to shake. The absurdity of the moment was not lost on her. Did she actually vibrate when he was near? Embarrassment washed over her. She wanted to tell him to stop where he was, to turn and leave, sparing her a less than dignifying moment. Instead, she stupidly challenged him. "I don't want you."

"Okay." he said and stopped moving. "Tell me to go," he said

"We have work to do," she said, really not wanting him to go.

"Tell me to go," he insisted.

"Don't tell me what to do." she snapped.

"Tell me to go," he said again.

"No!"

"Tell me to stay." He took a step closer, eliminating the gap.

"No." she said lamely.

"Please, tell me to stay." His hand gently gripped her chin and tilted it so that their eyes met. He bent and brushed his lips against hers, barely making contact. "Tell me to stay."

Now she was vibrating. She leaned in and pressed her mouth to his. She felt his hands under her arms, and then the floor disappeared beneath her. Her legs wrapped around his waist and his palms slid and opened up across her shoulder blades. His mouth opened with hers and a soft gasp escaped her. He tasted of fresh mint and sage. His tongue moved in and gently sparred with hers. He pulled away taking her bottom lip between his teeth and a small groan escaped his throat as he let go. He held her tight ,pressed his face into her warm neck and said again," Tell me to stay."

Her arms were wrapped around his neck. She didn't understand. Hadn't she said it? Wasn't it enough that she was in his arms? "What do you want?"

He lifted his head and looked at her, dark eyes clouded with passion. He kissed her again slowly, his lips soft and sure. She felt her body respond as he pressed in deeper, testing the strength of her. Then suddenly, starkly, his mouth was gone and her feet were once again on the floor. "I want it all, Timber." He looked down at her and shook his head. "I want it all and you can't even ask me to stay. I know I could take you." His voice was deep and husky making the statement much more erotic.

Her heart sank as he continued, backing away from her.

"I also know we would both have a great time, but tomorrow, could you look at me?" He shook his head. "I won't do that again. We've been there, and I have been wearing the goddamn t-shirt ever since." He turned, his back stiff, shoulders squared.

As he walked away, Timber was trying to make sense of his words. He was angry. She could hear it in his voice. She was still dazed from his kiss and he was angry. The strangeness was too much for her to grasp in the time it took him to grab his gun, slide it into his holster and get to the door. She followed silently, still rattled, not knowing how to respond. She thought maybe she should be angry, but in light of his anger she didn't feel inspired. She watched as he pulled open the door and turned to her.

" See you tomorrow at the office." He said the last pointedly. Timber felt her anger starting to rise. His voice was void of emotion, as were his eyes, eyes that had been filled with desire moments ago. Before she could respond, he was through the small passage and pulling the door shut behind him. It clicked into place and she walked like a zombie to flip the deadbolt into position. She hoped he heard it and read her silent message in the noise.

Chapter Nineteen

Blake was still frustrated. He couldn't believe that she so clearly wanted to be with him, yet she wouldn't allow herself to commit to any responsibility for that desire. She wanted to lay it all on him. He felt like time had reversed. He remembered clearly the bantering, the sexual tension, the fighting all leading up to the hottest night of his life. It had been so intense he had actually had a moment of fear. A feeling akin to terror had gripped him. It was unidentifiable after a while he guessed it was because he somehow knew that something so wonderful couldn't last. And it hadn't. Now, suddenly, he was reliving it all. He swore he wouldn't make the same mistake twice. If he ever had the chance, he would not be so blind. Maybe she really didn't feel the same way about him. Maybe she was simply physically attracted and that was the end of it. If so, he would find out and sever all ties. It wouldn't be easy; it was damn well a necessity. You just couldn't have sex and walk away from someone you were that crazy about, he couldn't anyway. The image of Detective Graydon appeared in his mind's eye and he laughed aloud. That guy could walk away from anyone. He probably hasn't had a true emotional response in his entire life. Blake sometimes thought if Carter Graydon had not become a cop he'd probably be a criminal. He had all of the characteristics, overblown ego, fragmented thought processes and he was most definitely unaware of others emotional responses.

Blake's radio came to life. "Detective Blake, there's a call for you. Camden Rythdale wants to meet at 16th and Sheridan."

"Great, I'll take it now."

"He says he'll be waiting. Do you need back up, Detective?"

"No, it's the realtor. Maybe someone in the neighborhood witnessed something."

"Okay, Detective. The address is..."

Blake typed the information into his console computer with his right hand and turned the wheel with his left, changing course. The address wasn't far and he needed to stop thinking about Timber. If he could just catch a break, grab the psycho that was playing with them, then he could concentrate on her. For now, the case was all he could handle. He knew from experience that if you didn't keep focus, bad things happened.

Ω

Timber made the decision to go see Blake at his home. After working with him and seeing him daily it became abundantly clear that they would not be able to continue as things were. She was hoping he would come around to her way of thinking. She was ready to admit how much she wanted him. It was obvious to them both. So why not enjoy the benefits of that attraction. It took a lot of thought, but after a few hours of unrest and a ridiculous amount of unnecessary cleaning, she decided to go and see him. They were both adults, why couldn't they enjoy some benefits. She needed to get this guy out of her system. Her clothing was chosen to take away any of his objections. She imagined his expression as he opened the door. She knew he could be stubborn. She was also reasonably sure that as much as she wanted him he wanted her more. How he had walked away, she would never understand. As she drove her fingers tapped the wheel nervously. She let herself consider the idea that he would send her away.

She groaned, thinking of the humiliation. Could they continue to work together if he was the cause of that humiliation? "Not gonna happen." she said aloud. The decision to dress up and try to seduce Blake was partially based on the idea that if she didn't stop obsessing about him she would let something vital get past her. She was fairly sure that that may have already occurred. Her hope was that they could work together and sleep together until they solved the case. *Then what?* she asked herself. And what if they didn't solve it? Many murders were never solved. What if this had a similar path to the BTK case out of Wichita? That case spanned thirty long years. Her mind began to cross off all of the possible scenarios and she had just convinced herself to go home when her phone rang.

"Byrne," she answered.

"Hi, Agent Byrne; this is Cable. Detective Blake got a call earlier today and hasn't checked in. The address is at Sixteenth and Sheridan."

"What kind of call?" This certainly changed things.

"Just a follow-up interview; it was with that realtor, Camden."

Timber knew the guy but was surprised by the development. As far as she knew they got everything they could from that and it was dry. "Yeah, I'm familiar. Was he supposed to check in?"

"No, but ..."

"It's okay. Thanks for the heads up I'll check it out." She didn't have time to chat if Blake was in trouble. She shook the idea away.

"Great.. Okay.. um…" Cable seemed unsure of what to do next.

"Go back to it, Officer," she said, stating the obvious. It still annoyed her how some cops were afraid to take a step without direction.

"Yes, ma'am."

Chapter Twenty

"It's cold in here." Timber looked at the steel-lined walls of the small, dimly lit room. A center bulb caused a cone of light to illuminate the center of the odd space.

"Yeah I can see that." Blake said blandly, his eyes set at her chest.

She looked down at her sheer red top. Hard round points pressed against the thin material, responding to the chill in the room. "You're bleeding." she said stupidly.

"I can feel it." His hand came up and wiped the streaks at his temple. He looked at his hand, obviously confused.

"How did he get the jump on you?" she asked

He seemed to smile, but it turned to a grimace as his fingers prodded the space above his ear. "The jump?" he said absently.

"Don't be difficult." she said, trying to distract.

Blake leaned against the wall and looked at her with a ridiculous pout. "I can be any way I want. I'm bleeding."

"Okay, be difficult, but let me look at it." Timber knew head wounds could look bad and be nothing; on the other hand… She shook off the thought and stood on tip-toe trying to see the bloody wound.

He leaned away from her. "Why? Are you hiding a med kit in that slinky top?" He raised a thick brow and inquired, "Hey. .. Why are you wearing that?"

"Well, I knew we would be trapped by a raging psychopath so I dressed for the occasion. Let me see your fucking head!" she yelled at him, her voice echoing off the walls.

"Potty mouth!" he said, and slid his finger over the strap of her handkerchief sheath, lifting it off her shoulder and then letting it drop just before it ended at her breast. It was a pretty, strappy, red top that covered her breasts and ended in a 'v' just below her navel. She knew it was sexy and she was pleased with his response.

"Come here and sit down." She motioned to a barrel-shaped container.

"Shouldn't we be trying to get out of here?" he asked as he sat down.

Timber nodded. "We will, but the blood is about to start dripping into your eyes. I really want to know if you're going to pass out."

"I'm not going to pass out. Head wounds bleed; it's not a big deal," he insisted

"Okay, humor me." she said and tried to get a better look without prodding. She lifted the hair covering the spot where the blood seemed to be coming from.

"So?" he asked.

"It's not that bad." she said, although she really didn't know that for sure. It was bleeding a lot and she couldn't see much in the dim light.

"I told you." he said.

She laughed keeping her tone light. "Aren't you glad I care?"

"No." he said "It's irritating."

"That's a weird reaction." she said, honestly surprised by his response.

"You don't care. You just want to jump me and walk away." he said, with a hint of anger.

"Jump you?" Timber needed to get his head into a better light. She wanted to see if it really was a superficial wound. She was warring with confusion by the turn in the conversation and the need to help him.

His tone seemed to change slightly, becoming dismissive. "Seduce me, whatever. The point is, other than my washboard abs, you don't give a crap about me."

"You have a very high opinion of your sex appeal." she teased.

"Do we need to keep having the same conversation? I'm bleeding. I can't deal with rehashing this crap."

"I thought you said you were fine." she said, then added "You don't know what I want, so stop acting like you have some wonderful insight into my psyche. Okay?" She was unprepared for his immediate response.

Blake grabbed her by the waist and pulled her into his lap. His hand slid down her bare back, opening to support her between the shoulder blades. She was shocked by the heat of his palm and the quickness of her response to it. He grabbed her waist band at the front of her slacks and pulled, his fingertips grazing just above her hairline. The sudden movement caused her back to arch, her head to fall back. His lips found the pulse below her ear and she shivered. He whispered against her neck, "See my point?"

"You are a mother fucker!" She scrambled off of his lap. He let go of her, allowing easy escape. He chuckled and she turned on him. "Why does it have to be all or nothing?"

"I think I deserve more than a bootie call." he snapped

"You are such a girl!" she accused.

"Ouch." He pressed two fingers under his right ear. The idea that he was checking his pulse made her nervous.

"A sensitive girl." she said acidly; nerves and adrenalin were mixing, she felt the beginnings of a headache.

"Watch it, I might cry." The sarcasm was deeply evident in his tone.

"Fuck off." she said softly. She was too far away now to see clearly. Risking the possibility of him grabbing her again, she stepped closer.

"You need a new line." he said and a column of blood began dripping onto the shoulder of his white t-shirt.

"Your bleeding is worse." she said.

"It's your fault," he accused.

"How is it my fault?" she asked. "I can't wait to hear this."

"My blood pressure is up because of that shirt."

"Shut up!" The blood was starting to freak her out.

"Why would you say that? You doubt me?" He swiped a hand across his brow; she saw sweat, perspiration in a room far too cold to allow such a thing in normal circumstances.

"Take off your shirt." she said, her hands were starting to shake and the headache was nipping at the base of her skull.

"Take off your shirt." he shot back

"No, I have no bra on." she said, smiling innocently.

He groaned, low in his throat and she was pleased to see his Adam's apple jump. "I don't mind." he said quietly.

"Stop it! I need to make a bandage for your head, to stop the bleeding."

"Your shirt would work just as well. Probably better. It is the size of a bandage."

He was wasting precious time bantering. Her voice rose. "That is very astute, Jackass, but then you would be too tempted and you might cross a line you don't want to cross."

"Good point." He grabbed the waist of his white t-shirt and pulled it over his head.

A gust of breath came out of Timber making an embarrassing hush sound.

"Thanks." he said, a small knowing grin curving his full mouth. It had been a while since she'd seen him shirtless; she didn't remember it being this nice. He was obviously working out regularly. His chest was broader than she remembered and there were small muscle lines dipping into his sweats at each hip. Those were definitely new. She realized she was staring and blinked, grabbing the shirt from his fist. She stepped in and grabbed his ear, turning his head so that she could see the wound just above his hairline, at the temple. A half inch gash opened the skin. It was bleeding profusely, dripping down his neck. He also had a few streaks on his forehead where it had dripped when he looked down at her, changing the blood's trajectory. She folded the t-shirt and pressed it onto the gash. His head tilted slightly under the pressure and she found herself staring at the line from his neck down his chest to the deep crevice in the center of his abdominal wall. Timber couldn't remember ever having such a visceral response to a man.

Her body began to hum and she said "Grab this and keep the pressure!" She stepped away so quickly he almost dropped the shirt.

"What's wrong?"

"You stink." she lied.

"Sorry, I was at the gym." he grunted. Well, that explained the running pants, tennis shoes and t-shirt. A man should not be allowed to look that good in such casual gear. In reality he smelled fabulous. Sweat mingled with a musky wood, mint and cinnamon. The flavored toothpicks to which he was addicted kept his breath always smelling and tasting of cinnamon and mint, one of many reasons it would be almost impossible for her to find him unappealing.

Timber quickly changed the topic, latching on to any possibility. "How did you get from working out, to being bashed on the head and locked in a storage locker?"

"I got a call." he grumbled.

"Another body?" The story was familiar.

"Yeah. You, too?"

"No. Cable called, said you hadn't checked in," She felt like an idiot. The call should have smelled of a setup from the start. Unfortunately her mind wasn't as sharp as it could be these days, too many distractions.

Blake sighed, "When I arrived, I was surprised by the lack of big whites on scene, so I drew, called for backup and then I heard a female voice. She was crying out. I entered the building and I am embarrassed to report, that is my last memory."

Timber looked around her. "There was no female here when I arrived, just you. Do you think it's another vic?"

"Maybe. Why did you come in here?"

"Your car." She hoped he wouldn't realize she had rushed in, fearing for his safety. The feeling that erupted from seeing him lying unconscious on the cement floor was not something she ever wanted to relive. "Cable gave me the address. So…"

"Did you see anything?" he asked.

She shook her head. "No. I entered, saw you and secured the scene. As I was checking you for a pulse, the door shut and the bolt slid into place."

"Why are you dressed like that?" he asked, tilting his head to the side as if trying to see her from every angle.

His sudden left turn staggered her. "That's what you want to know?" she asked, astounded by his undaunted focus on her ridiculous attire.

"Yes." he said slowly, scanning her from lips to crotch and back again. She felt naked under his intense gaze.

"I had a date." As soon as she said it, she knew she had him; his eyes squinted into dark slits, his posture stiffened and a muscle jumped in his jaw.

"Oh." he said in a tone that corresponded with his sudden change in mood.

"Really?" she smiled at him, deciding to share her plans and see where it took them.

"Really what?" he asked

"Oh. You said 'Oh'. Is that all you have to say?" she prodded.

He mocked, "Tell me his name so I can kick his ass. Is that better?"

Absurdly, she liked the way that sounded and told him, "Yes."

"So, what's his name?" It was his turn to prod.

"Robin Blake." she stated flatly and watched closely for his reaction.

He stared at her blankly. She could see his brain tick, tick, ticking away. A loud humming startled her and she turned toward the sound. "Shit!" she exclaimed, a form of realization setting in. Cold air blasted from a series of vents along the top of the square space. "Holy fuck nut!"

"Girl, you are eloquent." Blake said.

She turned back to him and asked astounded, "Do you realize what is happening?"

"I don't have brain damage." he said.

"Why are you so goddamn calm?" she demanded.

"Because, I had a feeling as soon as you stopped freaking out over me, you would freak out over the situation. One person losing it seemed like enough."

"So, this whole time I was worried about your bleeding ass, you knew we were trapped in a fucking death room?"

"That's dramatic." he said blandly.

"Well, I am dramatic!" she gasped as the air blew over her exposed skin.

He began to laugh, his chest rising and falling as his stomach muscles bunched in hilarity. Timber watched him her eyes wide, her breath quickly becoming visible puffs of smoke. "Crap! Stop laughing!"

He stood cautiously, one hand still pressing the t-shirt to his wounded head. His torso was long and lean. One shoulder had red smears that had seeped though his shirt earlier. Other than that, he seemed almost perfect. His pale skin was in sharp contrast to the dark line of hair that started at the base of his sternum descending, disappearing below the low slung waist of his running pants. As he moved, he seemed to regain his strength. With his free hand he reached out and gripped her high on the right arm. Gently but firmly, he guided her to the door. "Stand here for a minute." He let her go. She wasn't sure what he was doing. He walked around the room running his free hand along the wall, all of them cast in shadows. As if he understood her curiosity, he explained, "I'm looking for a thermostat. Maybe there's a temperature control." He sounded hopeful.

She couldn't help but be cynical "Yeah, then we wait and in no time the cavalry will come and save us before we starve."

"No worries. The world may accept my disappearance easily enough, but you are a Federal agent. Isn't there a protocol?"

She nodded. "I'm sure my SAC will send out a team when I don't check in. Question is, did I leave a trail of bread crumbs?"

"Did you?" He stopped and stared at her expectantly.

"Not exactly." She frowned, starting to grasp the enormity of their situation. "I called Patrolman Spokes and told him not to disturb me unless it was an emergency." She grimaced as she said the next words. "I said I needed twenty-four hours to work the case."

"Ah," he said, then clarified. "Everyone thinks you're at home, reading files and using your immense brain to crack the case?"

"Well, Cable knows, but I told him I would handle it."

"Nice."

"Yep."

"How often do you do that?" he asked, still walking the perimeter

"What? Go home and work alone?" she shrugged.

Blake nodded, obviously knowing the answer before she said, "In almost every case."

"Timber!" he exclaimed making her jump.

"What? I like to work alone." she defended.

"Have you read the definition of task force? Damnit, you are the perfect target. Why didn't I see this?"

"What the hell does that mean?" What the hell was going on? First he was blaming her and now he seemed to be swinging in an entirely different direction.

"I know you. I know what's happening; I should have seen this coming." Blake said.

"I don't know what the fuck you and your swollen ego are bitching about, but no one could have seen this shit coming."

"I should have. I've seen it before."

"What? Oh, with Dan? How could you see that? And what has that got to do with this?"

The look on his face said it all

"You blame yourself for what happened?" she continued.

"It's not a matter of blame, it's a matter of fact. I figured it out too late."

"No, you didn't! She's alive Blake."

"If you can call it that." he said.

"I think she might disagree and, anyway, you did figure it out. You knew where she was. When everyone else was fucking around with magic and mojo, you were the only one with any realistic solution."

He shook his head.

"Stop! Self deprecation is not sexy." Timber said

"Not really looking to be sexy." he said, a scowl distorting his face.

"Too late."

"So what you're saying is that this is your fault and not mine?"

"The blame game, I love it. Okay, for now, this is all my fault. I'm the dumb ass that got us locked in a freezer."

"Gosh, you must believe we're done for."

"Gosh?" she mocked, almost laughing, then shivered.

"Stop picking on me. I'm bleeding." he whined.

"That card is bent. Stop playing it. Anyway the bleeding should be stopping any second now. This cold is probably saving you from bleeding to death." Timber assured him.

He stopped walking and dropped his arm to his side in defeat. "No gauge."

"Bummer."

"Yeah. My head hurts."

She was worried. He looked too pale. "No wonder."

“I’m gonna sit down.” he said and she began to feel her stomach tighten at the idea he could be in real danger.

“Good plan.” she said, trying to keep her voice calm.

Pressing his back to the steel wall, he slid to the floor. “If we die I’m really going to have issues in my next life.”

She laughed. “You don’t believe in that crap.”

“Maybe I do, this seems kind of karmic. Two people I care about trapped by a nut in one lifetime. Not likely to be a coincidence.”

“I’m not a big believer in coincidence; you have to let that go. Plus you just admitted you care about me, better watch it. You may be losing too much blood.”

“The bleeding has stopped.” he told her and she wondered if he was lying.

“Great.” she said, choosing to believe.

“Yep, now I can live long enough to freeze to death.”

She shivered and he pulled her close so that her cheek was pressed into his warm chest. She was amazed that he was so warm; she knew it wouldn’t last long. The air was rapidly becoming colder. The blowing current may have stopped for the time being but it was only a matter of time before it started up again maintaining the frigidity of the space. She remembered a similar scene playing out on a soap opera her mom watched when she was growing up. The two beautiful people caught in the freezing room had been very cliché in their attempts to stay warm. Timber wondered if Blake had contemplated that alternative. His hands rubbed against her exposed back trying to create friction. She could feel the warmth slowly seeping from his form. “You should move away from that wall.”

“Not yet.” he said.

“How’s your head?” she asked and she felt herself starting to relax, listening to the thud of his strong heart.

“Better. The cold is helping.” he answered.

“That’s not going to last.” she murmured. She smiled, remembering that they had been bickering a few minutes before.

“I know.” he said. “We need to stay warm.”

"I can feel my heart starting to slow. I'm tired, Blake." She was so relaxed she couldn't remember why she had been irritated earlier.

He pulled on the string at her back and the small piece of material fell away. Without preamble, his mouth was on her, pulling a hard nub into his mouth. She arched in his arms, pressing closer to him and felt her body immediately start to warm. She still felt the sleepy drug of the cold; her blood was moving faster again, as his mouth pulled on her. His arms left her and his mouth disappeared. She moaned and then was lifted at the hips, her pants pulled from her. She shivered and looked up at him. He laid his bloody shirt and her pants on the ground and moved her to lay on them. He was still so strong, even with his blood loss and the cold. She briefly wondered if this was the right thing and then he was on top of her, his body heat blocking out all cognizant thought.

His voice was rough. "Sorry for the rush, but I need to move this along for the sake of time."

She didn't remember him shedding his pants, so she felt some shock as he entered her suddenly, filling her and causing butterflies to jump and dance deep inside as she stretched to accommodate his girth. He pulled away slowing and then entered again. Her breath caught and she cried out as he hit her in just the right spot. She gripped his hips and pulled him tight. He kept his movements slow and measured. Her heart was slamming against her chest as she looked up into his eyes. He was looking at her with awe. She turned her head.

"Don't do that!" he demanded. She looked back and was stunned by the open emotion there. Was he moved because he believed they were going to die? Their eyes locked and he continued his slow torment, stroking her internal wall, creating just enough friction to keep her on the edge. She clenched and wiggled beneath him.

"Stop that." he groaned. "I'm trying to make this last. If I come, I'm going to pass out and we are going to die."

Timber gasped "I can't believe you just said that."

He pressed inside her harder this time and she moaned. She was close to going over the edge. He reached behind her head and lifted her mouth to his. The kiss was hungry and deep; the whole time, he continued his slow onslaught. Timber felt the top of her head grow warm. Her center began to quiver and her mouth fell open in ecstasy. He licked her lips and her teeth, moaning into her open mouth as warmth washed from her center and around his hard shaft. He began to move faster, her body convulsing around him. She was wondering how long a person could come before he died of pure pleasure when another round of spasms caught her in their grip. There was a pounding in her ears, his mouth moved from hers and he stilled. "Do you hear that?"

"What?" she gasped? "I don't hear anything."

"Listen." he demanded.

She did. She could still only hear her blood rushing and the sound of her pounding heart. She clenched.

"Oh, God." He looked down at her in dismay and then moved away. She felt his exit as fully as she has felt the initial impact and it was equally devastating.

"No! …What?" She tried to grab onto him, but he was slick with sweat and her hand slid away. He was slipping on his gray pants pulling them up to cover himself. Stunned and shaken she pushed up on elbows and crossed one arm over her chest.

"Get dressed, the cavalry is here."

"Huh?" As suddenly as it had disappeared, her hearing was back. Sirens blared outside the door. How had she missed such a racket? She scrambled upright just as the door began to open. Blake moved in front of her as an officer and two detectives pushed into the room.

"Detective! Thank God. We got a call and uh …" the voice trailed off as he took in the situation.

The snickers were muffled, Timber was mortified. It couldn't have possibly been worse.

She wasn't sure which detective said it, regardless, it was clear that they had come to the obvious conclusion.

"Let's give Agent Byrne and Detective Blake a minute to straighten out before we uh.. save the day."

"Good idea," Blake said, and then to Timber, "Ya might wanna hurry."

As the noises continued outside, Timber rushed to get dressed. Blake tied the strings on her small top and she picked her gun off of the cold floor. As they were walking out, an ambulance came screaming into the lot.

"So," Blake said, laughter evident in his slow drawl. "You never really did explain the outfit."

"Bite me! Asshole!" she said and walked as far away from him and his amazing smell. She felt a small twitch and shiver inside and realized she was still at the end of an awe-inspiring orgasm. She shivered, shook her body and yelled over her shoulder, "I hate you!" She heard his chuckle and kept walking.

Chapter Twenty-one

“I’m leaving Blake in charge while I go to the lake.” Timber’s tone left no room for doubt about her intentions.

`“Is he up to it?” came the voice on the other end.

`“Yep, he’s great.” It was true. The head wound had turned out to be superficial. All of the real trauma had developed from other things.

“What the hell happened out there?”

She felt some shame at admitting the truth. If she knew anything; it was that her SAC could always see through her bullshit.

“I wasn’t thinking clearly and I let him get the drop on me.”

“You were thinking about what exactly?” he asked, pointing his tone like an arrow.

She felt her face go red and she was extremely relieved this conversation was happening on the phone. Timber knew there was no secret in the soup. This was an exercise in humiliation. She would normally balk at such an intrusive tone; unfortunately she was walking a fine line and didn’t need the complications of a suspension. She took a deep breath and dove in with the truth. “Sir, I was prepared for a much needed night off and I was focused on spending some down time with my” she paused, not knowing what to call him, “…lover.” She had decided blunt was probably the best way to go. “Anyway…” she rushed on, “I was on my way out. I had the task force busy with busy work and I wasn’t prepared for…oh shit…it was just a bad situation and I’m freakin’ embarrassed.”

“Seems to me,” he said, “That an agent should always be prepared.”

"No, that's a Boy Scout," she said. To her relief he laughed and she blew out her breath.

"Look, Byrne, you are going to be dealing with the backlash from this clusterfuck for a decade. I understand why you want to run, but I'm going on the record to say bad idea."

She started to argue, "I…"

He cut in, "I'm not going to stop you. I don't have a pony in this show. We have enough to cover you and the Bureau is not exposed, so go get your shit together and come back. Just get on with it."

Timber had a mixed reaction to his statement. She was relieved that he seemed to be accepting of her decision, yet he was mocking and derogatory in his delivery. If she hadn't been the person she was she may have taken more offense to his words. As it was, she recognized his tone and force and realized if the roles were reversed she would be reacting almost precisely as he was. She began to breathe easier and told him that she would clean up the mess when she got back.

He made a 'harrumph' noise and told her to keep her shirt on. The comment wasn't lost on her and she laughed as he unceremoniously ended the call.

"Well, shit," she said as she stared at the phone in her hand. She had dreaded this call, fully expecting it to be filled with recriminations and degradation followed by threats. To her immense relief, he didn't seem to realize the grand scale of the shit storm they were in for. Maybe it was for the best, maybe not. The reality was, eventually the media was going to glom on to the story and from that point on, her ass would be glued to her desk. Metaphor or not, if she was going to get away, now was the time. Plus, she missed her daddy and when a girl missed her daddy she began to make bad relationship choices.

Before she could slip the phone in her pocket it began to sing. "Come on!" she bitched and carried the conversation starter on to the next level," What?"

"What the hell fell in your soup?"

His voice did nothing to calm her. In fact, she felt pain behind her right eye and pressed her thumb below her brow. “I really can’t explain what is going on with me. Maybe it has something to do with a certain male pain in my…”

“Hey! Watch it; you know how sensitive I am!”

It was strange to hear him try to make her feel better. How dare he be sweet to her when she was angry and confused? “Stop that!” she demanded. “Anyway, I am leaving and…”

“Stop what?” he ignored her last comment.

“Being charming! It’s taking the air out of my…” She suddenly felt stupid and shut her mouth.

“Where do you have air? Are you gassy? This is probably too much information,” He laughed at her expense. Even under these circumstances his voice sent tingles across her skin.

“Oh, shut up!” she snapped.

The laughing stopped as quickly as it had begun, “Be safe and enjoy your trip. I’ve got it handled.”

“Thanks, Blake.” Her relief was short-lived.

“That said, I think you’re a coward,” he said.

“Lovely,” she mumbled and pressed ‘end’ on her phone. She stared at the dark screen and cursed, throwing the phone and watching it bounce, the cover snapping off and flying in two directions. The satisfaction was immense.

Chapter Twenty-two

The setting sun reflected off of the murky lake water. Stumps of black, rotting trees pierced its glassy surface. The images of dead things raced behind Timber's eyes. Even as she took in the dark beauty surrounding her, she couldn't shake the visuals that banged around in her muddled mind's eye. A creak behind her had her whipping around and reaching for a gun that wasn't there. She still wore her black slacks and button-down white starched shirt, but the gun holster wrapped around her shoulders and secured at her back was empty.

A deep chuckle made her stop her accustomed action and smile into the eyes of her father. Cal Byrne was a tall, barrel-chested man with pale blue eyes that crinkled at the corners when he smiled. His smile was large and came easy. He had shaved his head last year and although it made him seem just a touch more imposing, it suited him.

"Hey, Daddy," Timber said, and dropped her hand.

"Hi there, little girl." He moved forward and wrapped her up in his strong arms.

Her head rested against his solar plexus and she heard his heart beating steady and strong. "Right about now I'm glad for that rule," he said.

She lifted her head and looked up at him. "Oh come on daddy, you know I wouldn't have shot you."

He gently grabbed her shoulders and held her at arm's length. "You never can be sure of anything when you're surprised." He tilted his head and dropped his arms.

The rule at the lake was: no guns. It was a rule that could never be negotiated. Cal Byrne had four sons and one daughter; of those, three were in law enforcement and one was a firefighter. Save the firefighter, they all carried firearms on their person at all times, unless at the lake. Guns were put in a safe in the main cabin upon arrival. If that did not happen, you were subject to the 'Wrath of Cal', a rare occurrence and one to be avoided whenever possible.

"You haven't been here for a while. Not that I'm not tickled about it, but why are you here?"

"Needed to do some thinking," she said, and thought that seldom had truer words been uttered.

His southern drawl washed over her and reminded her of why she always came home in times of crisis. "Well darlin', whatever you want, you have it. I'm just glad you're safe. I was hearin' some whispers about some bad stuff happenin' up there in Denver. Are you on that case with those murdered boys?"

When she raised an eyebrow, he laughed and said, "Okay, okay, I won't ask any questions. You do your thinking and I'll send the boys out here when they get in." She groaned, the boys? The last thing she needed were her brothers swarming around her asking a million questions, being over-protective.

Her father grasped her hand, gave it a tight squeeze and let go. "You can handle it. You've been handling those boys your whole life." He turned and said over his shoulder "Dinner's in an hour, baby girl; catfish. So work up an appetite. You do your thinking. Take the kayak out, do whatever you need. You'll be alright."

"Thanks, Daddy." Timber shook her head in abject awe. Her father could make her feel so strong with just a few words. If it were her brothers standing in front of her, she would be questioned, pressured, then they would feel the need to go into a protection mode. The never-ending male need to fix it was an irritating experience she had dealt with for as long as she could remember. Not Daddy. Daddy believed in her. He understood her strengths and accepted that her stature was an illusion, not a billboard for an actual product.

"When your feelin' less like you wanna shoot something, you come on up to the house and see your momma." he ordered in his easy tone.
"Yes, sir," she said and laughed out loud. It felt good to laugh. Timber watched him walk down the dock. His gait was sure as he stepped off of the wood onto the grassy bank. Cal Byrne had recently turned seventy years old, yet he was as light-footed as he was light-hearted. Sometimes she was amazed by his age. He seemed like a young man to her, and although he was just over six foot, she saw him as a giant among men. She pondered more than once if that was why she hadn't had a lasting relationship. Did she expect too much? Were her standards too high? It was beginning to occur to her that she would never be happy till she met a man who lived up to her strapping daddy.

Timber turned and once again stared out over the lake, trying to work the problem. Things had gotten muddled. This killer was crossing all boundaries. Not sticking to any Modus Operandi and bodies were piling up. She was frustrated and needed a break. She also felt a sneaking specter of denial creeping around her edges. The real issue that had her running for the Texas border had not been a series of grisly massacres. That was something that she could handle. Given time, Timber had every confidence she would see what she was missing and everything would fall into place. The same could not be said for her tumultuous love life. Love life? Is that what she was calling it? The cause of her frustration and confusion was as simple as it was timeless. Passion, passion for something she couldn't have and passion for someone she shouldn't want. Robin.

"Robin Blake" she mumbled his name and an instant image of his coffee colored eyes, broad white smile and deep cleft flashed in her mind's eye.

She shook off the mental distress and decided to follow her father's advice. She walked to the garage that stood at the edge of the water and lifted the kayak off the wall. It was heavy and awkward, but after the almost monumental task of getting it off its hooks, she knew she was on the right path. Purpose was making her feel better already. She grabbed the strap at the nose of the small craft and dragged it to the edge of the water. She rolled up her sleeves while retrieving the oar and looked down at her slacks. *Oh well, no time to change.* She climbed inside and pushed off.

The oars felt good in her hands and as she paddled she felt her muscles pull, stretch then bunch as she fought the wind. Initially her mind raced with possibilities. She saw the bodies splayed out before her, felt the absolute terror remembering her fear for Robin and the utter confusion that these murders didn't match up on any level. Then there was the refrigerator. A trap set by a criminal madman had brought her more pleasure than she cared to admit. Just thinking about how Blake felt inside her made her pulse jump and her stomach tighten. The acceleration of her heart rate kicked up her speed and the small craft skated across the still water. As she felt the beads of sweat slip between her breasts, her mind began to clear. Body moving to the beating of her pulse, she began to push herself harder. Blake licking her open mouth, the taste of sweat and cinnamon as she lost herself to his powerful thrusts.

"Stop it!" she screamed and maneuvered the oar, turning the boat, changing course too quickly. Just as she feared she would capsize, a large black bird perched on a protruding branch took flight, its wings slicing through the air with a singular noise. The boat righted itself and Timber gasped at the beauty and the serenity around her. Slowly she began to rotate her arms, using the oar to propel her forward. She was careful to protect her shoulders, keeping the motion low and wide. Her speed increased and she somehow managed to keep her mind on problems with possible solutions.

By the time Timber reached the center of the lake, her midsection was burning and her thighs were tight. At times when her body was revved high, she found that her mind began to do its best work. The sweat dripped down her back and cooled her hot skin. She ran through the details of the case in her mind. The victims: all men; ages: across the board; different socio economic status, different skin color, different nationalities, different religions. It was as if this person was intentionally choosing victims as different as possible. *Could that be the key?* She lifted her oar from the water and coasted forward propelled by her past efforts. She said it out loud. "It's as if he's choosing different victims on purpose." She dipped her paddle in the water and began moving again.

Why? *Think, think.* First victim mutilated, second poisoned. Then gunshot .The words on the wall and the house that's not a home. Then there was the blood. Blood that matched none of the victims. And the apple. What was the apple? *Okay. go back,* she thought

She paddled harder. Someone was finding victims that were poles apart. Too different to be linked. Changing M.O., changing everything. Making contact with the lead detective, Then focusing on Charlie. Pulling in the media. Classic. *And what the hell was the apple about? And the quotes? What does that mean???* She was sure that the quotes and the apple had something to do with each other. At the moment the task force was focusing on the theory of more than one perpetrator. Every time the profile started to make sense to them, the M.O. would change completely. The only quantifiable things were the letters and box, all sent by the same person. She was sure of it. She was sure of it, but she was the only one. Timber felt like she was alone and losing ground every second. Silly considering all of the people working with her. Her arms pumped harder as she shifted her weight and used her right shoulder to press down and turn the small craft. Her left arm relaxed slightly as the boat turned in a wide ark.

An idea was brewing, an idea that felt crazy, but she needed to talk to someone, needed to bounce her idea off of an uninvolved party. As her triceps began to burn, she approached the shoreline. Her white cotton shirt was sticking to her skin; she felt great, invigorated. She slid the boat easily onto the beach, jumped out, pulled the rope to secure the craft and walked to the small wooden enclosed shower.

The stall was covered from all angles but Timber didn't bother removing her sweat-soaked clothing. She turned the knob and stepped under the spray. Due to the days hot temperature the water wasn't as cold as she would have liked, but it did the job anyway, slicking the sweat from her clothes and skin. She felt her heart rate return to normal.

"I should have known where I'd find you. You always were a shower hog!" The deep vibrato didn't startle her. She was as familiar with that voice as she was her own, and under any circumstance, all it could ever do was comfort and cheer her. She turned off the shower, stepped from the enclosure and jumped into her oldest brother's outstretched arms.

Undaunted by her wet attire and dripping hair, Brent lifted her off the ground, and turned in a circle. "Hey, sugar," he said, looking down into her face. "Dad said you were lookin' peaked and I have to agree." He dropped her to her feet and ran his thumb under her right eye. "There's darkness here; anything to it?"

Timber looked into his worried face and smiled. This is why she had come home, this is what she needed; people who understood her. But more than that, they all understood her job. Brent was her oldest brother; he had turned fifty this year, and he wore it well. His blond hair was still a full mass, disheveled as always. The crinkles around his blue eyes only added to his appeal. He wasn't a big man, and like her, he was a tribute to their mother's genetics. Wiry and short for a man, he reached only five foot-eight inches tall, still towering over Timber. Despite his size, Brent could easily hold his own with any man twice his size and half his age. He was the first in the family to join the force. Soon after, his younger brother, Trec, had followed in his footsteps. To the boys' everlasting frustration, the youngest had joined the fire department.

Brick Byrne was the brother Timber was closest to, despite the fact that he was the only Byrne to defect to the heroes' side. That was what Brent called him, 'Everyone's hero'. For a while, the siblings did their best to influence Timber in her career choice, but for her it was never a choice. She was a cop from the beginning. Mediating arguments between the boys, solving problems, finding things the family had lost and discovering which boy had wrecked the car. Trec was still pissed about that one. They called her the 'nosy detective'. No one was surprised when she joined the force. Although Brick did do his very best to send a load of guilt her way, lamenting the unfairness that already existed within the law enforcement household. The only sticking point with the others was that she had gone Federal.

Brent was looking at her with his patented concern, and for a moment, she felt guilt at bringing her worries home. He grabbed her by the hand and began dragging her up the small hill to the cabin. "You need some dry clothes and a hot meal."

She allowed herself to be pulled and relaxed into old roles as she teased, "Sounds good, Bossy."

He pulled on her arm hard, slinging her forward. She almost tripped as she shot in front of him. Just as she regained her footing he pushed her from behind and laughed as she ran up the hill out of reach of his irritating playfulness. As she pulled open the screen door it creaked loudly and Timber yelled, "Mom!" She looked over her shoulder and Brent scowled, "Tattletale!"

Ω

By the time dinner was over, her worries had subsided and she knew she had done the right thing by coming home and finding her center with her family. That sentiment was driven in with her brother's next words.

"Wait, so what you're saying is; the eyeballs were scooped out?" Brent said and grimaced, balancing the dinner plates and sliding them into the soapy water. He bent and kissed his mother on the cheek. "Great dinner, Mom. Thanks."

"Yep, clean." Timber said and skirted around him. She dropped two glasses into the water and slid onto a high-backed stool that sat around the large center butcher-block island.

"Were there any guts missing?" Trec asked, sitting and picking his teeth with the corner of a metal-pronged fork.

"Trec!" his mother snapped and turned, plucking the fork from his fingers.

"Ah, Ma, come on. We're talkin' about a murder; it's not gonna be pretty," he whined, a big grin on his handsome face. Trec was his mother's favorite. They all knew it, despite her vehement denials. They also realized it was due to the fact that he was the carbon copy of her one and only true love.

"He's right darlin'. Maybe we should go for a walk." Cal said sweetly to his wife and Timber saw the beginnings of worry in his eyes. Occasionally, her father forgot her mother's mammoth strength in favor of his protective nature. It astounded Timber how he could be so supportive with her and yet so utterly protective when it came to his wife.

The tiny woman lifted her chin and said defiantly. "I am not going to leave my kitchen just because the topic has turned ugly." She shrugged her small shoulders that Timber knew could hold up the sky and turned toward the sink, dipping her hands into the sudsy water. "You talk about what you want, I'm fine. Just watch your language."

All eyes turned to Timber and she threw her hands into the air. "What? Why are you all looking at me?"

Her brothers and father laughed loudly, but the only sign that her mother was amused was the slight telling shake to her back and shoulders.

"Anyway," she said, choosing not to take the bait. "Was there something missing? Not really."

"What does that mean?" Brick asked. He had a grimace on his face, like he might know the answer. Brick may be a firefighter, but growing up in a house filled with cops had given him a perspective that few had.

"Well it was there, but not where it should be." she said, using implication and swirling her fingers in front of her to signal that it was far too explicit to talk about in front of their mother.

On cue their mother spoke up "Peach cobbler?"

A chorus of "Great.""Yeah." "My favorite." "Thanks, Mom." echoed through the sizeable kitchen. She turned from the sink, a wide smile on her face and nodded. As their mother busied herself getting plates and retrieving the delicacy from the oven, Brent asked "Okay, so what's with the writing on the wall?"

"That is bizarre." Brick said.

"Familiar." said Trec.

"I was thinking that too." Cal piped up, looking more intrigued despite himself. Her dad had often complained that his kids gave him far too much to think about.

"How different was that one?" Brent asked. Brent was a chief now and close to retirement. Although he hated the idea of giving up the job, he hated riding a desk even more and was planning on buying a sailboat to live on. Timber knew he was still a detective at heart and often mused over why he had given it up for beauracracy. It was something he would never share. Seeing him now, chewing over the details she could see he hadn't lost his edge.

"Well," she answered, enjoying the give and take from fresh eyes. "That was the one where we found no body, so… very different."

"What about the other crime scenes?" Brick asked, trying to play along, but sounding bored as he jumped up to help his mother pass out plates of browned peach cobbler with vanilla ice cream piled on top.

"Body dumps." Timber said and smiled at her mom as she scooped up a large bite and stuffed it into her mouth. For a few moments all conversation ceased as the group fell into a haze of food-induced euphoria. The peaches were fresh, the cream thick and sweet; the combination of the warmth and cold made for a delectable decadence. The group moaned and grunted, making the matriarch swell with pride before she rubbed her hand over Timber's back and returned to her chores.

"That sucks." Trec said, referring to her earlier statement.

"He cleans them." Timber said around a full mouth of peaches.

"Well, shit." he said

"I said watch your mouth!" Eliza Byrne snapped.

"Sorry, Mom. Hey, I know what it is; you guys are dumb aaa…buts" Trec stumbled, yet managed to save himself. Timber snickered.

"Better, thank you." Eliza replied, satisfied.

"Why are we dumb butts?" Brick asked, a smirk playing at the corners of his mouth.

"The die pigs thing, it's the Tate-LaBianca murders back in like uh… 1929." Trec said triumphantly.

"'69 knucklehead." Brick said.

"Hey! You didn't think of it." Trec shot back.

"Sure I did, I was just bein' polite and letting you get there, 'cause I know you're getting old and shit." Brick said and laughed. He enjoyed flaunting his youth to his older siblings and found every chance to land a swift kick.

Timber thought it was his way of getting back at them for all of the 'hero' jabs.

"Ouch!" Brent said, taking the comment as a bigger bash to him considering he was the oldest.

"Can I just point out I am not the one with a foul mouth here." Timber said, pointing fingers at her arguing brothers.

"Noted." Eliza said

"Thank you." Timber said and made a face at Brick.

"That was Manson, right?" Cal asked

"Yeah." Trec said "I can't remember the case exactly, but I know there were two events related to the Manson killings. One was that famous director's wife and her friends and the other was random. I can't remember which scene had the writings, but it was definitely the Manson deal."

"How many people did he kill?" Cal asked before putting a heaping forkful of cobbler into his mouth. He seemed to be enjoying his time with his children more than the tasty treat.

"Manson wasn't actually at the first scene, he sent a few people from his cult to do the job. I can't remember the second one, I think he may have been there but he never got his hands dirty." Trec replied.

"I don't think he was at either scene." Brick interjected

"Hasn't he been in prison ever since?" Eliza asked, looking over her shoulder and adding to the conversation.

"Yep, he went down hard. He's a loopy fuuuhh.. fellow." Timber stuttered.

"Nice save."Brent said and laughed .

"So that phrase written in blood seems pretty pointed." Cal said

"I would say so." Brent agreed.

"Maybe it's saying there is more than one, a leader, pack situation." Brick suggested

"That's one theory," said Timber.

"But… you're not buyin'?" Brent asked.

"Nah. Doesn't feel right," she said.

"The de-escalation is what freaks me out." Timber admitted, and thought about the second body and how in comparison he was almost untouched.

"Yeah." Trec agreed.

Eliza turned and wiped her soapy hands on her apron. "Why does that freak you out?" she asked, using her daughter's phrase. It sounded odd to the younger woman.

Trec spoke up. "Well, under normal circumstances, yeah, but a serial, they get worse as they go. There's a need, a compulsion. When these crazies follow that compulsion they start to kill closer together, in that I mean, the time shortens almost methodically. For instance, they may start killing once a month, then once a week, maybe they kill two in one day. And they always get a little worse. This is all called escalation. We count on this, it means they get careless, the passion, the need supersedes all else and they makes important mistakes. Then, we catch them." Trec ended his explanation as he stood and walked to the sink. He slid his plate into the water, gently pushed aside his mother with his hip and despite her protestations, began washing the dish.

"Wow, Trec! Ever think of going Club Fed?" Timber said and rose to add her dish to the mix.

"Hell no! Anyway, Mom," he said pointedly, ignoring the jab. "If escalation doesn't happen, it means that it's all calculated. Calculation means more bodies, less cohesion and a psychopath much harder to capture."

"If this killer is copying an old murder, doesn't it make sense that the others might be copies, too?" Eliza asked as she took Trec's seat, allowing him to clean the remainder of the dishes.

"That would explain all the different kills." Brent added, nodding.

"It would also explain the de-escalation." Trec said.

"Holy crap!" Timber exclaimed, seeing the case from an entirely new vantage point.

"Now you just have to read up on every murder ever, 'cause if he copied the Manson killings he's not doing serials." Brick said.

"Huh?" Eliza muttered.

"Seriously? You have three cops for kids and you don't know the difference between a spree and a serial?" Brick said, sarcasm leaching into his voice.

"Hey, don't talk to your mother like that." Cal's eyes snapping.

"I know the difference, Brick! I just forgot. Anyway, I'm old, so I can say silly things."

Timber could see Brick was instantly contrite. The room was filled with moans and grimaces as they all denied that their beautiful matriarch was anything but youthful and perfect in every way.

"Gosh, Mom, way to garner some major compliments." Timber snickered and rose from the island. "Looks like I've got some homework to do."

"Grab your piece and I'll drive you to the library, they have those History Channel documentaries." Brent offered.

"Awesome, get popcorn." Brick said.

"Yeah! Byrne family movie night!"Trec added happily jumping on board.

"Do you want me to take notes?" Eliza offered.

"That would be great, Mom," Timber said and smiled, looking around the room at the faces, all of them eager to be a part of her dilemma. "I love you guys!"

"You better," Brick said, "'cause if it gets out that you just shared all this stuff with a firefighter and two civilians, your ass could be in a serious sling."

"Brick, I will wash out your mouth with soap if you don't watch it!" Eliza threatened.

Cal pushed away from the island and said "Come on, bride of mine, let's let the kids alone. I want you all to myself. I'll take you out on the boat."

Timber watched as her mother seemed to swoon in the gaze of her adoring husband. "I'll get my sweater." She looked at her eldest son. "Drive safe and remember to take that curve slow, I don't want another visit from Sheriff Lowe."

"God, Mom! You ever gonna let that go?" Brent asked.

"No." she said over her shoulder as she followed her husband into the cool early evening air.

Chapter Twenty-three

The four young girls sat around the small table and chatted, smiles illuminating their pretty teenage masks. That's what they were to her, masks. Everyone wore one, but teenagers were the nastiest. The lies behind the masks were enormous, and oozing with possibilities. How many times had they lied or stolen, probably from their own parents. She watched them laughing, their eyes showing little real emotion. Payton carried her tray to a nearby table. Her eye line was direct, so looking their way would not seem too overt. She was also close enough to evaluate the situation. The blonde pushed a strand of hair from her cheek and leaned over, showing off ample cleavage as she whispered loudly across the table, "That guy's looking right at you!" she exclaimed. The girl she spoke to was nervously chewing the nail on her index finger and was immediately uncomfortable. Her shoulders slouched, her eyes darted as she began searching for the allusive stranger.

Payton glanced at the man the blonde was referring to. He was looking, but only in a cursory way. He obviously had no feelings, other than disdain, for the small giggling band of hormones. Still the blonde persisted in teasing the other girl. "Come on, Shelly! Ya know ya want him. Oh no! Shelly has an old man boy-boy," she taunted.

Shelly spoke up, "Stop being such a bitch, Rachel!" Then she stood and walked around the table, bumping into the corner of a chair as she went. The two others began to laugh and commend Shelly for her comeback, while still playing up to the obvious leader of the pack. Lots of "ooohs" and "she got you's" erupted as Shelly angrily stomped away, turning a corner into the bathroom hallway. Payton watched the gangly teen. She was a pretty girl, tall, thin with long dark, curly hair. She was too far away for Payton to know her eye color, but she got the strong impression they were light, contrasting eyes. Self-confidence was the girl's problem. If she had that, she would easily overtake Rachel in the beauty department, throwing the group's dynamics crazily out of whack. Rachel obviously knew this and was doing her part to insure that event never took place.

Payton took a bite of the chicken sandwich and savored the rich flavor. There was nothing better than a 'Chick- Fil-A' sandwich and a large cup of milk to wash it down. She loved it here. The food court reminded her of high school. Good times at Schumacher High. She laughed at her stupid joke and almost choked on her chicken. She coughed and quickly sipped her milk before the piece of meat could lodge in her throat.

The girls sipped on long straws, enjoying the many flavors of the Orange Julius, already forgetting the torment of moments before. Payton contemplated going after the girl. She would be an easy target. She was alone, insecure and dying for a good slaughtering. *Don't all teenagers secretly want to die?* Payton contemplated that thought while chewing her food. She was ravenous. She began to take bites in rapid succession, filling her mouth even before she had swallowed the previous bite. Gulps of milk helped the process and soon only paper wrappings and the crumbs from her delicious sandwich littered her tray.

The three remaining girls pushed away from the table, one after the other. The loud scrapes of their chairs echoed off the walls of the large open space. They chattered, shoved each other and giggled as they walked away, leaving all of their trash for someone else to dispose of. Payton crumpled up her sandwich wrapper and dropped it on the center of her tray. She was not surprised that the girls had left their friend, if you could call her that. It still caused her to shake her head in dismay at their blatant disregard for human decency.

As she walked to the large trash can, Payton watched the girls walk into a small store erected specifically for the adolescent diversity. The space was a typical retreat with black-lit walls and bright colored gaudy decorations, to entice the brainless and titillate the retarded. She dumped the trash from the tray and slid it onto the top of the flat lid.

The store was crowded, so Payton knew it wouldn't be hard to blend in with the tight rows of belts, hats and overpriced tee shirts. Teen sweat permeated the air. The space was tight and Payton found herself breathing from her mouth as she pretended to contemplate the veracity of a poster in the far corner. Her thoughts were actually occupied by the voices to her far right. The girls talked about boys, the price of a pair of high-heeled stripper boots, whether they should attend a party at the end of the week and the merits of oral sex. They never mentioned their abandoned friend and Payton wondered how they would feel if they discovered her mutilated corpse draped inside their fancy car. The idea of the guilt and shame she could cause almost made her turn from the shop and seek out poor dejected Shelly.

No! That's typical, cannot be typical! she told herself vehemently, *refocus!* Shelly was never the goal. People like Shelly just needed a little help. Well… a lot of help. But they didn't deserve to die… now Rachel, on the other hand…that bitch had a world of hurt coming her way.

Payton left the store. The clerk glanced at her as she passed through the electric barrier, but turned away disregarding her existence as soon as he was sure she hadn't lifted anything from the premises. The mall was bustling now with early Saturday shoppers taking advantage of the late season sales. School would start soon, giving the Rachel's of the world a fertile breeding ground for their hate and focused humiliations. Payton felt reassured about her decision. Not only was she feeling good about the decision, she was feeling empowered by the idea of making the world a better place. Once Rachel was gone, maybe

Shelly would have time to see how beautiful she was without the blonde bitch's constant ridicule. Of course that could only happen if Shelly stayed alive long enough. The way the girl was acting, she was begging for someone to take advantage and change her small life for the worse.

Shelly was leaning against the corner of the long hallway leading to the bathroom, her back to the open space beyond. Her eyes searched the crowd, and in one palm she gripped a sparkling red cell phone. She looked lost and very alone. Payton groaned in disgust as she watched the girl bring up her pinky finger and begin chomping on the nail. Any man watching this girl would know she was easy pickings. Her friends had left her to fend for herself in a jungle of predators. Payton turned the corner and silently sent the young girl a blessing of good luck.

Chapter Twenty-four

The cacophony of voices filling the room was silenced as the impact of books on wood reverberated off the walls. Timber watched as all eyes turned to her and her empty box, its former occupants now sliding across the center table: the covers screaming for attention. 'BTK, Entering Hands' by John Leak, Ann Rule's 'Green River, Running Red', 'Criminal Behavior' by Curt R. Bartol and Anne M. Bartol, 'Unholy Messenger' by Stephen Sinular and Helter Skelter, a bio pic released to DVD in 2004. Among the hardback bound books and films, one stood out, sliding to the center of the mass. The title was lengthy, but summed up the topic accurately: 'The Serial Killers: the Sick Minds Behind the Most Gruesome Murders in America'.

Blake turned from the white board and stepped to the table; an odd mixture of anticipation, amusement and bewilderment playing across his features.

Timber avoided his eyes and addressed the room, making eye contact with several of the detectives and uniformed officers. She knew he would notice the deliberate avoidance, she couldn't help herself. Timber knew if she met his eyes, the night in the freezer would flood her memory banks. At that point she would begin to curse uncontrollably, stumbling over her words and every person in the room would see her for what they thought she really was, a pretty girl with no brains when it came to a swinging cock. On some level, she knew this was not a truth, but it was somehow better than the alternative. At least this was an idea she could be pissed about. The alternative she wouldn't, couldn't even contemplate.

"It's time to get into research mode, boys!" Timber said and spread her hands over the table. "This is a library of all of the biggest serial cases in the last thirty years." She smiled sweetly but her voice held a determination not to be argued with. "I expect you all to become very familiar with these cases, so get reading. I just spent 24 hours doing research. Your turn."

Collective groans erupted in the room.

Timber shook her head in disgust, "Come on! You can all read, right?"

Officer Cable asked, "Can't we just watch movies?"

She waved away the arguments. "Sure, Cable, you and Peterson can watch the movies."

"Hey, why does he get the pretty girl?" Detective Scott asked.

"Is that sexual harassment I hear?" Timber quipped, good-naturedly.

"No, ma'am." Despite the address, he seemed to be mocking her.

Timber blinked and shook her head, musing about the detective's unprofessional attitude and etiquette. His shirt was wrinkled and his shoes old and worn, one completely untied. She was tempted to make an issue of it but decided it wasn't the bureau's responsibility to make the locals look good.

"Well, maybe you should get to reading, Detective."

"Sounds good, Boss." A much younger detective standing in the back of the room said and pushed forward to look down at the table. He sounded genuine. This one was obviously new, probably on the job just long enough to get out of the bag, a term used by guys on the job to describe the four years required to drive the car. Most officers had higher aspirations; the 'bag' was where they all had to pay their dues. This one was fresh.

Timber smiled as he rummaged through the stack and grabbed the black book with the bright red letters spelling 'BTK'.

"Why are we reading about a bunch of locked-up or dead criminals?" Peterson inquired, pushing her ponytail over her shoulder, then began to twirl it into a bun at the back of her neck.

"Because, I am starting to find way too many coincidences and as we all know…" Timber waited and looked around the room, her eyes skipping over Blake.

"Coincidences, Schmoincidences?" Cable said.

"E-e-exactly." she pointed at him and drew out the word. "The message scrawled on the wall…"

"Pigs Die?" Peterson asked.

"Something like that. Remember the Tate-LaBianca murders?"

"I don't know about you, but I think that was a little before my time." Detective Scott said, rubbing his bald head.

A voice came from the back. "Really, Scott? You look like you could have been the lead detective."

The room erupted in a series of "Oooohs and aahhhhs."

"Yeah, old man. Why don't you fill us in on what Agent Byrne is talking about." Cable said sarcastically, playing into the oldest taunting game on the job.

"Yeah Scott, where are the field notes?" Peterson quipped.

"Ha, ha ha." Detective Scott said. "Anyway?"

"Anyway," Timber interjected, "we're going to discover if there are any more coincidences. Then we will work out a profile and go from there." Timber watched as they all stared at the table then back to her. For several seconds she watched as they all stood, not moving. "Today!" she said and was pleased when they jumped and then began grabbing books from the table.

"Isn't this a tad farfetched?" The voice in her ear instantly had her hackles rising. She took two steps to the side in defense. His hip slammed into the back of a plastic chair with metal legs, it screeched across the floor. She looked around to see reactions and everyone glanced away quickly. "Oh shit." she muttered, feeling clumsy and paranoid.

"What is wrong with you?" Blake looked down at her with the face of a man that appeared to have not been deep inside her less than seventy-two hours earlier. She felt nausea wash over her. She was getting pulled back in time. He was turning off again and she was on. More than on, she cringed. And he would never know it.

'Stop asking me that." she said, focusing on the case again, mad as hell that he was so much more composed that she could ever be.

"Do I do that?" He sounded so good; she remembered his breath in her ear, his taste in her mouth.

She shook her head hard, then nodded. She knew she must look crazy. "Yes, and it implies I am flawed."

'No, it is a question about your behavior." He tilted his head to one side and asked. " Everything okay, Timber? You are acting a little strange."

"My behavior?" She wanted to yell and scratch his face off. How could he not understand how hard this was? He was acting like he didn't remember. She kept her voice calm "What about your behavior?"

"What about it?" His innocent act was appalling.

"Well for starters..."she said, and then realized that she didn't want to have this conversation. He didn't want her. It was so very clear now. They worked together, nothing more. If she could only focus on that, everything else would go back to normal. Normal and consistent, just what she needed.

"Yeah?" he pressed

"Forget it." She felt tired suddenly. Her mind was full of case notes, stats and criminal personalities; she had no room for romance.

"No, really. For starters….?" He pressed, crossing his arms over his chest defensively.

"People are looking." she said, coming up with childish reasons to move the conversation away from where it couldn't go.

"Let them look. I ironed my shirt, I have a new tie. I'm good."

"You are a dick." she said, and looked at the bright red superhero tie in disgust.

"I am not. I'm considerate, trustworthy, intelligent and super good-looking," he said with utter confidence.

"Super?" she asked.

"Super," he confirmed, chest out, grin in place. A grin she would love to wipe off his face with the knuckles of her tight fist.

"You forgot modest." she said.

"Oh, yes I did, sorry, I am also extremely modest. So do you want to tell me why the war room is suddenly the Arapahoe County library, police branch, or do you want to fight?" He was beginning to see how angry she was.

"I want to fight," she said bluntly.

"Would you mind terribly if we did that later?" he asked in the same tone he would use if postponing a coffee date.

She wanted to let it go. Wanted for him to pack up his perfect face and his smoking hot body and get the hell out of her face, her case and her life. But she couldn't, so she said "When?"

"I could pencil it in for, I don't know, tonight around nineish?" He seemed serious.

"Okay." She replied, trying to match his tone.

"Good, now what's up?" His hands slipped into his slacks pockets pushing his jacket to the sides and showing of how nicely his shirt slipped into his pants with a flatness a teenage boy would envy.

She felt dismay at the errant feelings and tried once again to focus on the job "I think we have a copycat."

"Which pattern?" he asked interest obvious in his tone.

"That's where my theory breaks down. I see a lot of subtle notes but only one big melody."

"Music metaphors?"

"You are so quick."

"What's the melody?" he asked, playing along.

"Death to all Pigs."

"I remember that; is it the Tate thing?"

"Yes. In 1969, a group of men and women entered the home of a famous director's wife and killed her and a few of her friends. The director was out of town and subsequently became a suspect."

"Did they think, maybe a kill for hire?" he suggested.

"Exactamundo." She pressed a finger to her nose. "But they got over that when the cult killed again. Turns out that this crazy fucker Charles Manson was the guy behind it all."

"So because of the writing on the wall you think someone is using a script?" he asked.

"Why not?" she shrugged one shoulder and said "It has been done before; some fan following in a killer's footsteps to gain some of the gory glory."

He shrugged. "Any other similarities?"

"A few, but they're mixed together and you would be amazed at how many of these freaks do the same gross shit. But that phrase written in blood," she shook her head, "That is too much."

"What about that second one, 'for heaven's sake, catch me'. Was that it?" he asked.

" I don't know, I'm hoping the crew will figure it. I think it's a lead and I want to get the profiler in here. I heard the CBI has sent in their best."

"That's what I hear."

"Well, if she's so fucking good, where is my profile?" She was about to ask again when she noticed he wasn't looking at her. His gaze was locked onto something behind her.

"Well, I think it's in her hand," he answered, a smirk curving the corner of his upper lip.

"Has she been standing behind me while I'm bitching about her absence?"

The smirk turned into a huge toothy smile. "Yes ma'am'."

"Asshat" she said and turned to look directly at a tall willowy blonde, with eyes hidden behind glasses, her lips in a tight thin line.

"Whiner." Blake said from behind her, and started shuffling the books around on the table.

Timber glanced at him and said "Oh give it up. You're not gonna read anything. So don't even pretend." She looked back at the women standing impatiently before her. "You got my profile?" She wanted to add bitch to the end of the sentence, but felt it might add more stress to her day.

The woman seemed to get the implied word and shot a line of daggers from behind her red rimmed glasses.

Blake spoke up, ridiculing her behavior."Be nice! Agent Blake, this is Special Agent Sally Crane with the CBI. Agent Crane, allow me to introduce you to Agent Byrne." Blake maneuvered around Timber, managing to graze his hip against her. He shook the other woman's hand, then he turned to Timber. "While you were away, Special Agent Crane and I have been going over the scenes, notes and details."

"Is that so?" she asked dryly.

"While you were gone," he said again pointedly, "Special Agent Crane has been working. Don't you think we should pause and find out what she has come up with?"

"Of course, thank you Special Agent Crane. Your reputation precedes you. I look forward to hearing what you have. Excuse my earlier behavior, Detective Blake has a tendency to bring out my inner bitch." She knew that some sarcasm was still evident but she was hoping it was pointed in the right place.

"I understand," The severe expression melted away revealing an open, easy expression. Agent Crane pulled off her glasses and slid them into the pocket of her blue shirt. Timber was temporarily dumbstruck by the oddity of the woman's eyes. They were black. So black, in fact, she could not see where the pupils ended and the irises began."

"Hey, are you a demon? 'Cause we really can't have a demon working this case." Timber leaned in closer to the woman and squinted.

"Okay chucklehead" Blake said and laughed. "I'm sorry, Sally. She's kind of nutty."

"It's fine Robin. I like her. She's funny." Sally seemed genuine. Timber was still struck by her sudden appearance and was put off by their level of comfort.

"Awesome! We're all on a first name basis and I'm a funny chucklehead. Let's get to work." She pulled out a chair and flopped down on it. "Come on; show me what you've got."

As Special Agent Sally Crane moved to the board, she dropped a file on the small table in front of her and removed a hair tie from her wrist to tie back her wavy, long hair. Pulled away, her face became longer and her features more defined. She wasn't conventionally pretty, but she was striking in a way that startled.

"You better not be a demon." Timber said, only half kidding. *Anyway, who has a name like Sally Crane. That's not real,* she thought snidely, and felt a sting when Sally was immediately impressive. Her words were articulated well and her focus undeniable. What was odd and unbelievable were the theories. The first words that slipped from her mouth had Timber and Blake sliding to the edges of their chairs and several others in the room beginning to move within earshot.

"I believe your unidentified subject is a white female between the ages of 25 and 30, she will have a solid job, probably in the medical field or some form of life-saving institution. She has a psychological disorder, possibly schizophrenia that allows her to believe that what she is doing has purpose and value. She is not married and has a deep distaste for the male sex. This woman is trying to lead the investigation which means she has knowledge of the criminal justice field. She has gained control over many large men. This leads me to believe that she is persuasive and attractive. She used sex to lure her victims and there is defiantly a sexual aspect to all of the crimes. An important point, she knows that a profile will hit on the fact that she is a woman soon so I expect a female victim to show up to throw off any progress."

"A female usually kills males from same race. Males kill females from same race. This varies when the unsub is a homosexual or is killing along specific lines such as prostitutes or single mothers as an examples of such. Usually a victim matches the physical type of someone that may have scorned the unsub, as was the case with Bundy. All of his victims were young brunettes with straight long hair. These were the physical characteristics of a girlfriend who scorned and humiliated Bundy."

"But what about Agent Byrne's copycat theory? Wouldn't that negate any real suspect analysis thus creating a profile that represents the original killers?" Blake asked.

"Sure, if the copycat theory was solid." she said

"Hey!" Timber snapped.

"That's not what I meant." Sally said.

"No?" Timber was about to take a break.

"I'm sure she has an explanation." Blake said and shot a look in her direction that she knew well.

"I'm sure she does." she muttered.

"What I was trying to say is, look… The crime you were using as a comparison was Sharon Tate, correct? "

"Yes. " Blake confirmed.

"So, if this is a copycat, I would ask; where is the beautiful blond who happens to be twelve months pregnant?" Sally asked.

"Is she an elephant?" Timber said, mocking the other woman.

"It's an expression," Sally defended.

"Whatever." Timber was being petulant, but she did not like the theory and she wanted that to be clear.

"Maybe he was copying the other victims" Detective Graydon suggested.

"Okay, but my point is that if this were truly just about recreating the past, the victims would be identical or at least bear a resemblance. These crimes vary, yet all of the victims are male, white and between 25 and 45."

"I get it." Timber said grudgingly. She knew Sally 'Blackeyes' was on to something, but she didn't like it at all.

"I do think that this particular unsub is familiar with these crimes and maybe even uses them as inspiration."

"Inspiration?" Blake asked.

"I do not see it being the driving force." Sally didn't clarify her earlier comment, but it was clear the message was disturbing.

"What is the driving force?" Cable asked.

"Vengeance." Sally said.

"Vengeance?" Timber asked doubtfully.

"Yes, in my experience a person does not exhibit this extreme amount of overkill without some form of vendetta. "

Timber looked around the room. "Where the hell are Cable and Peterson?"

"Ridin' bareback?" someone suggested.

Chuckles erupted around the room.

Blake said "You sent them to watch the films on serial murders."

Timber nodded and pushed her hands through her short hair, "Great. That seems useless now."

"I wouldn't expect to see many more connections." Sally said.

"If you don't mind I think we will leave our options open." Timber practically snarled at the woman and secretly snickered as she took a protective step back.

"Of course. I'm here to provide an updated profile. If you need me, I'm a phone call away." Sally turned and began to walk away.

"Thanks, Sally" Blake said and looked at Timber, confusion on his face.

"Good luck Detective, Agent Byrne." Sally said as she exited the room.

"Thank you." Blake said again.

"Yeah, thanks." Timber said, not feeling grateful in the least.

"So should we keep reading?" Graydon asked. His manner and his tone caused Timber's ire to rise.

"Yes, I think that is appropriate. Take notes and if you recognize any duplication, highlight those. We will all meet back here at seventeen-hundred." As Timber finished her statement and moans about the early call erupted, her phone began to shrill. As if on command, Blake's phone joined in and soon all of the detectives in the room were looking at their phones. "Damnit."

Timber looked at the room of eager faces and groaned. "Let's try and make this the last one, shall we?" Timber grabbed her coat of the back off a chair and slipped into it. It was not needed; the weather was warm, she already felt a chill and knew before the night was over that chill was going to reach much deeper.

Chapter Twenty-five

As Timber stepped into the room, the first thought that struck her was that the space had no corners. From the outside, the house was a normal wood and brick structure; an average home, complete with rose bushes and a low iron fence. Yet inside, the shapes and decor were designed to astound. Shades of emeralds and blue, stars on ceilings, shapes of stucco and stone built into the interiors. A house refurbished with whimsy and skill. This one, the room of horrors, had not always been so full of color. Until recently this space, unlike all of the others, was stark white and furniture free. Timber gazed at the corner-less room and realized it was oddly tub-like. Spattered with dripping blood, the white walls gleamed against the burgundy as if proudly displaying proof of recent violence. Lying directly in front of her in the center of the small space was a body. More blood pooled around its naked form. The acrid smells of dispelled fluids filled the air, slid into her breath, slipped down her throat, found their way to the center of her gut and settled there.

A young woman naked from the waist down stared up with blood-filled eyes. Her startling gaze pierced Timber, screaming silently for release from the horrors that had killed her. A scarlet blouse, bunched up under the arms of the dead woman, blended with the crimson flow of blood that dripped from the damaged cloth. A jagged opening from breastbone to pelvis ripped into the pale flesh. Pieces of flesh were scattered about the floor. Slowly, methodically, Timber took in the scene. The hack and slash, the overkill, the blood on the walls, all of it was somehow familiar. This had happened before. She took a step closer and saw two things that made her retreat a few paces involuntarily. The first was the organs of the dead woman nestled against her ribs; and the second, the realization that the 'woman' was really a child, a child of no more than seventeen years of age. Footsteps behind her caused Timber to turn. She saw her own horror reflected in his dark gaze.

"Shit!" It came out in a gust of breath as if he had been holding on to it for days.

"I know." Timber said, then added, "she's just a kid."

"What?" Blake looked slightly dazed.

"A kid." she said again, "Look at her."

"Oh, God." He was perfectly still, his eyes the only movement in his tall frame. Timber knew he was already sizing up the scene, making mental notes, creating a scenario. But the primary response was disgust.

"Yeah," she said, agreeing with his useless statement.

"Whose house is this?" he asked.

"We don't know yet."

"Strange place." He looked at the high ceiling and back at her.

"Yeah."

"Who was first on scene?" he asked.

"Peterson."

"What's she got?"

"Nothing. I heard the call and arrived just after. She was securing when I pulled up. No witnesses so far. House was open, doors unlocked. Call came in from a pay phone."

"Really?" He turned his head, eyebrows raised in an odd expression of surprise.

"I know; amazing they still have those things." she said sarcastically.

"Ha, ha; I just meant that's… uhh.. What was it 'B.T.K'… didn't that bastard call in tips on pay phones?"

"Uh... I think he did or it could have been that other freak."

"Which one?" He looked at the dead girl again and the absurdity of the conversation struck them both at the same time.

They laughed and were startled by the sound of a loud female voice behind them. "You guys are sick! How can you laugh at this?" The officer had red rimmed eyes and a wet spot on the front of her otherwise tidy uniform. It was obvious she had been sick.

Timber felt bad for the woman, but knew if she was going to survive in this line of work, she would need to toughen up quick. "Just some humor to lighten the mood. Get the camera from my kit and document the scene. Get every angle."

"Yes ma'am" the officer said softly.

"And, Peterson...." Timber said; as the woman turned to face her, Timber slid a stern mask into place "Watch how you address superior officers, especially when you don't have all the facts." The officer looked sufficiently regretful and quickly left the room in search of the camera.

Blake smirked, "So, Sicko, ready to do this?"

"Funny" she said and moved forward, careful not to step in any of the blood, a difficult trick considering the shape of the room.

"Got gloves?" Blake asked.

Timber took two pairs of latex gloves from her pocket and tossed him one, both slipping the gloves onto their hands. She looked down at the victim on the floor. Something about this was so familiar. The body's position, the cuts, the organs laid beside the open gash. She stared at the macabre scene, mentally recalling the murder rooms she had come upon in the past. Her catalogue was large; yet try as she might, she couldn't bring up the image she was searching for.

"Does this strike you as familiar?" she asked.

"Not sure yet,... maybe"

Timber understood how these things could begin to bleed together. After a while the details of the past had to be put away. If you couldn't compartmentalize, this job could drive you crazy. Crazy was not a good place to visit, especially while packing a loaded gun.

Peterson returned and began clicking away, occasionally stepping in Timber's line of sight, then quickly retreating, as if afraid of being reprimanded. Timber could hear the patrol cars arriving outside, sirens blasting, tires skidding. The scene would be a mess soon, with cops everywhere. Every cop loved a blood bath. They may all groan about it and say it's the worst experience..blah blah blah. But Timber knew most people on the job had a fascination with the crime scene, a need to witness the carnage of man, just before slipping on their capes and going after the bad guys. The evidence was in the mass amount of blue-and-whites screaming to the curb outside. Timber shook her head and stood. "Give me the camera, I'll finish up here. Go out there and see if you can secure the front. Only let the task force in"

"What about..?" Peterson started to argue.

Timber could hear them getting close to the door. "Now!"

Detective Carter Graydon walked through the door just as the nervous female officer slipped out. "This is what they refer to as a blood bath," he said dryly

"Always stating the obvious, Detective," Timber said. She didn't like the detective and she hadn't been happy about him being on the task force. Unfortunately. his ability to do the job was in direct conflict with his personality. Detective Graydon was a slimy woman chaser who had no desire to hide his distaste for the same gender he so desperately pursued. His short stature and paunch only added to the bizarre combination. On the other hand, he was extremely intelligent and focused when it was required. His ability to do the job well was the only reason Timber tolerated the man.

He raised one eyebrow and Timber noticed his flat brown eyes were far too close together. He addressed Blake "You or Agent Byrne canvassed yet?" He said her name and rank with distain, making it all too clear he felt an equal distaste for her person.

"No," Blake said. "Been here maybe five minutes" As he answered, three more men entered. Two stopped short, staring, as the third turned and ran from the room, retching sounds punctuating his departure.

"Rookie." one of the men mocked.

Timber was irritated by the event. "Hey, asswipes, stop standing around and get on it! Talk to the neighbors. Find out whose house this is. Get a goddamn witness. And get the fuckin techs in here. Where is Cable?" she asked. The patrolman was on her team and should be on scene taking statements.

"Not sure, ma'am." an officer she didn't know said, and then asked excitedly, "Can I help?"

"Yeah," she said. "You can find Cable and tell him if he wants to keep his job he better get his ass in here."

Graydon turned away, mumbling something about bossy women under his breath.

Ignoring an all too familiar felling of repulsion, Timber turned her focus back to the scene, took out her notepad and began describing her impressions. Blake began barking out orders behind her

Chapter Twenty-six

Detective Carter Graydon was nervous, a feeling he was entirely unfamiliar with. He'd seen the case file and was beginning to make connections. The killer was not following any conceivable patterns except one. The possibility was terrifying. Had he somehow caused these bizarre events? Were his fingerprints on this case? He felt a shiver run down his spine and the tiny hairs on the base of his neck tingled; too many coincidences, way too many. He began looking through his notes again and grabbed a folder off his desk that contained his class preparations for the last several lectures. Manson, BTK were the last, his mind swam as he glanced over his notes. He knew he couldn't wait any longer; he had to tell someone his suspicions. He felt sick to his stomach as he reached for his phone.

The loud chime of his doorbell stilled his hand. Who would be coming by at this hour? He looked at the clock, 12:15, just past midnight. He slipped on his robe covering his boxer shorts and thin tee shirt and headed for the door. As he opened it he was more startled by his visitor than he'd expected to be.

"What are you doing here and why are you dressed that way?" He took in the short, dark wig, sexy red dress, fishnet stockings and garter belts, peering just under the hem of the too-short dress. "I was in the neighborhood and wanted to stop by"

"This isn't a good idea." Despite his better judgment, he felt his body reacting.

"Why? Don't you like me?" she asked, pouting seductively

"Of course I do, but .." He needed to make that call, but maybe in a minute…

"But nothing," she purred. "I'm here and no one has to know."

"What are you out doing dressed like that in the middle of the night?"

"I lied before." She stepped closer, her voice and eyes playing a dangerous game ."I dressed for you. I came over here directly; I wasn't in the neighborhood."

"Really?" The danger of the situation was slipping away quickly. She was right, who would know?

"Yeah really" She was illuminated in the doorway and it occurred to him that neighbors may see.

He shook his head. "I can't do this now; I have something important I need to do."

"Will you do me next?" she asked sweetly, making it all the more dirty.

"Look, let me make this call and then we'll talk," He waved her in and shut the door.

"I don't want to talk," she said, stepping over the threshold and pressing closer to him.

"Okay, let me take care of this and we'll see what happens next." He knew what would happen next. His reaction to her was all physical.

"Who are you going to call?"

"The FBI," he said, turning from her so he could think.

"Why?" she asked, the purr gone now.

"I don't think it's a good idea to discuss it now."

"Why?"

"Because it's a chain of command thing." Despite her attire and the feeling she initially induced, he was losing interest.

"So?" she snapped.

Now all interest faded and he turned from her, "So I'm really not going to do this."

"You figured something out?"

"I think I have. I hope I'm wrong."

"Come on. Detective... share." The purr was back and this time it was ridiculously obvious.

He scoffed and turned to grab for the phone as she reached out wrapping her hand around his. He felt a small pinch in his arm and realized she had stabbed a needle into his flesh and depressed the plunger in one swift movement. He jumped back dropping the phone and stared at her." What the fuck!" He grabbed her by the upper arms and lifted her off her feet. A small smile fluttered on her lips. "What did you just give me?" he demanded.

She shook her head slowly. He watched her face begin to swim in his vision and his arms lost their strength, dropping her back on her feet.

"What did you do?" he asked and heard the slur in his voice. His heart should have been beating fast in terror but he felt it keeping its regular cadence in his chest and realized he had been given a powerful quick-acting sedative. He fell back and she grabbed his arms, gently guiding him to a large chair. His head felt heavy and he was confused by the sudden turn of events.

"Have you spoken to anyone about your suspicions?" she asked in a sweet voice.

"No, was gonna call Agent Byrne... need to tell her... need to" his voice trailed off. He wasn't afraid, he felt better somehow.

"Where are your class notes?" she asked and he could hear an urgency and wondered why.

He answered her, "On my desk, I need to talk to Byrne, need to help."

"No, I don't think you'll be doing any helping."

He watched as she lifted the hem of her dress and revealed the tops of her legs; her garter belt hugged her slim hips and framed her. Unencumbered by panties, he could see she was clean-shaven and tiny. She straddled him and he felt her pull open the slit in his boxers and take hold of him. He felt himself grow in her small hand and he groaned. He knew he was in trouble. Things were foggy and he felt as if he were encased in lead, wading through a bog, but his mind grasped the severity of the situation; yet he still felt the blood pumping to his cock as she gripped it hard and began to stroke.

His head fell back and it occurred to him that he was being raped. She released her grip and lifted herself up over him and sat down slowly pressing her wet center against him. He felt a moment of panic as he started to press inside her and then his foggy brain lost the feeling as her tight sheath slipped fully over him. Again he heard himself groan and he managed somehow to lift his head enough to look into her glazed eyes. She looked absolutely mad. Her hands came up and wrapped around his throat closing off his airway. He gasped for air and struggled against the drug-induced lethargy. He grabbed her fingers and tried to pull her hand away. She moved on him, up, down, slick and wet, he felt completely out of control. Then her hands left his throat and he gasped as a rush of oxygen filled his tortured lungs. Amazed that he was still erect inside her, he watched in horror as she reached inside her bra and pulled out a small knife. She grabbed a handful of his hair and yanked back and in one quick motion sliced him from ear to ear. The pain was hot and quick. He went limp inside her as his warm blood spattered her smiling face

Ω

The words written on the walls shocked Timber to the tips of her toes. They were a repeat of a previous scene; one that had her believing the killer was recreating old crimes. 'Death to pigs.' She stood and turned in a wide circle. The blood, the cords tied in knots and scattered on the bare tile, the pillow covering the victim's face. She moved closer in slow motion, one step at a time. If what she was considering was true, then all of her investigation was lost in a sea of bullshit. Her vision became dark, the tunnel of light leading from her to the victim. She moved as if in a daze. She knew what she would find. Knew with a certainty that her nights were going to be longer and her confusion deeper.

The tunnel vision continued as she moved slowly toward the brutalized man lying dead on the floor. Next to his head lay a large lamp; the glass from the broken bulb crunched under her foot. Under normal circumstances this would alert her to the issue of contaminating a crime scene. Based on her visual assessment of the scene, Timber lost all desire to protect the evidence. Her only desire was to get to the body, lift his shirt and see if her suspicions were correct. Her knees bent as she came closer to the body. Her right hand reached out, the tunnel vision became tighter. Circling her fist as it gripped the hem of his green t-shirt, she slowly pulled it up, lifting and sliding it away from the sticky bloody skin of the dead man. Etched in his stomach— deep enough be easily be read— were three letters that made the skin on Timber's back want to crawl off.

She had said it before but now it had to be believed. This was not an original murder. Not only had the perpetrator repeated the words this time, he had gotten all of the details down.

"Hey" The voice ripped into her visceral consciousness. She turned and looked up.

Blake stood in the doorway, his eyes worried. His eyes searched her face "Been yelling at you for a few seconds, Byrne. You ok?"

She looked at him and shrugged, her fist still tightly wrapped up in the dead man's shirt. She looked back at the word etched in blood and said, "We are in so much trouble here."

"Why?" Blake started to walk into the room and stopped a few feet from her. "Shit!"

Timber was glad she didn't have to explain; she knew she would be doing a lot of that in the very near future. She watched as Blake took in the scene; the lamp, the cord tight around the deceased man's throat. The blood on the cords; tied and left on the floor. And then the large man's stomach and the obscene word 'WAR' deeply carved into the flesh. His breath escaped him in a great gush as he finally realized what they were up against. "LaBianca" he stated, confirming that he understood her distress. This is much more accurate.

"Yes" she sighed, "and that means..."

"Yeah, we could be screwed here. How many people know about the last one?"

"Your guess is as good as mine; we have been keeping the lid pretty tight but you know how that can be."

"Yeah, that blue blood brothers crap. Cops stickin' together." He shrugged.

"Have you ever seen this kind of duplication?"

"No. but my guess is we're being played with and this bastard knows what were thinking before we think it."

"Or bitch." Said Timber.

"Come on, do you really believe that?"

"After this there isn't a lot I wouldn't believe."

" Really? How weird is it that the profile tells us that this isn't happening just about the same time that it does?"

"Not that weird; just means your girlfriend was wrong."

"Jealous?"

"Yes, terribly."

"Good. And she wasn't wrong; she called the next victim perfectly. Let's canvass."

"Okay, maybe today is our lucky day."

"Nah, that was Friday." he said, referring to their moments locked in a refrigerator. Considering his distant behavior, she was surprised at the reference.

" Maybe when we catch this fuck you can buy him a gift. After all, it was his idea."

"Her." he corrected.

"Shut up, Robin." She started to turn from him and was stopped, just for an instant, by his deep voice.

"I love it when you say my name."

Ω

A knock at the door brought her head off the pillow. Earlier Timber had come home with one focus. She pulled off her clothes, stepped into a hot shower and tried desperately to erase her confusion. She had come back from the lake so sure that she was ready to wrap up loose ends and walk away once and for all. Maybe she could talk to Danielle about her unit in DC. Moving could be good for her. As she stepped from the shower, her skin red from the scalding water, she felt better. As she slid between her clean white sheets and pulled the fluffy comforter over her shoulders, sleep gripped her and pulled until she gave in. Now, as the sudden noise jerked her from oblivion she cursed and sat up. She jerked open the door and Robin Blake stood in the doorway. "I'm here to fight. Didn't we have an appointment?"

Chapter Twenty-seven

Timber gazed out at the faces looking back at her. She knew she wasn't alone. Blake and Danielle stood beside her, providing a stable base. Despite the long night before, where nothing had been solved, yet much had been said, and done. Timber put that from her mind. As the lead in this investigation the pressure to move things forward, to delegate and make things happen was tremendous. The last thing she needed was instability from a transient physical relationship. She started the conversation by asking for affirmation that her people were behind her.

"Yesterday I gave you some material to familiarize yourselves with. In the interim we had a couple things come up. Our profiler has had time to get up to speed and she will be speaking to you shortly. We also had a female victim which seems to back up the profile. And there was the copycat LaBianca. I'm going to assume you've all read the case files and are familiar with the crimes in question?" As she waved at the board, a murmur filled the space, detectives and uniformed officers all asserting their understanding of the horrible atrocities taking place. There wasn't a cop in the room that wasn't taking things seriously, using every spare minute tracing down the psychopath that was now terrorizing their city. Their dedication showed in their bloodshot eyes and rumpled clothing. But the real truth came in the form of crass jokes and inappropriate jabs at one another, a cop's way of coping. "So let's have it."

Officer Cable spoke up, reading from a small note pad. "So, we have the lipstick killer, William Heirens. They called him that 'cause he wrote messages in lipstick. One of them matches our scene."

"The house?" Danielle asked

He looked at her for a moment, seemingly mesmerized, then shook his head once and said, "Yeah, he wrote the same message we found on the wall, in lipstick."

Timber grinned at his response to Special Agent Devon, but it quickly died as the details of more atrocities kept coming. He continued to read his notes "Harvey Louis Carignan killed only women. He used a hammer while he forced them to perform oral sex."

"Wasn't he afraid they'd bite it off?" Officer Sebastian asked.

"Yeah, it gave new meaning to the phrase blow…"

"Shut up, Cable." Timber said

"Sorry." He looked embarrassed for only a second, then continued. "Bundy, well we're all familiar, anyway he used, um, handcuffs, tape, strangulation, some rape and a lot of bludgeoning. All the victims looked like his ex-girl friend."

"So he stuck to a very specific type?" Blake said.

"Yep." Cable nodded, and continued "The Manson murders fit the scene and one fits the victim exactly. The word 'war' was carved in Leno LaBianca's abdomen. The 'W' looked like two 'X's' that made the "W" just like ours. The rest of the scene is the same. It all matches up from pillow to table lamp. Somebody spent some time on this one." Cable sat back and gazed at Danielle.

"We looked up Kenneth Allen McDuff, Douglas Clark and Bianchi. We found similarities in the vics but it's a bleed over." Sebastian said, pulling out his notes. "The most bizarre is the female. She was found on November 9th. According to forensics, she had fish and potatoes in her stomach and she was eviscerated."

"Mary Jane Kelly was discovered on November 9th, the last victim of 'The Ripper'." Peterson added.

"Last meal fish and potatoes?" Timber guessed.

"Bingo." said Sebastian.

"Wasn't Mary Kelly's face mutilated?" Blake asked.

"Yes, I think the coroner called it hacked beyond recognition," Peterson said, grimacing.

"I remember seeing the photos; that's a pretty accurate description." Danielle added.

"We obviously don't have that here." Timber motioned at the board.

"Maybe that would be too obvious?" Peterson suggested.

"In a few minutes our profiler is going to come in and lay it out for you. I was pretty skeptical at first, not because I don't believe in a good profile. I am true believer, I was skeptical of this particular profile." Timber told the group confidently, willing to admit when she was wrong.

"Not anymore?" Blake asked.

"Not anymore," Timber chose not to take the bait. "She has some great information so pay attention and take notes. I have also received a call from a retired profiler. He was previously with the Washington, DCPD. I received a call from him last evening. Sounds promising. Any of you know Leo Marks?"

"Only by reputation," Blake said.

"Then you know he could be helpful. He says he has some information. I'm meeting with him soon. He's a professor teaching Terrorism and Criminology at DU."

"Doesn't Carter teach abnormal psych there?" Sebastian asked.

Officer Peterson spoke up, "What was the name of the street of that house where the girl vic was found?"

Timber glanced at the woman, her severe face showing little emotion, a vast difference from their previous encounter.

Timber nodded in recognition of staying on point. "Miller Street." she answered from memory.

"Ya sure it wasn't 'Court'?" Danielle asked.

"I think it was Miller Court." Blake said and Timber nodded, remembering the odd, round, blood-spattered room.

"What's the connection?" Danielle sat on the edge of the table and stretched out her long legs crossing them at the ankles. She seemed so comfortable in her skin. Timber wondered why she was noticing such trivial things. Her level of distraction was astounding. She glanced at Blake standing in the front of the room at an angle. He had one hand shoved in his front pocket, the other absently sliding along his bright red tie adorned with artwork depicting a black woman with white hair floating on the surface, blue sparks shooting from her palms. She looked away and asked Peterson, "Why is the address important."

"That's where Mary Kelly was discovered, Miller Court."

"She's playing with you." Special Agent Crane said matter-of-factly as she stepped into the room, her dark eyes taking in the room and its occupants. Timber could see her sizing up each member and filing her judgments away.

"Welcome Special Agent," Blake said, a smile on his lips that irritated Timber enough that she wanted to grab stupid Sally by her long blonde hair and bitch slap her.

"Thank you," Sally said, and Peterson, speaking loudly, asked the question that was on all of their minds, "You said 'she'?"

The profiler used a middle finger and pressed her glasses up on her thin nose. She held her leather briefcase by its thin strap and spoke in a relaxed tone that belied her stiff demeanor. "Yes," she confirmed. "Some of what I have here we have discussed earlier; you're unsub is a female, approximately thirty years old. She is extremely intelligent and well-versed in serial and spree murder cases. She is attractive, although not conventionally so. She does not call undue attention to herself. She can entice a person's confidence so she is well-spoken and well-educated. She is single and probably has a steady job. She is playing a game and believes she is far superior to all of you. She does not believe she will be caught and she probably has an end game."

"Why do you say that?" Detective Scott asked, sounding unconvinced.

Sally answered straightforwardly. "The way the victims are all very different and the types of body dumps and variation mean this is all based on calculation instead of typical motivators, such as revenge or sex or power. These crimes suggest a game. A game has an end with a winner and a loser."

"Hopefully we are the winners." Danielle said, an odd tone embedded in the statement.

"That is the hope." Sally agreed. Then added "The unsub will have a history of abuse in her past, probably sexual, although she will not advertise this. Those close to her may never know this has occurred. She may have been raped and never reported it. The crimes that were sexual in nature were carried out without hesitation. This would suggest an aspect of enjoyment or purpose, although she probably tells herself this is not the case. She came from a single parent home or was raised in foster care. She is compulsive, but hides that side of her behavior behind a pragmatic attitude."

"What does that mean?" Officer Cable asked and Sebastian laughed.

"Shut up man!" Cable said, "I want to be clear."

Sally nodded, "Clear is good. She pretends her actions are motivated by events around her that she has little control over, while in reality she often reacts before she has time to consider the consequences. She will live alone, have no animals and she may have a secret addiction to pain killers or alcohol."

"That's weirdly specific." Peterson said skeptically.

"Haven't you ever seen those TV shows where they practically know what color the killer's pubic hair is?" Detective Scott asked, making a derisive snorting sound.

"Those shows are all crap and you know it." Cable interjected.

"Well, apparently not!" Scott said waving his hand toward the woman providing the information.

"You're a prick ya know that?" Peterson said then sneered, "And where's your asswipe of a partner?"

"Watch your mouth rookie or I'll watch it for you."

"Is that a threat?" Peterson asked, her eyes snapping . She seemed tense and Timber was worried about the unprofessional behavior.

"Shut it!" Timber yelled "If you don't want the CBI to bust in here and take over, stop acting like baby cops and listen up." Timber turned to the special agent and caught a big grin on Danielle's face before she asked the profiler, "Anything else?"

"The incident with Detective Blake indicates the unsub is volatile and connects you directly with her survival, I would be very careful if I were you, Timber."

"Noted." Timber said, and saw Danielle's smile disappear.

Sally continued, turning to Blake. "The reporter she has contacted"?

"Charlene Morgan." he said.

"Yes. She will need some sort of protection."

"I'll contact Nick." Blake said.

'Nick?" Sally asked.

"Nicolas Devon is her Significant Other." Blake said.

One eyebrow rose over the top of her red-rimmed glasses and she swallowed loudly. "Oh, that's very significant."

"Who is Nicolas Devon?" Cable asked sitting up straight, seeming more engaged suddenly. Peterson looked pissed and Sebastian was cleaning dirt from his fingernails with a car key.

"The rumor is he's ex-CIA. He runs the local newspaper now; he's gone legit." Scott said. He didn't sound convinced.

"The CIA's not legit?" Cable asked.

"Not the way Nicky boy did it." Detective Scott said.

"That's enough." Danielle's voice was husky and resounded throughout the room. The impact was instant.

"Sorry, Danielle." Scott looked at the floor, a scowl on his face belying his words.

Danielle stood, pushing her weight from the table and addressed Timber. "Nick is a respectable citizen with no ties to any enforcement agency at this time. Charlie will need a car."

"Really?" Scott said, derision dripping from the word.

"Yes, and you; I don't know your name, but Nick is my brother and I can give you some inside information."

"Cool." he said in the same tone.

"Don't call him 'Nicky'. That could be very detrimental to your health."

Scott rolled his eyes and scoffed, although it was clear Danielle's word had the affect she had intended. He glanced down at his notes and grumbled incoherently for a moment before saying loudly, "Are we done here? Can we get our assignments and move this along?"

Timber couldn't help herself. She said, "Yeah, Scotty, take your ass to Miller Court and re-canvass the neighborhood. Ask if anyone saw a man with a cane and top hat on the night that Rachel Keelee was killed."

"Huh?" Cable said, looking from Scott to Timber.

Peterson laughed and smacked her partner in the arm "That's what Jack the Ripper supposedly wore, dork."

"Don't call me a dork," Cable said.

"Why?" Peterson asked innocently, pushing her chair back and slipping her flashlight into its holster.

"'Cause, it means whale dick." he said, standing with her

"Does not," she said unbelieving

"Yep," he assured her and she patted him gently on the same shoulder she had smacked earlier.

"Well, I sure won't make that mistake again."

Timber laughed aloud at the implied insult and the rest of the room joined in. The earlier tension dissolved and soon chatter filled the space. Blake informally handed out assignments and an agreement was reached to reassemble at 7 p.m. for debriefing.

Chapter Twenty-eight

"Where the hell is Graydon?" Blake asked as he pushed open the doors that led to the war room. Timber sat on the edge of the table staring at the board. Her attention was barely diverted by his angry words, her eyes glued to the images tacked to the large white surface. *What am I missing?* This was not his purview, profiling. Still a part of him felt like Agent Sally Crane was off base, even though the rest of her equation was anything but. How had she known a woman would be the next vic? There were no indicators pointing to a women being next on the agenda. Timber remained where she was, focused on the board, ignoring his question. "Did you hear me?" Blake said loudly.

"Yeah stop your yelling; I'm trying to think!"

"Well, think about this. Detective Carter Graydon wasn't at roll call."

"And?"

"Well as long as I have known him he's never missed a role call."

"Seems about time then," she said, still looking at the victims that littered the macabre collage.

"I realize you don't like him," Blake said.

"That's very astute of you."

"Despite those feelings, we need to find him."

"You don't think there's a bit of an overreaction happening?"

"Have you forgotten the refrigerator?"

"I'm trying to."

"Ouch."

" Suck it up, Blake. Walking wounded doesn't suit you."

" I'm not... man, you have a way of getting me completely off track." He spun in a wide circle and addressed the rest of the room. "Anyone seen Detective Graydon?"

A chorus of 'No' and 'not today' echoed in response.

He turned back and shrugged at Timber in an 'I told you so' manner. She slid of off the table and put her hands in the air. "You got it. Let's search for your missing asshat detective, because that's a top priority."

"Good, I knew you would see it my way." Blake smiled like a big dumb ass.

"So I assume you have called his cell?"

He looked at her and she felt bad for assuming such incompetence and worse for vocalizing the thought. She was expecting him to say something snide despite the fact that the look said it all. As he turned away she followed. Her thoughts, racing around working on achieving supremacy, ranged from the dead girl sprawled on the floor of a random home in a random neighborhood, a profiler that seemed to know everything and nothing and a detective causing a problem by choosing to be irresponsible. Timber picked up her pace keeping up with Blake's long stride.

"When we find your AWOL friend, are you gonna cut him loose?"

"Depends on his reason."

"Really? So if he has a good enough excuse he can do whatever."

"Not excuse, reason. If he has an excuse, I'll cut him loose."

"So where to first? His house?"

"Yeah, then we'll check the bar on 6th and Speer."

"Yuck. He hangs there?"

"A lot of us do."

"You hang there, too?"

"Sometimes and why do you keep saying hang? I go there occasionally for a drink. Get in the car."

Timber asked, "You're driving?"

"Do you know where Carter lives?"

"I'm FBI, it wouldn't take long."

"Waste of time."

"Sure. I'll feed into your paranoia and we'll go check on your errant boy."

"Thanks."

"But when we find him nursing a hangover, we go back and figure out what nut fuck is creating a gorefest all over my city."

"Deal. Now get in the car!" he demanded. She raised one eyebrow as he slipped into the car saying, "Please!"

Timber opened the door as he started the car. Her feet were barely inside as he sped away from the curb. "Hey, freak!" The door slammed shut from the momentum. "What's your damage?"

"My gut is telling me something is wrong. I don't have time to banter with you."

"So, instead you're trying to kill me?"

"Kill you? I wasn't aware it would be so easy."

She laughed at the creases developing on his forehead and the tension in his chin. "You are really worried?"

"What part of this doesn't seem real to you?" he asked.

"Why Graydon? If something is going on, why him?"

Of all people, Graydon seemed like an odd casualty. "I don't know. Why me in a freezer? Why all men and then suddenly a woman?"

'Yeah right, let's just get there." Suddenly Timber felt uneasy.

"It's close."

Ω

The door to the house at 3861 S. Dartmouth was red. This was the reason that the bloody handprint wasn't visible until Timber was a few steps from its glossy surface. She stepped to the side, motioned to Blake who flanked her and slipped her Sig Sauer from its holster. Her pulse sped up as it usually did in these situations, but this time there was a difference. This time the feeling spread just a little more to her center. Behind the door was a comrade. Like him or not, he was a fellow warrior and she had a deep suspicion she was looking at his life force smeared on the front of his dark red door. Her left hand reached out and slowly and pressed down on the handle's lever. The mechanism responded without much pressure releasing the door, opening it inward. She steadied her gun and called out "FBI!" then waited. After only a moment she rolled into the doorway and was stopped cold by the scene. Carter Graydon lay on the floor of his tiled foyer his pants pulled down around his thighs. His eyes were open and he appeared to be looking at the ceiling. His throat had been cut. The laceration so deep Timber could see bone. There was no expectation of life here. She moved past the gore noting the arterial spay on the wall beside his corpse. The meaning was clear. Graydon had died from that wound. No poison was used to end his life. Someone had overpowered him and slit his throat. These thoughts were racing though her mind as she ran from room to room Blake hot on her heels. She cleared each one knowing beforehand that the detective's killer was long gone. Finally, the house secured, she dropped her gun to her waist as she bent at the knees, dropping her head for just a moment before looking up at Blake. Her sadness and guilt were glaringly clear. "Call it in," she said and watched as he turned and pulled his 'walkie' from his belt.

Timber found herself kneeling beside the fallen cop. She looked at the wound, the position of the body, the blood spatter. There was a footprint in the thick liquid. Hand print and smear on the wall just inside the door. The hallway was full of droplets, probably from the tip of the blade as the killer left the scene. Despite the terrible thing that had happened here, there were several things that caused Timber to feel hopeful. This was a body leave. Unlike the previous victims, this body was not moved. That meant they had a primary crime scene. Even the girl had been killed somewhere else and then an elaborate stage-set had been put in place. But not this. This was an original.

This hadn't been carefully laid out like the others. The kill seemed to be the only purpose here. But why? Why kill Graydon? Why not come after her or Blake. After all, the refrigerator bit had failed so why not come again and finish the job? The answer was obvious, if not logical. The unsub was playing with them. Doing what sociopaths did. Exploit their power. Play on the control. If one of the leads ended up dead who would he play with? But why not kill a street cop? Why Graydon? What did he know? Or was it simply a roll of the dice, a game of chance? Timber didn't think so.

Blake's voice cut through her thoughts. "CSU is on the way."

"Along with half the force, I'm sure."

"Yep, probably."

"We better get busy if we want to preserve anything."

"Okay."

The next ten minutes Timber and Blake spent stringing police tape and taking pictures of the scene. They were still carefully documenting every detail when the sirens began screaming within earshot. Blake was looking pale and a little green. She was worried that he was going to blame himself for this and she was determined not to let that happen. As the first car pulled up onto the lawn, tearing up the grass, its driver's only focus the man inside, Timber grabbed Blake by the shoulder and pulled him out the front door. "Come on, big boy, let's get some air"

Her fingers gripped his shoulder using all of her tensile strength to guide him through the front door. A patrol officer pressed past her about to ask a question. His mouth shut when he saw the look Timber shot in his direction.

Blake's eyes were hard and hollow; she glanced away and removed her hand from Blake's shoulder. She wanted to comfort him, to assure him there was no way he could have stopped this. No way could he have assured a different outcome. She was trying to find a kind way of telling him these things when he turned from her and walked away. She watched the car door open under his large hand, the running lights flicker on and the engine revved before she fully realized he was leaving. “Hey!” She took a few steps before the lawn curled up around the rolling rubber of his tires. “Fuck!”

“Care to share, Agent?” Danielle’s appearance didn’t surprise her.

“Fuck no! Care to suck my…”

“No need for that.” Danielle said.

“There’s no need for this.” Timber was angry and feeling useless. She didn’t need to feel anything. She wished for the kind of focus the other woman possessed. “I assume our team is about to get bigger.”

“Yeah, I expect to get a few calls.” She would undoubtedly be receiving word within the hour that the CBI was moving in.

“Let’s wrap this so we can get to the grit of this mess,” Danielle urged.

“Sounds good.” She stood staring at the tread marks in the grass.

“Might be quicker if you stick around.” Danielle’s open palm pressed on to her right shoulder.

“I know.” The contact made her feel less alone but did nothing to ease her concern.

“He’ll be okay.” Danielle said.

“I know.” The thing was she knew very little.

Timber marched back the way she had come. She tried to erase the image of the vacant look behind Blake’s eyes as he drove away. She knew him, knew him well enough to know he would be okay. But it wouldn’t be from an understanding or an acceptance. It would be from putting it away and focusing on the problem at hand. If he did that, when he did that, he would be okay. Timber stood on the porch of the pretty house and looked at the ugly sight through the window. CSU had arrived and were bagging and taping evidence. A detective stood next to the body, a sketchbook gripped in one hand, a pencil moving over the page. Peterson snapped pictures of the body while Cable used a measuring tape to accurately document the scene. The surreal nature of the moment wasn't lost on her. She saw it all, the dead man on the floor, the blood on the walls and the wallpaper. It was little clocks etched in shades of browns and gold. The clocks seemed to scream at her that time was running out. Time, wasn't that what it was all about? Time. Salvador Dali drew clocks, melting clocks. Had he seen the world as she was seeing it now? She squinted, witnessing the clocks begin to melt. She could see the time melting away, figuratively and literally. What was happening and why couldn't she see it?

Chapter Twenty-Nine

The fear of imminent, universal danger trickled over the students in the room as the film played on the white board. The movie showed terrorists touting propaganda and jihad children waving guns in kindergarten classes. Katie watched in horror as thousands of people chanted, "Death to America!" The mantra sent chills down her spine in a slow moving arc.

Leo Marks sat at the back of the room, tipped back in his chair, cowboy boots stretched out in front of him, crossed at the ankles. Katie glanced back over her shoulder and took in the professor. His dark hair was short and messy. His mustache was too long, reaching down to his chin on both sides. She remembered someone saying it was a "Fu Manchu." His eyes and their exact shape were somewhat a mystery, because thick eyeglasses always hid them. The glasses themselves, like his unusual mustache, were antiquated. Every time Katie laid eyes on her instructor, she was reminded of the rollicking seventies, where men looked up to Starsky and Hutch and women feathered their long, flowing hair. Despite it being somewhat theatrical, the look suited him.

As the film came to an end, Leo stood and began to ask the class about their feelings on its integrity and substance. After a long and rather heated discussion, of which Katie held a central voice, the class came to a close. Books being shoved into backpacks, keys being pulled from pockets and purses were a few of the noises that accompanied the end of every class. As these trademark noises began, Leo raised his hand, preparing to issue a reminder to those in the Crime Club. Crime Club was a group of like-minded individuals that spend one day a month enveloped in the criminal justice genre and all that that implied. Sometimes the club went on tours of mortuaries. They learned how to properly handcuff a suspect and once Leo had taken them to a shooting range. They hadn't been allowed to shoot a gun, to Katie's immense disappointment. They had watched and learned about gun safety and things of that nature. The club was an interesting addition to the education process and Katie always looked forward to it. Although sometimes, as in the case of the shooting range, the experience didn't live up to the hype.

She stopped preparing to leave and listened raptly to his announcement. As Leo Marks spoke, Katie's heart rose to her throat and her fingernails bit into her palms. "For those of you attending the meeting this week, we will be discussing the murders that have been occurring throughout the city. As some of you know, I am consulting with the task force and I think I have come up with a significant theory." He was so pleased with himself. A wide smug expression pulled at the corners of his mouth. "With any luck, it may lead to a break in the case."

A soft excited murmur came from the students still in attendance.

Leo shook his head, "Of course, I cannot discuss my findings with our group until I have updated the task force, but I'm calling the lead detective as soon as I leave here and will be cleared to share by the time our group meets."

Katie spoke up "How can that be? Don't you have to wait to share theory and information until the case is closed."

"That is correct" Leo smiled confidently "But with what I have, that shouldn't be a problem."

Another student spoke up, but Leo waved his question away." Nothing else today; save your inquiries until our meeting. Have a good night." He began packing up his brief case as the students filed out, talking excitedly amongst themselves.

Katie remained seated until all of the other students had left and the door swung shut behind them. She stood, placing her hands on her desk for support.

"Leo, I've been working on a paper for my psychology class on this serial murder and I was wondering if you could give me an opinion on my theories."

He was clearly irritated. "Katie, I told you, I can't discuss this now."

"I know that, but you can talk about my paper." she quipped, her heart still lodged in her throat.

"Isn't your paper on the case?" he asked, a sharp point to his tone.

"Yes" She needed him to be a little irritated. She wanted answers. She needed to take him by surprise, if the answers didn't calm her.

"Well then, I can't discuss it," he stated flatly.

"Oh… well, I was just gonna tell you, I think it's a CJ student." She watched his reaction to her statement.

"What?" He appeared stricken.

Shit, she thought, this is bad. She pressed, testing her theory further."And I think the differences in the crimes aren't because they're confused or trying to find their groove. I think it's intentional to throw off the cops" she rushed on, watching his expression. "And they know how to do it, because they study criminals" She chanted inside her head, *Tell me I'm crazy! Tell me I'm crazy!* She liked Leo, really liked him. Sadness moved in her somewhere as she considered the inevitability of this moment.

He didn't tell her she was crazy, as she knew he wouldn't. His eyes were slits now and Katie knew; she wasn't wrong. He was too close. Her heart regained its normal pace as calmness washed over her. Her gaze was sharp and the air inside the room became heavy. She could feel the atmosphere thicken, as it always did in these moments. She heard Leo ask, "How did you come to these conclusions?" he demanded to know.

"Why? Are they the same as yours?" She tilted her head demurely and winked at him

"Close, very close." he replied slowly. She could see his brain, tick, tick, ticking away, trying to find a solution to this bizarre situation. Somehow a student had come to the same conclusions that he had labored over, paced the floor and lost hours of steep over. She could see it all on his face, etched into the lines around his eyes. She squinted at him, looking deeper, seeing what only she could see.

"But you have something else, something that will blow the case open?"Katie asked. With his next action, Katie knew she was correct. Knew with a certainty that if she didn't act quickly this man, this lousy retired profiler, would be her undoing.

Leo opened his briefcase and began searching inside, while his attention was diverted, she slipped her hand into the backpack and slid out the long pearl-handled knife. This had been a present from her grandmother ten years ago; a gift meant to hang on the wall in celebration of another man's victories. She gripped it tight and wondered how many men's blood had slipped down its long blade only to end in the palm of their killer.

She saw his deep exhalation as he located his paperwork on the case. She giggled. The sound was close to hysterical, harsh and shrill.

His head came up at the sound.

"I didn't steal your papers." she said, and took a few quick steps in his direction. "I would never do that." He hadn't noticed the knife. She could see him trying to evaluate the situation, to gauge its magnitude.

"I'm so sorry. I don't know what you have but I can't risk it leading to me." Katie said.

He moved his head as if to shake it, then stopped and looked directly into her eyes. "Why would…" he stopped and his eyes grew wide as he obviously realized the full implications of the situation.

Katie lunged forward, plunging the pearl-handled blade deep into his mid section.

Eye widening, teeth gritting, Leo grabbed her shoulders and pushed. As he did this, he stomped down hard on her left foot. She felt and heard the bones fracture in several quick snaps, like twigs from a brittle tree. She bit back a startled scream, held tight to the handle and fell back, landing firmly on her buttocks. Katie watched as Leo fell back against the wall and opened his mouth to yell out. She jumped up from the floor and shrieked as pain, fire and ice, tore into her injured foot.

Immediately she dropped back to the floor, a moment before his boot landed under her chin. Her teeth slammed together and blood filled her mouth. Still conscious, she wondered how she had made such a terrible, obvious mistake.

Leo may be a professor, a profiler, but he had also been Detective Marks, a decorated police officer. He wasn't one of the ashen, soft, useless men she'd dealt with in the past. This one was trained and accustomed to pain. He'd taken a thick heavy blade to the stomach and still he moved toward her. As blood pooled and streamed, still he stood; no, not stood, walked. Fear and pain, a universal motivator, stirred in her. She rolled onto her stomach. As the tip of the leather boot came into view, Katie reared up and plunged the blade into the top of his boot, through the skin and bone, slamming it into the floor beneath. A guttural scream filled the room, like a siren waking Katie to the danger she was in, which had nothing to do with the battle she was currently waging.

She moved across the floor on her stomach, rolled over and pulled herself onto her shaking knees. The sight she saw shocked her enough to make her choke on the blood in her mouth. Head bent forward, balancing on her knees, she spat a mouthful of crimson onto the tile. As her eyes came up she looked into the gaze of a madman, blood dripping from her blade he now held. His teeth were showing, in a wide snarl. As he moved, blood trailed under his injured foot. He was dragging his foot a little and as he spoke, she realized they were the first words he'd spoken since she'd stabbed him an hour ago. Wait... it wasn't an hour, it was seconds, only seconds, and now she was about to lose it all. A stupid mistake.

The dripping, bleeding madman said, "You're the one. Why?" As the last word still echoed in the small classroom, streams of slick, dark, blood, fell from his open mouth.

His eyes widened, and as she watched, it seemed as if bones had been extracted from muscle tissue in one fluid movement. He fell only a few feet from her, the blade clattering onto the ceramic tile and spinning away. She watched in shocked fascination as it came to a stop an inch from her fingertips. Streaks of the professor's life force accompanied its journey.

Katie turned her head left and then right, trying to establish where the loud keening noise was coming from. Had the fan in the central AC unit collapsed? Her nerves were raw and the sound was excruciating. Her jaw hurt where he had slammed his oversized boot into her face. She could feel the swelling already beginning.

She pushed off of the floor and leaned her back against the wall. *What was that noise?* When the noise changed to a whimper then a gasp, Katie realized that it was coming from her. Blood spattered the walls and covered her clothing. She knew her DNA was everywhere. She remembered spitting blood on the floor. The keening began again. *Think, think!*

She crawled toward Leo and began searching his pockets. He had fallen into a contorted bloody mass on the floor. She had a hard time getting her fingers into his pockets. Front jeans nothing. She turned him and was startled when his head fell to the side and smacked against the floor. His red-rimmed eyes stared at her. Stopping, she leaned in and looked at him. His glasses had fallen off during the fight. Funny, she hadn't noticed. His eyes were brown, like honey. Some people would call them amber but Katie liked honey. Whenever she heard the word 'amber' she thought of mosquitoes trapped in that hardened stone waiting for the collection of dinosaur DNA.

So stupid, how a crazy movie could change someone's view of something so easily. She reached out and pressed her index finger against the soft skin beneath his left eye. So soft, she marveled at how she had never noticed his lovely honey-colored eyes. The left one had a tiny fleck in it and she leaned in closer. Rings of gold and almost, but not quite, brown, captivated her. She could see he was no longer there. No life waited to re-ignite within the honey whirls. The same finger that rested on his face reached up slowly and rested against the surface of his open beautiful eye. As her skin met the surface she was surprised at how dry it felt. She expected it to be slick and moist with tears. It was also harder than she had imagined. The surface firm and not spongy as she had somehow been led to believe. She pressed against the eye and was surprised again by how it moved as a whole and didn't indent under her finger. She wondered if more pressure would do the trick. Would the eye pop? What did the inside of an eye look like?

The last time she'd dealt with this, she had just scooped the eyes out she hadn't touched them. But this was different. She knew him; she liked him. Yes, this was different. She grabbed his eyelid pulled and watched as it popped down over the violated eye. She fell back so that she was sitting on her heels and looked at him. Leo marks was winking at her. She laughed. He had been a funny guy; she liked it. Plus she knew it made a sort of sense. He dies with a secret. Wink. Wink. Now she just had to find the secret.

What had she been doing when his eyes distracted her? She grasped for it in her mind, *what, what, what*! *Keys! Okay!* She began the search again. After checking the body several times, she decided to look in the brief case and there they were; two sets of keys. Katie knew he locked up for the faculty some nights. Sometimes he even let class out early so he could take care of the chore.

Okay, first cultivate a plan. She turned off the light and locked the inside door just in case. Pulling off her jacket, she used it to mop the blood from her mouth and hands the best she could. Her hair was long so that should obscure any security guards from taking a close look at her swollen face.

She grabbed her book bag off the desk and emptied all of the professor's paperwork and laptop into it. Removing the small penlight and jump drive from around his neck, she draped them around hers. Backpack in place, she peeked out the door. The hallway was empty; she slipped through, locking the door behind her.

As Katie drove, she contemplated how she would move forward. There were ten hours before the campus awoke and the room that had become a slaughterhouse was opened. The body would have to be moved. But how? And even if she moved the body, they would know where he was killed the minute they saw the room. Everyone in his last class would become a suspect.

Nothing to be done about the mess but I can at least get rid of all of the evidence. She dropped her car off in the parking lot of a gas station, went to the restroom and looked at her reflection. Surprisingly she didn't look frightened. She looked exhilarated. Washing her hands and face she laughed as an idea struck her.

Chapter Thirty

Timber looked around the small classroom and shook her head.

"So, whatever happened here, it wasn't fun."

"Really, you come up with that idea all alone or did God whisper to you?"

Timber shot a quick glance at the agent. "Ah, shut the fuck up, Stanley!" she snapped. Timber had worked with him before and she liked him, his shaggy haired good looks reminded her of her brother.

She laughed as he yelled "Hey!" He hated when she used his first name.

"Yeah yeah, Officer Travis," she amended. "You first on scene?"

"No, Ma'am."

She cut him off, "Is that bleach I smell?"

"Yeah, and ammonia" He stood taller and pushed out his chest, sounding pleased with himself

"Really? You can't mix those, should we be in here?"

Travis looked unsure for a moment then placed a hand over his nose and mouth. "I don't know, first guy passed out, second guy found him and well… I can't." He started to laugh and Timber got the picture quickly. Timber took a scarf out of her kit and pressed it to her nose. "So our killer comes to a college campus, has a bloody romp, takes away the 'who', the 'what' and leaves a message about the 'why'? She motioned to the white board and the blood smeared in a cryptic message.

. for the life of the flesh
is in the blood

"What does that mean?"

Something about it pulled at her. A memory, flashes of the other scenes. She shook it off and focused on the obvious.

Travis spoke, breaking in with what was clearly evident, "Well, at least we know 'where'. Think there's any trace left?"

"I doubt it." Timber said blandly, looking at the smears on the tile and walls. "Find out who was in this room last. Hopefully there's enough to blood type. Damn tile, if this was carpet we'd be golden."

"Maybe the grout." The voice was new and familiar; she hated how it made her blood hum. She kept her back to him and answered in a carefully neutral voice "Maybe."

"How many students you think attend these classes?" Blake stepped closer to her as he spoke.

"Don't know, maybe thirty."

His deep voice was a silk ribbon sliding along her spinal column. *Focus!*

"Hey," She gave an order and evidently regretted her tone, "Get a list and start calling. Anyone not picking up the phone, let me know ASAP."

"Will do… Boss." The sarcasm was strongly laced within each word.

She chose to ignore it and continued. "Find out what the class was about." She stepped back to the white board and looked at the message.

"You do realize this is a partnership?" he said. Humorous undertones played within his words. His obvious ability to find amusement in the situation only made him more appealing. Why couldn't he be alpha male and piss her off? That would be so much easier.

"Travis?" She mumbled the officer's name.

"Yes, ma'am?"

"Remember what I said before?" She couldn't believe her first response to the scene had been so off.

"Huh?" he stumbled to catch up.

"I was wrong… it may have started off differently," she paused, looking around the room, taking in the deliberateness of the streaks, the spatter on the ceiling. She shook her head slowly, sadly realizing the truth. She continued, "But in the end…. this was fun, fun with a purpose." The message, it wasn't a cry for help. It was a justification. A resounding verification that the end was not neigh."

"Huh? …Oh." Timber looked over her shoulder. She took in Travis, his wide eyes finally understanding her meaning.

Timber addressed Blake who was looking at her with a kind of undisguised frustration and awe. "Get the photos and meet me for coffee, I have a theory I'd like to discuss."

He nodded and gave her a lopsided grin.

As she walked out, Timber heard Blake speaking to the techs, authority and professionalism apparent in his resonating tone, something she never felt when they shared proximity. She knew it would take him awhile to get the evidence checked out properly and find out the details of the last class. In the meantime, she contacted the only person who might have the answers she needed.

The crime scene investigators were making their usual destructive run through the room, scraping up grout, pulling prints off the smooth tile floor, mostly partials and shoe prints, Spraying Luminal for blood trace, which was lighting up the room. Whatever happened, it had been brutal. The suspect hadn't taken the time to clean much, just poured the noxious combination over the evidence and smeared it into a macabre painting. Blood spatter covered the walls but the consistency was wrong.

Chapter Thirty-one

Payton paced the small space, throwing her hands into the air. She realized that she was acting crazy and she said aloud, "I'm not crazy, I'm not stupid," then felt like she was articulating something of importance. She stopped, listened and said "Stupid, stupid, stupid." Was she stupid? She started pacing again." I'm not stupid, I'm smart!" But, she had made a mistake, a vital mistake. Sweat trickled between her breasts and she felt a drop slide down the hollow in her lower back. The small bead felt like a bug crawling on her skin and she shivered. *It's so out of hand. What the fuck was that profile all about?* She thought she had taken care of things with the nosy cop but no! They had to pay attention to that blonde skinny bitch from the CBI . She would be caught now, caught before she had time to do the one kill this had all been about. The one kill that she needed.

I'll just do it now. Now would be okay, wouldn't it? She could drive to his house and pretend like she wanted him back. She could beg, get him to let her in. It would be easy. Then she would stage the kill, this time an original. No notes, no games and she could walk away. The test was soon, she qualified now. The test and Kiernan, that's what it was all about, take care of Kiernan and take the test. A new life awaited her and she was shaking with anticipation.

She imagined how he would look when he saw her standing at his door. The vision was visceral. She could smell his cologne; see his dull blue eyes, the dark hair peeking out of the neck of his white t-shirt. She imagined wondering what she could have ever seen in this man and then he would exhale in awe and tell her how beautiful she was and how much he missed her. *Ahh,* she would remember, *this is why I cared for you. I saw myself in your eyes and I was lovely there*. Payton shook herself and sighed; the imaginings were very real as if she were remembering, as if it had already happened. Then she sighed. "If only I were that lucky." As much as she despised the bastard that had ruined her life, she was not looking forward to the mess she would create while seeking her needed revenge.

Chapter Thirty-two

"Toxicology came back." Blake handed her an envelope and pressed past on his way, purpose in his step.

She looked at the envelope figuring it was easier to ask than to read while chasing after Blake. "I was wondering why tox was taking so damn long. What's the situation? Pig's blood?"

"Unfortunately, no" he said, pressing a button on the wall. The small square lit up and she wondered why he was choosing the elevator over stairs.

"Human?" she asked watching him tap his foot impatiently.

"Uh huh." He mumbled in agreement. The doors slid open and he slipped inside.

"Which blood? she asked, following.

"Both." he said and looked up.

"So both the empty house and the blood in the apple were both human."

"That's what I'm saying."

"Just clarifying."Timber watched as he fidgeted and shoved his big hands into his pockets .

"There's more." He continued.

"Okay." She wondered if what he was about to tell her could have anything to do with his behavior.

"They match."

"What?" The strange words and the fact that they were in an elevator had her off kilter. "They are the same blood?"

Blake smiled at her. "Repeating what I'm saying with different words doesn't really change anything." Condescension peppered his tone.

"Are they really a match?" she asked, "and why are we in an elevator?"

"Why would I lie?" he asked, ignoring her second question.

"Anything else?"

"Male, iron deficient with a high amount of neurotoxin." His voice was deeper than usual, a little raspy and his color was off.

"Crap." Timber said. "He was getting sick or he was sick and he was trying to hide it."

"Yeah."

She allowed the misconception. "So there may be a vic alive out there somewhere?"

"Could be, but I doubt it." The doors opened and he stepped from the elevator, his hand sliding along the wall in a subtle bid for support. She pretended not to notice the bead of sweat that appeared at his hairline.

"All right." She said and slowed her steps "The kills are vicious and calculated but the last two scenes were frenzied. Even if this feeakazoid was keeping someone alive, it's been too long and in my estimation, fury outweighs any ability to calmly keep a hostage."

"Makes sense, but a hostage?" he slowed, matching her step. He seemed relieved.

Timber wondered why he had such purpose. Despite his green pallor, he moved without pause. "Okay, wrong choice of words. I don't think that the person that the blood belongs to was ever going to survive."

"Agreed." he said "So now the issue is; who is it?"

"How are you?" she asked and wasn't surprised when he abruptly stopped in midstride and turned to her.

"Left turn, Clyde?"

"I know, sorry. I'm just concerned." she said, feeling awkward about the idea that he may realize how true those words actually were.

"Don't be. I'm good." The tips of his fingers pressed against his forehead and came away moist. He looked at them with contempt.

"Fuckin' liar." She was thinking he would need rest and that was going to make life difficult when he interrupted her thoughts with his characteristic sarcasm.

"That helps. And is it possible for us to discuss why you feel the need to say fuck so much?"

"It's cathartic." she defended.

"It's trashy." he shot back and began walking again.

"Fuck off."

"Will do. How do you kiss your momma with that mouth?"

He was walking fast again and it occurred to her that she had never realized how large this building was. "Gosh, Barney, I've never heard that before."

As they arrived at the garage door, she realized they were leaving and he started to ask again "Seriously what's…"

She interrupted "There's been a study done recently. It concluded that when a person uses profane language they can deal with pain better."

"No shit?"

"No shit." she said, then asked "where are we going?"

"So why are you in pain?"

She said "I'm not." His hand shot out and he pressed his remote. A double beep accompanied the action and headlights flashed.

He turned to her and stared. He looked like he was considering something profound then said "Okay, then your argument is sinking in the stupid pool."

If he didn't look like it might kill him, she would consider hitting him with her gun. "Remember what I said earlier?"

"Fuck off?" he said and opened the door to his car.

"Yeah, that."

"Got it."

One leg was entering the vehicle, the other on the doorsill when Suzette's voice interrupted them and caused the conversation to cease. "Are you two having sex yet? I only ask this because if you're not, all this arguing is a waste."

Timber scowled and turned her back to Blake. "Jesus, Zet, let it go!"

"Nope."

"Anything new?" Blake asked and removed himself from the door's opening.

"Sure is. COD is exsanguination, but the most interesting part was what was left behind."

"Left behind?" Timber asked.

"Detective Graydon has sexual intercourse as he was dying." the medical examiner said

"As he was..." Blake started to confirm.

"Dying. His testicles were full of spermatozoa and there was vaginal fluid on the surface of his penis."

"I guess that solves the gender mystery." Timber said bitterly.

"I'd say that's one for the profiler." The words should have been more triumphant, but he just sounded tired.

"Damnit!" Timber was angry about her mistakes and angry about the death of an officer but now she was going to have to work without Blake. He was obviously getting sick, and considering it was flu season and she couldn't manage to keep her hands off him for any period of time worth mentioning, she was going to have to send him home.

"Why does it matter?" Zet asked.

"Can we find out more about that blood?" Timber asked.

"I could run it against the DNA database but that's full of convicts and the victims haven't exactly fit that profile. Plus you know that takes forever." Zet said.

"Well there really hasn't been an accurate profile. Unless you're a profiler." Timber said.

"Why are you so pissed?"

"Never mind." Timber said. She was already contemplating how to get Blake home and Danielle more on board. "I think that apple is the key. Something about that apple is gnawing at me."

"You should let him gnaw at you…" Zet laughed at her joke.

"Zet, you… are a fucktard!" Timber snapped.

"That's new." Blake said

"Really, Timber? Fucktard? Now she's just making up words." Zet said, looking at Blake, a big grin adding to the joy on her face.

He shrugged and scratched behind his left ear, trying unsuccessfully to fight back a smile. "Well." he said, "She is in pain and apparently using foul language makes it more bearable."

Zet laughed, the sound light and full of life, completely out of place in the current climate. "That's original." she said.

"Hey, I'm in the room." Timber complained.

"We know." They said in unison and Timber suddenly felt like she was in a bad situation comedy.

"Geez guys, can we focus on the dead?"

"Any ideas on where to go next?" Blake asked as if he hadn't been on his way somewhere specific only moments before.

"Well, I was thinking," Timber said. "We could go back upstairs, sit and stare at the board some more, then suddenly one of us, probably me, will suddenly figure it all out. We'll jump off the table, run out this time taking the stairs and solve the crime. Amazingly, when we arrive the suspect will confess in a long diatribe leaving nothing to chance."

"That sounds good, let's do that." he said and started to get into his vehicle again.

Zet pulled her gloves off and snickered. "I saw that episode. You forgot to mention the cavalcade of evidence piled in the front room of the suspect's house."

"I have a meeting with the dean of the college; you coming?" he asked, looking at Timber through the window of his car.

"Sounds boring." She knew she couldn't let him go alone, especially considering he appeared to be about to spread a gross plague to an entire university.

"It will be. Unless she turns out to be our guy." he said.

"I'm in. Just the possibilities are fuckin' awesome," she said and grabbed the handle to the car door.

"I can't believe that you guys aren't screwing." Zet said

Blake startled Timber by leaning out the window and saying boldly, "We are." His tone was deadpan and there was no mistaking his sincerity.

She started to deny it, but decided quickly it wasn't worth it. Instead she said "See ya, babe."

She cringed as they pulled away, Zet yelled behind her, "Timber Byrne! I am gonna kick your white ass for holding out on me."

By the time they pulled from the garage into the day-light, Blake was laughing and shaking his head. Timber turned on him. "You just couldn't stop yourself."

"Nope and maybe it wouldn't be an issue if your friend could mind her own business."

"We both know that's never going to happen." Tim-ber said.

"That's what I thought, so I took the wind out of her sails."

Timber made a scoffing noise, almost snorting; she covered her mouth, her eyes widening. Amazed by his naivety, she asked "You don't realize you just blew a hur-ricane into those sails?"

He shook his head, still in denial. "Nah. She'll stop asking if you just tell her we got together and it wasn't spectacular, so we let it go."

His words sobered her and she suddenly felt nau-seated. Her throat got tight and her mouth dried up in an instant. His words echoed in her ears getting louder as she looked into his deep brown eyes; *it wasn't spectacular.* She felt like she was going to lose her lunch all over his shiny black shoes. She knew her feelings were written all over her face but couldn't hide it. She couldn't pretend his words hadn't ripped at her. Timber watched his face in horror as he realized what she was feeling. Her cheeks became hot; she whipped around staring out the passenger side of his car. She felt his eyes burning into her back. She pressed her head against the glass and used her angriest voice: "Let it go Blake, I have shit to do and I don't have time to rehash our icky past."

His voice was raspy, revealing too much and yet nothing. "I never said icky, I…"

She cut him off. "Shut it! I don't care. And I swear to God if you touch me right now I will rip off your balls." She kept her head down and her eyes averted. Being trapped in a vehicle moving too fast to jump out, she waited, embarrassed, trying to gain some composure. She pictured the most graphic crime scene she could imagine and tried to channel her frustration. The woman lying cut open on the ground, a sick homage to Jack the Ripper; she realized that something must be broken in her to need such a memory. But her survival had always relied on her focus and at the moment that was being seriously tested. Why was Zet being a pest anyway? She knew how much the whole guy thing made her uncomfortable. What was she doing? The image of the murdered girl with her intestines spilling out over her hip bones had begun to fade, but Timber pulled it back and focused. The stage setting, the blood, the walls and the floor amidst all of that the girls face was the most shrill, screaming for her to keep the memory, not as an escape but as a fuel moving her to find the bastard that had stolen a young life. She silently promised that young girl, who once had a universe of possible options, that she would find the bastard that had torn the life from her. She vowed to no longer care about the trivial, useless crap that was her love life and give herself completely to the case. Her head came away from the glass and turned. He was looking at her, his mouth slightly open, his eyes slightly closed. Timber had to separate herself from him. She had done it before it was time to do it again. Tension filled the small car. "We need to add Graydon to the board and talk to the profiler. Something is different."

"I agree." he said stiffly

"Good, when I get back, I'll add him and we can go over the details."

"Cable can do that; it'll be done by the time you're back."

"Maybe." She knew he was pissed. That was good. If he was angry with her he would be less likely to reach out to her. "Drop me anyway. You can interview the dean. You don't need me."

The statement meant more to her than he could possibly know.

He turned to her then glanced away, avoiding eye contact. She knew she was being a wimp, but she didn't care, she felt trapped in the car, caged and angry. Timber knew if she stayed in the car for much longer she would say or do something that she could never take back. A bead of water appeared on the windshield, then another. Within moments the sheets of moisture were being pushed aside by the wipers in long strings of glistening silver and grays. When had the sky turned gray? A clap of thunder shook the atmosphere and the rain began in earnest. This didn't seem like a typical rain for this time of year. Its torrential nature and pounding announcements were more like an east coast storm than the usual drizzling Colorado fare. Traffic began to slow and Blake moaned in disgust. Timber leaned back against the seat and rubbed the heels of her hands into her eyes. The ride to her car had just gotten longer. Luckily Blake didn't seem any more interested in talking than she was.

Chapter Thirty-three

The world was a dark and murky place. The lines were blurry and frayed. Tendons felt like guitar strings, tight and ready to pop. When that happened, the pain would only suppress the longing for solace momentarily. Then the agonizing truth would return and with it the realization that, without the guitar strings holding it all in place, she could lose her grip on the world. The knife slipped from her bloody palm into the dark water below the rotten bridge. She wondered what would happen if the wood gave. Would she crack and shatter on the rocks below? Would she break like glass or bounce around, ricocheting off the waves and the power of the current? It didn't matter now. The knife was gone, the blood on her hands remained. For a second she considered climbing over the ledge and slipping into the cold and darkness. The blood would wash away, and only then she would be clean. She needed to be clean.

How long ago was it? Had she ever been clean? The memory of all of the men who had put their hands on her. At first she hadn't minded so much. After a while she managed to forget. It was what was referred to as compartmentalization; a skill. But now, now the memories swirled around each other. Now the dirt from all of them crusted her like a rotten skin that she couldn't tear away. The water looked so good. The water promised to break the skin from her frame and make her clean again. But, not today, today she had things to do. Today, she would finish what she started and maybe the skin would fall away without the bath. Maybe.

The exhilaration was gone now. The passion was starting to slip away. Now she was just pissed. Now she wanted some form of revenge. Marks was a casualty she hadn't counted on, a small complication that had ruined everything. She spit on the ground and felt a tooth shake in its soft resting place. She had scooped out his amber eyes and rolled them around in her palm like thick soft marbles. The knife she threw away had come in handy, especially when she sliced the veins away from the backs of the slick eyes. Once, years before, she had taken up crocheting. It focused her and allowed her to meditate, to keep her hands busy while her thoughts roamed freely. Slicing up Marks had been like that. Idle hands are the devil's workshop. That was what her grandmother said once, just before she grabbed a chicken by the neck and ripped it from the ground. Payton's childish vision had watched in fascination as her grandma's thick arm whipped around, turning the feathered beast in wide circles above her head. The chicken's body had flown to the ground as moisture that Payton hadn't been able to identify spattered her face. The chicken hit the ground and dust popped up around it before it gained its footing and ran in a wide circle. Payton rubbed the back of her small hand across her eyes and watched in horrified awe as the headless chicken fell to its side, blood flowing from the place where its head had been. As instructed by her Grandma she walked to the dead bird and picked it up with both hands. As she carried it into the big white house she wondered what horrible things the devil could do. Now years later her hands had stayed busy while her mind needed to be clear. After cleaning things up she was clear again. Clear to pretend that everything was okay, even while she wrapped her hands around the neck of a chicken. As the hours passed, her phone rang and buzzed with unanswered text messages. As she stepped into the flow of her hot water and blood and tissue washed down the drain, she thought about the muscle and sinew on Leo Marks. Alive he had been tough, dead even tougher. Her hamstrings were tight and sore from pulling and hefting his weight. She wondered if the crime scene techs had found the brain tissue on the stairs yet.

The sound of the water beating against the shower wall was comforting and steady; her head tilted up, her hands moved over her wet head and down to her neck. She rolled her shoulders and felt the tension begin to slide away. She was bruised. Her mouth was swollen and her ankle throbbed. She felt lucky that she wasn't broken. She was alive. Now was the time to clean up unfinished business. She considered her options and smiled, the action causing a small spiral of pain in her left cheek. She thought about Kiernan and how he would look. What expression would he wear on his deceitful face when he looked into her vengeful eyes? Would he shut the door in her face or would he invite her in?

She stepped from the shower and grabbed a thick white towel from the hook on the wall and pressed it into her face. The clean scent and soft texture soothed her. But as her eyes closed, a flash of red swam into her mind's eye; she saw herself slip a knife into the stomach of a dark-haired man. The blood slid down the hilt and splashed onto the floor. She pulled the towel away from her face. Her hands began to shake, she recognized the dark man on the end of the blade. Flashes of skin, his voice crying out and the blood, so much blood. Why was she having such vivid fantasies?

She pressed her face into the soft towel again. The flashes resumed; she was at the door. Now he was there, letting her in with a smile. She entered and slid her hand across his chest as she passed. It was warm and firm under her palm. But when he grabbed her wrist and jerked her toward him, she looked into his face and knew she had him where she wanted him. The vision was so real it took her by surprise to feel the water cool against her skin.

She wasn't standing in Kiernan's living room, she was naked and wet, water dripping down her legs, a towel pressed to her face. What was happening? Her plan was to catch him by surprise; to use him to finish the plan with his blood. Why would she imagine it any other way? Maybe she should rethink the plan. Was her subconscious trying to tell her something? Was she supposed to spare him, to make things right?

Payton bent at the waist and wrapped her hair in the towel. The water was cold on her bare skin but she liked the feeling of air drying. She always felt like she was spreading bacteria on her clean skin when she didn't let the air do the job. She stared at her image in the mirror and smeared a thick cream into her damp skin. The water made the lotion slide over a larger area without soaking in too quickly. As she bent to reach her calves, another flash had her reaching out to grip the counter. The knife slipping into his stomach just above his pelvic bone. A loud grunt and her perspective changed; she was looking into his eyes, his mouth stuffed full with an orange ball gag, the studded leather reaching around the back of his head. She looked down and felt her lips curve as she pressed the knife deep and ripped upward, his muffled scream erupting as if coming from the gushing gaping wound.

Payton blinked rapidly and rubbed the back of her right arm over her eyes. Despite the chilly air and wet skin, her upper lip was sweating. Her body was shaking and she took a few steps back and sat down on the edge of the porcelain tub. "What the hell?" she said, wishing there was an all-knowing voice that could answer her and explain why she was imagining a death that hadn't happened yet. Even stranger, if it had happened it wouldn't have happened the way she was seeing it. There was a plan. The plan was almost complete, despite the complications of Graydon and Marks. She shivered, a cold sweat beginning to seep into her skin and slide along the bone structure. Despite her sudden discomfort she continued to sit on the cold porcelain. Her tailbone, starting to ache, pressed on the hard surface. Without warning the stomach acids and coffee that once resided inside her splashed onto the tile leaving an acidic burn along the roof of her mouth.

Her swollen lips and broken skin warmed. Blood began to slowly slip down her chin as the wounds reopened.

Chapter Thirty-four

"What is, 'for the life of the flesh is in the blood'?" Blake sat in the rolling chair, his thumb pressed into the cleft on his chin. He was thinking in his usual introverted and musing way. He asked the question almost as if he were asking himself.

Timber pulled out a chair; the metal legs scraped on the hard floor as she spun it and straddled the small seat, crossed her arms along the back of the headrest and looked at the lines and words that covered the whiteboard. The connections between each victim, the odd words scribbled on walls and the visuals, would make even the most seasoned law officer cringe.

She answered "I'm not sure, but I think it's a Bible verse."

"The blood…" he mused.

"Do you think it's a coincidence that we're talking about blood?"

"Not a big fan of coincidence." he said and stood up. He began to pace, first looking at the initial kills and staring at the photos like they would soon begin to talk to him. She knew the scenario well, had seen cops staring at the same evidence for months desperately hoping that eventually the one clue they had somehow missed would jump from the page, in an epiphany only equaled by the greatest of history's storytellers. Unfortunately, it rarely worked that way. Still, optimism remained as he paced, reenacting a play as old as time.

"Are we talking about the blood at the scene?" she asked.

He shook his head, "I don't think so."

She nodded in agreement. "I think this is about the apple."

"That would make sense."

"The apple." he said and she saw the obvious nature of the symbol now so clear.

"Why didn't I see this before?" She shook her head in irritation.

"You?" he asked.

Timber clamped her front teeth together and pulled back her lips in a caricature of a smile. She said "Yeah, me. I'm the smart one."

He turned and crossed his arms in a defensive posture. "Oooh wow."

His reaction to her teasing was humorous. "Okee dokee, so let's stop focusing on my brilliance and get back to the fuckbag sending us on a live crossword." Timber said.

"My goodness it took all of sixty seconds before you reverted to form." he said

"Form?" She leaned back, gripped the back of the chair in her palms and arched her eyebrows.

He nodded. "Yes, 'form'; everyone has one, and yours includes expletives and unnecessary profanity in both extreme and tranquil circumstances." He explained this, as if he somehow knew her better than she knew herself.

"Tranquil?" Timber scoffed "At what point have you seen me tranquil?"

She was immediately alerted to a difference in the conversation. The mocking tone was gone and in its place was a melancholy that contradicted their previous banter.

"There was a time. Of course, it was a while ago, But, I looked into your eyes and saw unequivocally the most tranquil look I've ever seen."

"Oh." *Holy crap, he is too sexy to be real.* She couldn't manage to look away as he continued. She was mesmerized by his voice and words.

"And to make my point, I'll add the best detail." He arched a brow and lowered his voice to almost a whisper.

"Your mouth dropped open and in the most soft and gentle tone you muttered… 'Fuck'." His lips curved in a mocking grin and Timber felt her stomach do a little flip as she was unexpectedly jerked back to the memory of that moment. Time had passed, but nothing marred the image of his amber gaze as he looked into her eyes. She felt her cheeks get hot and she groaned. The sound was mercifully more disgust than she felt, belying any idea that she remembered what he was referring too.

"I did not!" she lied easily.

"Oh yes, you did." he assured her.

"Come on, how you can remember that?" She was skeptical even though his recitations of her actions were etched in her mind as surely as if they had been burned into the backs of her corneas. But, could he really feel the same? Was it possible that despite all that had transpired, all that she knew, that she had been wrong all along?

"I remember every second of that night." he said

A depth in his eyes made her uncomfortable and she quickly looked away. "You are such a girl." She mocked.

He laughed. "I know and you're such a guy."

"What does that even mean?" She stood, at the same time pushing the chair away.

Blake sighed, "I don't know. I'm just playing along."

"Shut the fuck up." Timber said, turned her back to him and took a deep breath.

"Imaginative."

"You are so irritating. Can we focus on the case?" she said, even as she headed for the door.

"Sure. We were talking about the blood."

"Yeah, so why the cryptic bullshit?" She turned her head and motioned for him to follow.

"Where are we going?"

"To see Danielle." she said.

"Where is she?" he asked.

"Why is she at the Marriott and not at Nick's?" They began jogging up the stairs in tandem.

Timber took the steps two at a time to keep pace with his long stride "I think Charlie was driving her crazy."

"Not Nick?"

"Nah." she said, gasping as she pushed open the outer door. "Nick's overprotective, but barely around. Charlie has started sniffing around the case."

"Crap."

"You said it, Bucko."

"Bucko?" he queried.

"I'm trying to watch my mouth." Timber searched the lane of parked cars for hers and came up empty.

"I'm touched, but don't go changing." Blake said.

"Ha, ha. Smart ass." She turned and shrugged her shoulders in confusion. "Where's my car?"

"That's my girl. You parked on the street."Blake said.

"Really?" She couldn't have been that distracted. "You let me run around…"

He muttered a curse and grabbed her arm. "Come on, we'll take mine."

Timber was immediately aware of the heat of his palm and the firm grip of his fingers on her upper arm. She allowed him to pull her while considering the implications of her heart rate acceleration.

"Why are we going to see Danielle?" he asked letting go of her arm and motioning her to his car.

The loss of his touch helped her ability to focus and she shook her head appalled by her inability to control her ridiculous reaction to him. She opened the door and slid into the seat. As the engine revved to life she said "Hampden and twenty five. It's the Four Points."

"Isn't that a Sheraton?" He glanced at her as he pulled from the parking lot.

"Yeah, sorry. It was a Marriott once, anyway…" she looked at him pointedly, "Danielle has access to some contacts that might help us."

"Contacts you're not privy to?"

"No, I have never had these kinds of contacts." she said and considered her next steps carefully.

Blake's eyebrows drew together. "Correct me if I'm wrong, but aren't you and Special Agent Devon the same pay grade?"

"Yeah, but this is a whole different sack o' sticks." she said and pulled her phone from her jacket pocket. "Just trust me." Timber had an idea that had started to germinate while watching Blake's frustrated marching in front of the board. As they had headed for the car, the idea had really begun to take form. They had the answer in their hands. It was really only a matter of using the resources available to them. As she listened to the phone ring on the other end, her excitement at the possible outcome became almost physical.

A deep feminine cadence came on the line. "Special Agent Devon."

"Hey, Dan. It's Timber. Blake and I are coming by."
"Sure. Is everything okay?"

"It will be, as long as you play ball."

"Great, no pressure." Danielle sighed.

"You may be our last hope." Timber said into the phone and winked at Blake; he smiled.

"That's dire, and a little dramatic."

"Serial murder brings out my inner drama queen." Timber said.

"Room two-thirteen." The phone call ended without ceremony and Timber knew she had expressed the importance of their visit.

"That was deep." Blake said.

Timber grinned and said "She directed us to her room, not the bar; I think I made my point."

Danielle opened the door and backed away. Timber walked inside and plopped down on the corner of the closest queen-sized bed. The room was adorned in dark wood and variations of deep brown and beige striped accents. It was a pleasing affect and Timber realized she had never been in one of these rooms. The hotel had been the epicenter for many meetings over the years but they had all taken place in the bar below.

It was clear Danielle had made herself at home. A small frame sat on the desk; in it was a five- by seven photograph of an attractive middle-aged man that Timber didn't recognize. She raised an eyebrow and no sooner had she realized what the photo meant than Danielle flipped it over with thumb and forefinger and leaned against the desk, blocking its existence from view.

Blake walked to the far side of the room and looked out the large window. Timber was nervous regarding what she was about to ask and she knew that at least initially, there would be resistance and possibly even denial. No time like the present. "So we need access to the DNA data base."

"You have access to that." Danielle replied, her dark brows rising in a scrutinizing expression. Timber understood the significance of her next request, but she needed to step across the line that had been drawn long ago by agencies in their field.

"That's not the one I need access to." Timber said and bounced herself back an inch further on the bed, expelling a little of the pent- up energy she was feeling.

Blake turned around, an inquisitive look covering every aspect of his expression.. "There's another one?" he asked softly as if he somehow knew the question was delicate.

"That's a rumor." Danielle said, but Timber saw the truth in her light gaze.

"Okay, so let's discuss the rumor and how, if it were true, it could put an end to these murders."

"That's quite a conclusion." Danielle said, "I want to help..."

"So help." Timber said.

Blake continued to stare his eyes going from Danielle to Timber. Timber could feel him sizing up the possibilities and gauging the reactions.

Danielle sighed. “Look, even if I knew what you were talking about, and I don’t,” she waved her hands in the air, pointing at the air ducts and electronics. “That is completely out of my purview. I’m not CIA. I have about as much power as a gnat when it comes to that kind of intelligence.”

“Nick was CIA.” Blake said, exposing the elephant in the room by stating the obvious.

“Shit! Really?” Danielle dropped her hands and sent them both scathing looks. “You know how this works.”

Timber understood that she was being sent signals, but like Blake, she felt Danielle was overreacting, so she chose to ignore them.

“I know it’s a lot,” Timber said, “but we need help. If we can’t identify the blood in that apple, we may never get this fuck nut.”

“How do you suppose I get access to this?” Danielle looked from Timber to Blake, “And even if it were something I could verify, how do we get it to work for us?”

“Well,” Timber said “I think you give the profile we’ve worked up to Nick, tell him the situation and ask him for a favor. We need a name. That’s all.”

“That’s all?” Danielle said, sarcastically. “Do you realize how difficult it is to distance oneself from the Central Intelligence Agency? Do you have any idea how hard he worked to get out?” Danielle asked, shaking her long hair in frustration.

“No.” Timber said “But it occurred to me that Charlie is wrapped up in this mess and if he feels she is in danger, he may be more willing to close ranks.”

“That’s low.” Blake said

“Yep.” Timber agreed.

Danielle lowered her head and rubbed her palms against her closed eyes. “Do you think Charlie’s really in danger?”

Blake spoke up. “Well, the crazy bitch locked us in a freezer…”

"Point taken," Danielle sighed. "You two need to leave."

"Hey!" Timber complained. "I…"

"No, this conversation is over." Danielle pushed away from the desk and walked briskly to the door. She pulled it open and waved her hand toward the opening. Her meaning was clear and her eyes were full of warning.

Timber jumped off the bed and walked out the door. She knew what had happened and hoped Blake would follow. As she continued down the hall, the door to Danielle's room slammed and Blake asked from behind her: "So that was weird; is she really pissed?"

"No. I think that was for show." Timber felt a small dose of adrenalin and wondered if more was coming. *How had Danielle known she was being watched?*

"So who does she think is watching?" Blake asked.

"Who the hell knows? But, I bet every time the name Nick Devon is muttered, someone, somewhere perks up their ears."

"No way. Really?" Blake seemed skeptical.

"Don't you know the history there? The guy was a ghost. A ghost that became corporeal."

Blake snickered. "Huh. That's an awesome metaphor. You should write that down."

"Thanks."

"Anytime. So what does it mean…exactly." he asked.

Timber laughed, she loved talking to him sometimes, and his dry wit was contagious. "He did wet work for the CIA. Anyway, that's the rumor. Of course, there is no real documentation on the guy because, well, they don't leave paper trails."

Blake scoffed. "Sounds like a damn nightmare. What if he got in trouble?"

"Then he's screwed. You ever see that movie 'Mission Impossible'?"

"Sure, I love Tom Cruise. He's little nutty, but awesome!"

Timber looked at him disbelievingly and he shrugged his big shoulders in defense. "Anyway," she continued, "That's not all fiction, and disavowal is a real thing. Screw up while on a mission doing something sketchy and you're on your own."

"That sucks." he said.

"Sure does." The elevator was opening as they approached and two men in dark suits stepped out. They didn't pause as they passed, walking purposefully in the direction of Danielle's room. Timber turned her head and followed the progress. "You don't think…?"

Blake looked alarmed and pulled his phone from his jacket. He pressed a number and waited. " "Danie… oh… Okay meet you there." He pressed 'end' on the phone and grabbed Timber by the arm and ran for the stairwell door. As he pushed it open, she stumbled after.

"What … what?" She kept her voice just above a whisper as they ran full-tilt, down the two remaining flights of stairs and burst into the lobby. He pulled her into a coffee shop on the ground floor and moved quickly to the table furthest away from the entrance. The sounds of polished shoes on carpet, running fast, startled Timber into a sort of shocked silence as Blake slid into a booth and lifted a menu, pulling her in beside him. He whispered in her ear: "Danielle said to get out now and she would meet us at the station."

"She really was being listened to." Timber said. It was an obvious statement but she felt like it needed to be said. "How the hell did they come back so quick?" she wondered.

"Well, based on my new knowledge that movies are real, I would say that they opened the door with their magical CIA key, saw that she was gone and did a little math. It's not hard to figure out that the couple walking down her hall were the voices they had just been listening to."

"You should be a detective." Timber mocked and pressed her palm against his chest just above his heart. She was pleased to feel it rapping against her hand. At least she wasn't the only one worked up. The motion was part that and part to keep a small distance. The way he had her gripped around the waist, without some balance she was going to be pressed fully against him.

"Yeah that…or a screen writer." he chided

"So what now?" she asked.

"Funny, you should ask me. Aren't you the fed?"

"Yeah, we are a bunch of tight-assed attorneys and accountants. What the hell do I know about espionage and black bag operations? Shit!" She felt responsible for Danielle's safety and knowing that Blake felt a sense of responsibility for some past imagined wrong, she began beating herself up for acting on another dangerous idea.

"You need to stop watching TV." he said

"I know!" Timber moved her palm and allowed him to pull her close. He continued to pretend he was reading the menu. His heartbeat did a little leap in acceleration and she grinned against his chest. "How long do we pretend we're not law enforcement and hide like chickens?" she asked

"I'm good with being a chicken. I think we should hang here a little longer and then call a cab," he suggested and gripped her tighter; she didn't complain.

"A cab?" Just as soon as she asked the question she realized why. "Oh yuck, this is going to be a fuckin' nightmare."

He shook his head, a gesture she felt more than saw."No, I don't think so. They probably just want to find out what we're up to. It's not like they can whack us for asking questions."

Timber pushed away from him and looked up at the smirk on his face. "Why are you so cheery? We were almost accosted by the CIA and we're hiding in a hotel and you're grinning like your digesting a damn canary."

"First off, if I were digesting a bird of any kind, I don't think I would be smiling; and second, I was digging the opportunity to have you so close without rules or drama."

"You don't find this dramatic enough." she asked aghast.

"It's different. This kind of drama I'm built for; problem, thought, consideration, solution."

Timber squinted at him and asked "So, you're saying that with me there's no solution or …"

He loosened his grip and waved at the waitress. "Ah, Damnit. You're ruining it. Stop analyzing everything." As the waitress approached he asked "Ma'am, can we get two coffees and if it's not too much trouble could you call us a cab."

She was an older woman, mid fifties with gray hair and a weather-worn look. Age had nothing to do with a woman's reaction to a charming, good looking man. Timber made a gagging sound as the woman practically swooned and said, "Yes sir, I'll get that right away sir." She lingered a moment, touching her hair and smoothing her apron. Then feeling better about her appearance, she smiled and turned to do his bidding.

"Gross!" Timber said and completely extracted herself from his grip.

"What's wrong now?" he asked innocently.

Chapter Thirty-five

Nick burst into the room, a look of anger so evident on his beautiful face that the incongruity was staggering. Timber stared open-mouthed at the male version of her friend. Timber had never met the editor of the paper or his alter ego, the super agent.

He was taller than Danielle and decidedly more masculine. His jaw square and his nose broader, but the azure blue eyes and coal black hair along with the deep Native American skin tone was exactly the same. Timber had never seen diozygotic twins look so identical, especially considering the opposite sex issue.

"Do you have any idea the shit storm you've brought down on me and mine?" Nick Devon stormed.

"Uh…I think Genesis is responsible for that." Timber said ruefully.

"Bullshit, Agent Byrne! Yes, I am aware of who you are and I am also aware of how you bullied my woman!"

"Really?" Timber found it funny that he called Charlie his 'woman'. "So, does she like that moniker?"

"You want something from me?" he asked, his body shifting from vibrating anger to an odd calm. Timber could see his power, it emanated from every aspect of him. Normally she would jab away until she pushed him to a breaking point, just to find out what that breaking point would be. As much as she felt a certain disappointment at the inability to experiment with a professional killer, he was right; she needed information and help. If she didn't tread very carefully she could lose him. Even her fun wasn't worth that.

"Yes, I need your help." She smiled and tilted her head to the side.

He laughed, a deep mocking sound, "Transparent, but better."

"Glad you approve," She added *asshole* silently and hoped it came through in her mind.

"What do you want?"

"Come on, we're playing games now?"

"I want you to tell me what you want. I think, after bullying Charlie and inconveniencing my sister, I want a little respect and consideration. I think you're not accustomed to dealing with people that stand up to you." He looked her up and down as if analyzing her by appearance alone. Then he said in almost a whisper, "Odd."

Timber bit her tongue to keep from telling him to take his big swinging dick and shove it up his ass. She snarled instead and said, "Fine, you've insulted me. You're bigger and badder and you're a man, so wow! That's just an obvious point. Also, I'm a terrible bitch and I owe Charlie an apology, even though I've probably saved her ass several times, but whatever!" Sarcasm dripped from her tone and she stopped talking to take a deep breath. She knew he was beginning to simmer again so she clamped her mouth shut and scowled at him. Man, he was the best-looking thing she had ever seen. She wondered how Charlie could stand being with someone hotter than her.

She shook her head and turned away for a moment, pretending to riffle through her desk drawer. Her hands were shaking and she realized if she didn't get her anger under control she was going to need to calm down or she would lose her chance. She wished that Blake were here. And where the hell was he? *Deep breaths! Deep breaths! Don't call him a limp dick. Focus on your verbal judo.* Hadn't she learned how to de-escalate a situation?

He interrupted her musings. "Byrne!" She whipped around. "You still here?"

"Sorry, I was looking for this." She pulled the slip of paper from her desk and slid it across. "This is the profile of DNA found in some evidence. It's very important that we find this guy."

"How important?" His tone was calm and showed no evidence of the tension she knew he was feeling. It was obvious he wanted her to beg and she was getting more pissed by the second.

"Jesus Christ, are you always like this?" she barked.

"As far as I know," he smiled. His perfect white teeth irritated her even more. *Why don't he have a big chip in his front tooth and why the fuck is he smiling?*

"I need you to use your database and find this guy." she said.

He stared at her and somehow his smile remained in place, even though his eyes remained cold and hard.

"You're really pissed about the Charlie thing."

"I'm not pissed. I'm feeling a little retributive at the moment. But pissed isn't really the right word." As he continued speaking, Timber started to detect a slight accent, maybe British? Weird. Then it was gone.

"Okay," she said slowly and sat in her chair, giving him the dominant stance of standing over her and looking down.

He remained just inside the door and gripped his hands behind his back in an almost military stance, feet hip width part, eyes hard, face having lost the smile, waiting.

"What can I do to get what I want? You're here, so you're either gonna kick my ass or you're gonna do what I want. But my guess is that I'm going to owe you."

"Good guess." His tone was dry.

"So, what?"

"First, you're going to respect Charlie." he said.

She laughed, and seeing his look, she clamped her mouth shut and said, "Okay, dude, really, I can't just respect someone."

"Fake it." he snarled.

"Fine!" she said, in the snottiest tone she could muster.

"Danielle's off the case. Send her home."

"Wh…have you met Danielle?" Timber asked, shocked by his demand.

"It's non-negotiable." he said.

Timber was aghast, "What do you think she's gonna say about this?"

"You're not going to tell her."

She made a loud noise in her throat that came out without her notice.

His eyebrows raised, "Problem?" he asked.

"No. Nope," she lied. "I will show the utmost respect for Charlie. I will sit down with her and give her an exclusive the minute the case is cleared. I'll tell Dan that we don't need Danielle and funding is chipped away because of bureaucracy. I will lie down and kiss your ass. Just give me a name."

He walked slowly to the edge of her desk and reached into his front pocket. It took all of her will to stay put. This man had the darkest presence she had ever experienced wrapped in the package of an Adonis. She could only imagine how dangerous this man actually was. The reputation definitely matched the man. A small yellow slip of paper was pulled from that pocket and dropped on her desk. She looked down in awe at the name scribbled on the sheet – Alexander Kiernan – and below a social security number.

"Are you kidding me?" she asked.

"Not something I spend a lot of time doing," He turned and walked to the door.

"Hey! I just gave this to Danielle this morning. How is this possible?"

"Part of the deal is no questions. Unless you want a repeat of the Four Points?"

"Yeah. What the hell was that…"

"No questions."

She shrugged, "Whatever, thanks."

"Don't thank me, thank Danny. And Byrne?"

"Yeah?"

"Don't forget our agreement."

Timber shivered as he walked out the door and pulled it shut behind him. She had the oddest feeling she had just come very close to something dark. She wondered how that could be, wasn't this guy a good one? She looked at the paper lying on her desk and was almost afraid to reach out and touch it. Timber laughed at herself, grabbed the paper, stood and rushed to the door of her office. As she passed several people in the hall it occurred to her that Devon had burst into her office with no badge and no visitor advanced notice. The thought made her stop in her tracks and look around her. "What the fuck?" she said, causing several people to stop and look at her. A chill went through her again and she rushed to the elevator. She decided against the stairs – way too creepy.

Chapter Thirty-six

Robin Blake was incredulous "We mentioned that we wanted access to a secret CIA database and moments later agents show up and Danielle disappears. Then she shows up the next morning, picks up the profile of the blood from the apple and four hours later Nick shows up with a name?"

"That's about the size of it," Timber said.

"Danielle?" Blake asked.

"I'm not talking," Danielle replied. "I contacted my SAC who made some calls. I'm off the hook as long as my lips stay zipped."

"Damn! Well, I'm supposed to cut you loose," Timber said.

"What?" Danielle actually stomped one foot. They all stopped moving and stared at her.

Timber was the first to break the silence and it came forth in a snort and a cough. Blake joined in, chuckling and eventually Danielle's scowl vanished and she laughed at her juvenile response. "Sorry," she said, "I feel like I'm six again and Nicky is trying to boss me around. He loves playing the Big Bossy Brother, and he's my twin, damnit! Why does he think he can do this? Did he tell you not to tell me? Did he threaten you? I'm going to kill him!" She stopped and took a deep breath and stared at Timber expectantly.

Timber wiped her moist eyes and said, "Oh, are you done? I don't think I've ever heard you say that much at one time. You okay?"

She looked at Blake leaning in the corner, a smile on his mouth, but something else lingering in his eyes. Just as she was going to question his expression Danielle said, "I'm fine, please answer the question."

Timber felt terrible as she opened her mouth and did what she usually enjoyed. She told the truth, "Yes, he threatened me. It was vague but pointed. He also made it very clear that I was supposed the keep my fucking mouth shut." As she said the words her gut did a funny little twist. Danielle was beginning to look nervous. Blake was pushing his hands so deep into his front pockets that they were disappearing at the wrists. Timber shook her head, "Fuck, am I in deep cow shit?"

Blake shrugged and kept his hands in his pockets, looking uncomfortable.

Danielle shook her head, "No, you're fine. What did he say about Charlie?"

"I agreed to an exclusive."

A gust of air blew from Blake's lips.

"Oh, shut up!" Timber snapped. She was embarrassed by the entire subject and she refused to allow this man to intimidate her. She looked at Danielle and Blake, the trepidation on their faces and again her gut jumped. She looked at Danielle, "He's not gonna have me whacked, is he?"

"No, he may kidnap and torture you, but he'll leave you alive so you can remember him."

"Awesome," Blake said.

And Timber said," Ha ha," knowing in a deep uncomfortable way that Danielle's words were only light on the surface.

Danielle waved away the thought, "Look, I'm not going anywhere. I'm going to run the name. I'll be back and we'll track it and crack this bitch wide open."

Timber grinned, "Stop trying to talk like me. You suck at it."

Blake nodded, "Yeah, it is bad. Please, never again."

Danielle nodded and grabbed the yellow slip of paper that Timber now held in front of her. "Don't worry. I'm gonna handle it, it's cool." Before Timber could consider Danielle's action more carefully she was out the door.

"Do you think I'm in danger?"

"Yes." he said.

"How can you say that?" she asked.

"You asked."

"What are you doing?"

"I'm going to take care of something before I lose my chance."

"Why would you lose…" His mouth was on hers, one of his arms pulling her off her heels and onto her toes. All of her weight was somehow gone and she felt almost as if she were floating. His lips were warm and firm. She knew this was where she belonged, wrapped in his strong arms, being kissed like he thought it would be their last. Her chest began to hurt as the kiss deepened and her hands slid into his thick hair. An emotion she was completely unfamiliar with filled her and she felt a tear slip from the corner of one eye.

He must have felt the moisture because he pulled away and looked down into her eyes. His emotions were there, raw and visible. He smiled a slow smile that reached his eyes long before the motion of his lips was complete.

She opened her mouth, "I…"

His finger came up as if to silence her and she clamped her mouth shut. The teardrop was at her chin and he caught it and lifted it between them as if it were some precious diamond. Then he rubbed it between thumb and forefinger and made a fist and slipped it into his pocket. It was the most absurd moment, the act of keeping her tear as if it were some treasure that could be captured and yet it made her love him more; more than she realized she could love. She wanted to tell him. She wanted to apologize. She wanted to take it all back, to…

"Not now." He gave her back her weight and took a step back. "After. We'll talk after. Acceptable?"

She nodded and was astonished that she no longer felt any embarrassment or animosity. She wiped any remnant of the tear away and smiled. “Okay. But I have a lot to say.”

His smile grew, “I’m sure you do. But let’s catch a killer.”

“Fuck yeah!” Timber felt happy and when his deep laugh filled the small room that joy doubled.

Chapter Thirty-seven

Danielle's voice came over the line, "It's the parent's house. Apparently he's been missing for a few months. There's a report but we missed, probably because they're in Albuquerque."

"Who is he?" Timber asked.

"Nobody really, just some guy. He had a career as a tech geek at some computer outlet and he took tap dancing."

"Gay?"

"Don't think so. Not all tap dancers are gay."

Timber shrugged, "Sorry, I'm from Texas."

"Anyway, if Nicky contacts you, lie. I told him you kicked me and I need to get back to Roger, so I went back to D.C."

"Did I mention Roger is an awful name?" Timber said, smiling.

"Shut it, Byrne."

"So call me when you land."

"Will do." Danielle confirmed.

"Hey, I've been meaning to ask. How did you get out of that hotel room so fast?"

"I have a bat cave," Danielle replied.

Timber laughed asking, "Under the Four Points?"

"You never know."

"Be safe." Timber said.

"Always am."

"Liar."

"Ouch."

The phone call ended and Timber considered what she would say if Nick Devon called. She decided she wouldn't answer.

"It's a Bible verse all right." She looked up. Tall, dark, dimpled, and looking tired with stubble peppering his chin, Blake practically danced with excitement. "That means the apple is probably a biblical thing, too."

"So, like what Adam and Eve? Is she taking revenge for the Apple debacle?"

"Debacle?" Blake moved into her office and closed the door behind him.

"Yeah, because of that stupid apple, women have gotten a bad rap for centuries."

He shook his head in what looked like bewilderment, "Yeah, that's why."

"Was that sarcasm?" she asked, squinting. She was so glad she realized she loved him. Looking was so much more fun now. He was luscious.

His lips twitched and he turned his head quickly as if he heard her say something that she hadn't actually said. "Can we stay on point?"

"Sure," she said and let her gaze linger from chest to crotch and back again. This was going to be so much fun!

"Stop that!"

Her eyes snapped to his, "What?!?

"The apple."

"The apple?" she asked, suddenly lost.

He spoke slowly, "It's from the Old Testament."

"Oh. Danielle found Kiernan." said Timber.

"Cool. We need to have an update, I'll call the team."

She stood and said, "Great job, good idea, you get on it, Big Boy." While she was talking she moved quickly and pressed her entire body to his, standing on her tiptoes. She grabbed his head and pulled it down to hers, then very gently took his bottom lip between her teeth and pulled. He made a noise in his throat and before he could do more she let his lip go and ducked under the arm coming around to grab her. "No time! Call the meeting. See ya' soon!" She practically ran from the room laughing. As she reached the end of the hall and realized he wasn't behind her she slowed. Something felt odd and she looked over her shoulder. It was pretty quiet but she felt like she was being watched. An instinct told her to run but she ignored it. She was in the offices of the FBI, safe and secure. Then the image of Nick Devon strolling into her office came unbidden to her memory. She turned again. A part of her wanted to go back and check on Blake. She forced herself to keep walking. This case was making her paranoid.

Chapter Thirty-eight

Danielle sat in the living room of the Kiernan's lovely home, sipping from a dainty tea cup. It was some sort of chamomile blend and was really awful but she couldn't bring herself to complain. The couple sitting on the sofa opposite her looked as if they had lost their son today instead of months ago. The once well-kept couple was now a red-eyed mockery of what they once had been. Photos of past bliss and family traditions filled the walls and were scattered about on surfaces of mantles and side boards. "Can you tell me a little about Alexander?"

The woman set her cup on the silver tray and smiled weakly, her husband squeezed her hand, "He is our only child. I know he's an adult, but he's my baby and always will be." The hand squeezed again.

"He just turned 30 this past summer. I gave him some lilacs to plant outside his home. He bought his first home this year and…" she sniffled.

Lilac, Danielle noted on her pad, "We didn't have an address for his home." she said

"Oh, he still used ours."

"Why?" Danielle couldn't imagine why a grown man with his own address would still use his parents.

"It was that girl," her husband said snidely, "That girl's a menace and he didn't want her coming around."

Danielle looked at the couple. Both had seemed to shift in mood, "Girl?"

"Yes," the woman said, "Payton."

"Or Katie," the husband chimed in, a certain mocking quality to the word.

The woman nodded, "She used different names and if you used the wrong one she would become angry."

“She was crazy, that’s all there was to it. We tried to tell Alex, but he wasn’t having it. Not until she killed Fred. Then he was done.” the husband added.

Danielle straightened, “Killed Fred?”

The woman seemed to catch on first and shook her head. “Oh…Fred was his dog. He was beautiful and they were very close. He was a golden retriever, Alex had him for five or six…?” She looked at her husband.

He nodded, saying” Six years. That crazy bitch killed Fred and left a note that she did it.”

Danielle felt her heart thudding, this was the right track, “Alex didn’t press charges?”

“No!” he said, “He lo-o-oved her.”

“Don’t be rude, Ray,” the woman said and patted his thigh.

He complied and leaned back, “He said he wouldn’t see her anymore but that he wouldn’t put her in jail.”

“She came by here a few times looking for him.”

“Do you have a picture?” Danielle asked.

“Of that…” his eyes widened in insult.

“Ray!” the woman chastised. She stood slowly and walked to the mantel. In a small frame was a picture of an average looking man with wide eyes and full cheeks. His face was happy and one arm disappeared out of the frame. She slid off the back, “I loved the look on his face in this picture. It reminded me of when he was a boy. I couldn’t help that it was because of her.” She pulled out the picture and unfolded it.

Danielle gasped. She felt as if she were going to pass out. The edges of her vision turned black and she reached out to balance herself.

“Young lady, are you okay?” the woman asked.

Danielle gasped, “I need to make a call.”

Ω

“Where the fuck is Danielle?”

Blake turned to the voice and was shocked to see Nick standing on the street, fists balled at his sides. He knew what that meant and when a man like Nick was barely containing himself; things were far from good.

"The last I heard she was coming back from Albuquerque. I've been trying to reach her."

"Albuquerque?" Nick came closer and cold air plumed like smoke from his mouth. Blake was accustomed to towering over most of his contemporaries, so when Nick stepped closer he was reminded that this wasn't the case, taking away the advantage he usually felt. An ugly sense of déjà vu came over him as Nick looked at him accusingly, "Did you send her to Albuquerque?"

"No," he denied, "Get in if you want, I'm going to the airport."

Nick grabbed the door handle and jerked open the passenger door.

Blake felt nausea settling in his middle as he turned the key and the engine revved to life. He couldn't contain his curiosity. "Why are you here? You couldn't possibly be this compulsive about her."

Nick scowled at him, his eyes throwing sparks, "I knew Byrne couldn't keep her mouth shut. I have never trusted her. She is far too small."

Blake blinked, "That's irrational."

"Am I wrong?" he asked, "Did she keep quiet?"

"No, I was referring to the small comment."

"It's true. She's a gremlin."

"Gremlin?" Blake laughed, "Really."

"I did some research for Charlie and I looked up a few things that worry me."

"Just a few?"

"Well, first remember that letter, the one where Genesis named herself?

Blake nodded.

"Those numbers we couldn't identify. They are the call letters of a radio station KAKE."

"Aw, shit," Blake said. That had never occurred to him.

"That's the station that the BTK killer sent his messages to. Also, that life is in the blood crap."

"For the life of the flesh is in the blood," Blake quoted.

"Yeah, it's Old Testament. Leviticus 17:11. It is a rather broad interpretation. Some people say it just means don't eat meat or you'll roast in Hell."

Blake glanced at Nick, and despite his words and the casual way he spoke he was extremely serious. He looked back to the road and listened.

"But the way I read it and the more strict interpretation is a sacrifice will be made to atone for your sins."

Blake said, "A sacrifice in blood."

"That is the message," Nick replied solemnly.

Blake drove; thinking and waiting. He knew there was more. There had to be. Risking life and limb, he once again brought up Danielle, "This is good intel and don't think I don't appreciate it but…"

"Why am I chasing after my sister even though she's a grown woman with Special Ops training?" Nick asked rhetorically.

"Yeah, something like that."

"I have a message for her," he said vaguely.

"Does it have anything to do with you killing Timber?"

"No. I have a bad feeling she's going to need saving, not killing."

"I really wish you hadn't said that."

"Why?"

"I have the same feeling," Blake said.

Chapter Thirty-nine

"Do you smell that?"asked Cable.

Peterson nodded, as Timber and Cable stepped through the front door. The most profound thing was the blood spray on the walls. The smell in the room was a mixture of urine and lilac, an odd combination that both nauseated and irritated the senses. Three tables arranged inside the front room had vases with rotted stems of lilac soaking in murky water. The air conditioner was running. a soft whir keeping the air a chilly temperature . Timber shivered, but it wasn't from the cold. The front room bespoke of horrors that had happened recently enough that the senses could detect them without much imagination. The wood floors were chipped and nicked in several places. It would be impossible to tell without crime scene techs but it appeared to Timber that a brutal homicide had happened in the room she now stood. "I smell it." she confirmed. There was no expectation of life so there was no rush to bust though the house or break down any doors. The room could be processed with precision. Timber, Cable and Peterson carefully traversed the room, walking its edges and avoiding any contamination or possible transfer that could confuse the issue later on. Timber pulled her phone from her pocket. Peterson screamed and just as Timber was turning to respond…darkness.

****

Her head hurt, her right leg felt odd and numb, a throbbing in her hip caused her to roll away from the pain.

A voice she recognized spoke to her in a soothing tone, "Stay still, your leg is broken."

"Danielle?" Timber couldn't remember her last moments before unconsciousness. The voice of her friend confused her and the idea that her leg was broken brought her instantly into a more conscious state. "Are you fucking kidding me?" She sat up and her stomach roiled causing her to groan and gag.

"She drugged us. Relax; if you move too quickly the results are bad. Trust me; I have the evidence on my clothes and hair to prove my point."

Timber braced her head with her hands and in doing so realized they were secured with metal handcuffs . "Fuck me!" She was starting to feel a pressure in her leg and turned her throbbing head in the direction of Danielle's voice. The tall beautiful brunette was sitting on the floor, her back pressed against a metal column, her hair and clothing drenched with moisture, "Why are you wet?" Timber asked.

"The bitch hosed me down when I puked, although she missed some spots. I don't know whether to thank her or not. What do you think?"

Timber stared at her, amazed at the attempt to lighten such a horrific moment. " Son of a cunt fuck! How did this happen?"

"I am not sure how you ended up here. I heard some noise and you came flying down the stairs. I have to tell you, it was nasty. I heard your leg snap…twice."

"Great!

"Yeah. I guess it was too much trouble to carry you so she chucked you." Danielle said morosely.

"I'm not a softball!"

"You're kind of the size of one."

"Are you trying to make me laugh?"

"Would you rather cry?"Danielle asked

"Why aren't you freaking out?" Timber said and choked back a sob of pain.

"Been here before, that time was worse."

"Why hasn't she killed us?"

"I think she is trying to finish something."

"We are part of a plan?"

"That is my guess."

"How long have we been here?"

"Not sure."

"I'm going to need pain meds soon."

"Figured."

"Are you hurt?"

"No, just humiliated and wet."

"Good."

"Do you have a plan?" Danielle asked.

"I have a broken leg."

"And I'm incredibly damaged."

"Come on! You're like the strongest person ever!"

"That would be you, Timber."

"Is this gonna turn into a fuckin' 'love-in' cause I think I'm gonna barf."

"Your leg?"

"That and you."

"Fuck you."

"Oh ! You kiss your brother with that mouth?"

"Ha ha."

"You think we're gonna die?"

"No way."

"What happened, Danny?

"I went to his parent's house and there on the mantel was a big smiley picture of Peterson and Kiernan in San Diego on vacation."

"Vacation in San Diego? The water is so cold."

"That's what you have to say?!?"

"My leg is really starting to hurt."

"You need to take off your belt, you're bleeding badly."

Timber looked at her leg. She had been avoiding that visual even though she knew it was inevitable. One bulge on the lower part of her shin was visible through the thin material of her slacks. "That doesn't look good" she said, hearing pain twined around each word. "Did you say Peterson? As in my 'task force Peterson'?

"You just got that?"

"Where's Cable?" Timber felt dread that overwhelmed the pain for a moment.

"Dead. He came down the stairs after you," Danielle pointed.

Timber followed the gesture, but quickly looked away. If he wasn't already dead, the fall would have done the trick. His head was turned at a sickening angle, the neck obviously broken.

"Where's Blake?" Danielle asked.

"He went to the airport to get you."

"Why would he do that? I left a message on his home phone that Peterson was involved and to come here."

Timber turned her head and puked. It was mostly acid and burned all the way up and continued to burn afterward. "We had a task force meeting where we gave everyone an update on the progress and your trip to Albuquerque."

Danielle groaned, "Peterson was in the room, wasn't she?"

Bile tried to rise and Timber swallowed," She's on the task force."

"Why here?" Danielle mused aloud.

Timber knew she didn't expect an answer but it seemed important to try, "Cable found the address; said it was a new purchase so that's probably why it didn't show up earlier."

"So Peterson fed him the address to get you here." Danielle concluded.

"But why?"

"To kill us."

"Good guess, stupid cunt!"

Timber began choking on a blast of cold water pounding her cheeks and forehead, her only thoughts consumed by the cold and pain that lassoed through her skin.

Gasping for air she turned her head away and the punishing liquid disappeared as quickly as it had begun.

"Throw up again and I'll drown you. That's gross."

Timber coughed and gagged, terrified that her last act would be regurgitation. "Valerie," she coughed.

"Don't call me that! My name is Payton. Payton!" her teeth bared as she raised the hose.

"Okay, Payton," Danielle said, "What can we do to help you?"

Payton laughed. Timber could see she was wearing a wig. Unlike her own ashy hair, her wig was almost yellow and cut with thick bangs. She wore red lipstick and a tight black dress. Her heels were easily five or six inch stilettos. "Do for me?" she asked in a silky voice. "You can die." Then she dropped the hose and sat down on the last step, draped her legs out in front of her and propped them both on Cable's head.

Timber looked at the macabre scene and almost laughed.

"I always hated him."

Danielle said, "I've been on this for a while now and I'm having a hard time following."

Timber understood instantly and joined in, "Yeah, what the fuck?" She knew that they were in the worst situation with no paddle in an uphill hell stream. The only thing to do was keep the psycho talking until an opportunity presented itself. At that moment, a sharp pain hit her from groin to toe and she cried out.

"Spasm?" Payton asked conversationally.

"I guess," Timber moaned, trying not to look at her leg.

"I'm gonna marry Roger," Danielle said out of the blue.

Timber laughed and she thought maybe she cried a little. "What about Garrett?"

Peterson asked, "Is he the guy in the coma?"

Danielle nodded and they both watched in horror as she crossed her ankles on Cable's head.

"Who's Roger?"

Timber answered, "Her boyfriend, but if you kill us she'll never get the chance to say 'I do'."

"So this Roger asked you to marry him and you ran away to your coma boyfriend?"

Danielle cringed and nodded.

"Maybe I'll just kill her," she motioned to Timber, "She looks close anyway."

Timber really didn't know how to respond. Her intellect and negotiating skills were taking a hard second to the throbbing agony of broken bones on cold concrete.

"You guys ever see someone…have their eye popped out?" She sounded excited and Timber was sure she was going to yack again. Time for the hose.

"Fuck, you are one crazy bitch!" She was never good at holding her tongue and the terrified look in Danielle's eyes did nothing to help it now. "Jesus, she's a freak show!" Timber yelled.

Danielle shook her head, "She's in shock." she said, defending Timber, obviously hoping for mercy.

Timber retorted, "I am not. I'm just over…"

"Shut up!" Payton took her high-heeled shoes off of Patrolman Cable's head and stood, clamping her hands into fists, "Shut up! Shut up! Shut up!" She bent and pulled off one heel and then the other. "Do you know what kind of damage something like this can do?" She sauntered over to Danielle and pointed the heel at her. Then as they both watched, the slinky stance and the hip thrust changed. Her hand and the shape of her mouth went from pouty and sultry to thin and tight, her eyes cleared, focused, and she seemed to slump in her shoulders as she turned and looked around the room.

"Katie?" Danielle asked.

"Yes?" A meek voice came from the mouth that was somehow no longer Payton.

"Who the fuck is Katie?" Timber demanded, angry, confused, and just a little disoriented. A part of her believed she had passed out and another person had entered the room.

"Shut up, Timber," Danielle urged.

"Timber… that's an odd name."

"Thanks," Timber said, pain now clouding it all. The edges of her consciousness were red and a pulsing was added to the mix.

"I mean no offense." Katie said sweetly, a soft smile on her crimson lips.

"None taken," Danielle replied and Timber thought it was very funny that Danielle was answering questions directed at her.

"Where's Alex?" Katie asked.

"You don't know?" Danielle responded.

"Who's Alex?" Timber asked, although she was sure she should know this one.

"Where's Alex!?!" she screamed, and threw the shoe at Timber. It hit her in the center of her chest and bounced away. Timber giggled and wondered how bad things were going to get.

"I think Payton killed him," Danielle said.

The new one, Katie, Timber thought, yelled, "No! No! That's last. Last! Not. No, I decided no." Katie stared at Danielle and said, "You're lying!"

Timber felt like she was watching a dark theatrical hell version of Sybil. Only she was starting to believe that maybe she was the crazy one because Danielle was talking to Katie like she wasn't actually Valerie Peterson, an officer for the Denver Police Department. She wondered if Blake had any idea that he had three girls in one working for him. She started to feel a bubble of laughter and suppressed it quickly, remembering the last time. The pain wasn't worth it.

"I'm not," Danielle said. "I wouldn't lie to you. Payton lied."

"No she didn't! Shut up!" Katie ran the three steps to Danielle and slapped her hard in the face. Timber watched in awe as Danielle met and held the other woman's stare, even as an angry red handprint appeared on her cheek.

Timber closed her eyes. "We are so dead," she mumbled and an image of her Daddy appeared in the void of her addled consciousness saying, *'don't give up, Sugar, don't ever give up'*. She opened her eyes, pushed down the agony shooting up her spine and asked in a calm voice, "What did you mean, "That's last"?"

Both of the other women, so focused on each other, seemed startled by Timber's voice.

She swallowed and reiterated, "That's last. Earlier you said 'that's last'. What did you mean?"

Katie seemed to forget Danielle, "I love Alex," she said simply.

"I'm sure you do. What happened?" Timber hoped the story was long, though she didn't really know how long she could stay engaged.

"I loved him," she said, then seemed to notice there was something unusual on her head. She scratched at the wig, shifted it and finally pulled it from her head. The transformation brought home a point for Timber that she knew but hadn't really seen until now. Peterson, with her thin ash blond hair and pale face, Peterson, the cop. The wig was dropped and she pulled the band off as well, allowing her hair to fall about her shoulders. "We were so happy. Then his dog died and he said I did it, but I didn't kill his dog. I loved his dog." She seemed to fade away, looking off to the left, "He said he saw me do it." She looked at Timber beseechingly, "Why would he say a thing like that?"

Timber could easily imagine the psycho, both she had met earlier, killing a dog. She could only imagine what it must have been like to witness your lover killing your dog. She shivered. She tried to sound reassuring when she said, "Maybe he was confused?"

"He lied. He didn't love me and he said if I didn't leave him alone he would ruin me."

Timber was beginning to see it. Peterson was the one he was with. He had to know she was a cop. If he went to the cops, even if he wasn't completely believed, there would always be a shadow. She had to have known that. Was he even aware of Katie and Payton? She asked the obvious next question, "Why did Payton kill the dog?"

Katie started to deny. She shook her head and rushed Timber, who cringed and closed her eyes, waiting for the blow. When it didn't come, she listened. Breathing, heavy and close; eyes opening, she saw Katie had sat next to her and was holding one of the shoes she had discarded earlier. "Alex said I need help. He said that Val and me, we could stay but Payton had to go. He didn't like her; he said she was a whore bitch."

"Yuck, that had to hurt."

She shrugged and turned the shoe in her hand, "She can't help it, being like that is all she knows. She's been selling it since she was little; it's all she knows, she's been selling it since she was little. It's how we survived."

Timber's mouth fell open, "You're telling me she was an actual whore?

Katie grimaced, "She hated that." She shook her head and said, "No. No. No." Then she met Timber's eyes. Katie's were sympathetic, "Better be careful. She really doesn't like you."

"Great." *The rabbit hole doesn't get much deeper than this,* she thought and glanced at Danielle.

"I gave her some more stuff." Katie said.

"What? When?" Timber assumed she meant some sort of drug, an idea that terrified her, especially since, unless she had lost some serious time, the effects of whatever it was had acted fast.

Danielle's head lolled to one side. She was obviously unconscious.

Katie held up a very small syringe. "Analgesic. Don't worry. Anyway, it's you I want to talk to."

"Why do you want to talk? Why did you have to drug her to do it?" Timber realized she was beginning to slur her words. "Where's Alex?" she asked.

"Alex is here." Katie said. He's here but I don't want to kill him. I don't want to. I love him."

"So Payton wanted you to kill Alex?"

"No. No! She was gonna do it. She promised. He loved me."

"I got that," Timber said and grabbed her head with her palms.

"Payton said no one could find out about Valerie. Valerie is the important one, she always has been. But Alex found out about me and he told me he loved me. Valerie thought they broke up. I kept coming over. He called me Katie. He'd say 'Katie, Baby, I love you, you're my sweetheart.' Then her eyes glazed over and she said "NO!" very loudly, pressing her fingers to her ears. It was over quick, but somehow she was still Katie. Katie telling her story. Katie on the edge.

"Katie, was Payton's prostitution the way she found her victims?" Timber asked.

"Sure. The plan was brilliant at first. Kill some guys, and then add Alex. She wanted to do that for me. He hurt me. But then some of Valerie's teachers started to get wise so Payton had to take care of things, even that detective teacher. He was almost exactly right. He knew Genesis was a dissociative and he knew she was a cop. He was going to go to you and propose testing – brain testing – for the task force."

"Ah…" Timber said, "He knew you were on the force."

She kept shaking her head," It wasn't me! It was her. It was her!"

Once again, Timber's eyes slipped shut and she considered slipping away. She felt like she could.

"I'm gonna give you something. Payton's coming back and you're gonna need something." She stabbed a needle into the leg just above the thigh muscle. It made her twitch in reaction but the edge of the pain was gone in an instant.

Timber wanted to tell the woman to 'Fuck Off', to punch and kick and scream. She wanted to drag herself from their situation by her nails at the walls, but she couldn't. She was terribly injured and assessed the injury because she was being drugged. "This sucks!" She hadn't realized she said it out loud until it was out and Katie said "Yeah" in such a sweet voice that tears started to form in Timber's eyes, although she was sure she wasn't crying.

"When Alex found out, he thought it would be cool to date three chicks at once. Didn't really turn out that way. Payton told me that it was time to kill him and I was like 'Not yet', 'cause maybe he didn't mean it. Maybe he likes all three of us. But he didn't like Payton."

"Can you make her leave?" Timber asked.

"No, no. Payton takes care of us, all of us."

"Peterson has the job, what about her?"

"She needs Payton too. She would never have gotten through Post training without Payton. We all need her. She's the strongest. But Alex, he didn't believe, so we were…" she paused, "We showed him."

"What did you show him?" Timber asked.

"Wait, maybe not yet. We are going to show him."

"I think Alex Kiernan was murdered upstairs in his front room, stabbed and mutilated and then hidden somewhere in this house."

"SHUT UP!" Katie stood and shook her hair, she pulled at her dress and she put her arms out and turned in a circle. When she faced her again Katie was gone and she found a small foot poking into the breaks in her leg. She gasped. "Stop that! Why were you poking at my wounds?" Payton was back and Timber had no idea how to proceed.

"Did you kill Alex?'

"Sure as fuck did," she said. "That bastard wanted to kill me so I killed his ass first. Katie and Val don't know. Well, really, Val doesn't know much. Just that we're setting it up and she's gonna bring it down."

"You mean she's gonna solve the case?" Timber was lost again.

" Yes, yes, yes. Stay with me. We all have needs. Valerie needs to be a cop, but not just any cop; she needs to be the best. I need to get rid of Alex and Katie. Well, we'll work on her later. We get what we want."

"But how is she gonna solve the case without sending herself to prison?"

"Oh, yeah. Well, we had a fall guy and we been planting stuff and he was gonna go down." She sounded different now, not as assured, almost rambling. Timber asked what happened.

"I had to kill him!" She shook her head, "He didn't have to be such a great detective, he was retiring."

"Oh Jesus fuck! You were setting up Graydon. He figured you and you killed him."

"That's the whole game, baby. And now I gotta kill you, too, and get you out. Maybe I'll find a trail to this house and feed it to Val. She can find you and still be a hero."

"Val doesn't know?" Timber asked.

"No, nosy. Val is our protected, I am the protector and Katie is the victim."

"Shit," Timber muttered.

"What?"

"I was hoping for a guy who could kick your ass. Watching you kick your own ass might just make this day better." It only took a moment for Timber to realize she had gone too far. The heel was coming at her eye fast. "STOP!" she yelled and it did, then Payton was beside and behind the ridiculous weapon. The tip of the metal spike was so close she could feel it brushing her eyelashes.

"I've popped out a man's eye. I stepped on one; it rolled for a minute then it popped like a water balloon filled with Jell-o. But I've never stabbed one out." Her grin was maniacal. She was going to do it. This one-in-three was going to fulfill a new experience on her fucked-up wish list and Timber found she was almost too tired to care. She wondered if Blake would love her with one eye and one leg. She started to laugh. She laughed so hard tears rolled down her face and Payton pressed the heel against her eye.

The fluid that hit her face was not what she had expected. It was thick, wet, and smelled of fresh blood and death. The smell of gun smoke made her aware that someone had just shot the back of Payton's head off. In effect all brain, face, and bone had exploded onto and into Timber. The body was lying half on her and she was about to pass out from the pain when she saw Blake holstering his gun. "Help!" was all she could say.

"I'm here, baby, where are you hurt?"

"I think I have psycho brain in my mouth."

"Gross. Sorry, any other angle and I would have hit you."

"You couldn't say "Freeze?"

"She was about to blind a federal agent. I shot first."

"Oh."

Nick Devon came into the space, cursing, "Where is she?" As medics were loading Danielle onto a stretcher, Nick asked, "Why is she out?"

Timber answered, "Analgesic. It's in the body's pocket." Blake helped lift Payton's dead form from Timber and put her on another stretcher.

Nick looked at Timber's injuries. You'll limp for a while, but you'll heal. If you didn't have gray matter dripping out of your hair, I'd kick your broken ass."

Timber lifted her head, "Bring it! If you can't control your sister and your girlfriend, then I can easily kick your ass. I don't care who you were before. Now you're just an editor so get the fuck out of my face!"

As she spoke his eyes widened, but he seemed more amused than irritated.

"And tell Charlie she gets her exclusive and it's better than anything she could ever have imagined!"

Danielle moaned and he rushed away.

Blake stepped up, "I guess you told him."

Timber smiled and said, “I’ve got his number.”

“Yeah, what’s that?”

“He can’t be mean to women, he was raised right.”

They both looked at the worry on Nick’s face as he watched his sister. Blake looked at Timber, “I love you. You’re not walking away from me again.”

“I won’t be doing any walking for a while.” She grabbed his head and they kissed deeply. Nick was saying something. They pulled apart.

“She’s awake.”

Timber was relieved, “Good.”

They heard her ask Nick, “How did you know? I told you I went home.”

“Well I believed you, I don’t know why,” he scowled at Timber. “Anyway I needed to find you and it turns out you lied. So I followed the investigation, plus a few of my men.”

“You have men?”

“Never mind.”

“So why did you need to find me?” Danielle asked groggily.

Blake and Nick looked at each other, “Well, you might as well know now. Garrett’s woken up.

“Well, Fuck!” Timber and Danielle said, in unison.

One Month Later

Timber sat on the bed looking down at the cage around her leg. It still amazed her that the six rods were screwed into her bone. A tray sat on the bed, a paper open to the latest Charlene Morgan story.

Ω

Alex Kiernan was found stuffed in his own freezer. His body showed signs of struggle and he had been stabbed fifty-seven times, his genitals removed. The story left out where they were later discovered. Several other bodies were found buried around his property, all men in various stages of decomposition. The part about Valerie – Katie – Payton and her Dissociative Identity Disorder took up most of the narrative, sensationalized as only a newspaper could. Timber had to admit Charlie had produced an ongoing piece of journalism, even delving into the past of the Peterson clan that was some pretty dark stuff.

Ω

Danielle was torn; curiously, she hadn't left Garrett's side. They all knew things were about to get complicated. Regardless, Timber wasn't worried. She had her family, and as much as Nick could push an agenda, he never really pushed Danielle.

"Hey sweetie, why are you out of bed?"

Timber grinned at the tall man with the goofy Spiderman tie. “I’m bored,” she whined.

“I have a perfect remedy for that.” As he moved over her, careful to avoid her leg, she knew that she was as happy as she had ever been.

“Kiss me, woman!” he demanded.

Timber was thrilled to comply.

THE END

Maybe…

MEET OUR AUTHOR

SAMANTHA (SAMMY) SHU

Samantha Shu lives in the beautiful mountainside city of Denver, Colorado. Samantha has completed three mystery novels, seven children's books and several short stories. From mystery thrillers to children's picture books, her prolific writing style crosses genres successfully and enthusiastically. Recently, Samantha completed her bachelor's degree. Her major, Criminal Justice, was chosen to do research for her books 'Blood Line' and 'Bloodthirsty'. On March 11, her goal was achieved and she graduated with honors. Samantha's published works include, *'There's a Season For All',* a children's fantasy picture book released in 2006; *'Blood Line'*, a mystery fiction released in October 2009, which is a prequel to *'Whispered Dreams'* released in November of 2008 and *'Bloodthirsty',* her newest novel. *'Bloodthirsty'* is steeped in realistic dramatic scenarios. Samantha's books can be ordered from her publisher, Argus Enterprises International, Inc. at **www.a-argusbooks.com**

As a consequence of her education, Samantha's villains are based on actual criminal personalities. Samantha writes for four hours each day and focuses her attentions between her first love, the written word, and her education. Samantha's love of writing is evident in her detailed and vivid style.

In her spare time Samantha enjoys swimming, skiing and martial arts.

To discover more about the fascinating new star of mystery, Samantha Shu, visit her at **whoisshu.com.**

www.ingramcontent.com/pod-product-compliance
Lightning Source LLC
LaVergne TN
LVHW020709110826
845149LV00012B/2177

* 9 7 8 0 9 8 4 2 5 9 6 9 4 *